PUFFIN CANADA

HAMISH X AND THE CHEESE PIRATES

Comedian SEÁN CULLEN was a member of the highly influential musical comedy troupe Corky and the Juice Pigs until 1998. His stage and screen credits include CBC's *Seán Cullen Show*, *The Tonight Show with Jay Leno*, the Showcase series *Slings and Arrows*, and the Toronto stage production of *The Producers*. He is the winner of two Gemini Awards.

Also by Seán Cullen

Hamish X, Book II:
Hamish X and the Hollow Mountain

Hamish X

and the Cheese Pirates

SEÁN CULLEN

PUFFIN
CANADA

PUFFIN CANADA

Published by the Penguin Group

Penguin Group (Canada), 90 Eglinton Avenue East, Suite 700, Toronto, Ontario, Canada M4P 2Y3
(a division of Pearson Canada Inc.)

Penguin Group (USA) Inc., 375 Hudson Street, New York, New York 10014, U.S.A.
Penguin Books Ltd, 80 Strand, London WC2R 0RL, England
Penguin Ireland, 25 St Stephen's Green, Dublin 2, Ireland (a division of Penguin Books Ltd)
Penguin Group (Australia), 250 Camberwell Road, Camberwell, Victoria 3124, Australia
(a division of Pearson Australia Group Pty Ltd)
Penguin Books India Pvt Ltd, 11 Community Centre, Panchsheel Park, New Delhi – 110 017, India
Penguin Group (NZ), 67 Apollo Drive, Rosedale, North Shore 0632, Auckland, New Zealand
(a division of Pearson New Zealand Ltd)
Penguin Books (South Africa) (Pty) Ltd, 24 Sturdee Avenue, Rosebank, Johannesburg 2196,
South Africa

Penguin Books Ltd, Registered Offices: 80 Strand, London WC2R 0RL, England

First published in a Puffin Canada hardcover by Penguin Group (Canada),
a division of Pearson Canada Inc., 2006
Published in this edition, 2007

6 7 8 9 10 (WEB)

Manufactured in Canada.

Libray and Archives Canada Cataloguing in Publication data available upon request.

ISBN-13: 978-0-14-305311-8
ISBN-10: 0-14-305311-6

To the real Hamish X,
my hero

Hamish X

and the Cheese Pirates

A Note from the Narrator

Hello and welcome to the book. I hope you enjoy the adventures of Hamish X. As narrator, my job is to tell the story in an exciting manner, to keep the audience interested and entertained. Sounds simple, doesn't it? Well, it isn't. If narration were easy, anyone could do it. As it stands, every narrator must undergo a vigorous training and certification program. For example, I have attended the Advanced Narrator's Certification College in Helsinki, Finland, where I received the highest score in the history of the facility. Lucky you!

A few bits of business before we get to the story:

Throughout the book you will encounter tiny numbers in the text. These are called "footnotes."[1] If you see a tiny

---

1 Hello. It's me, the narrator again, only down here at the bottom of the page. In the footnotes I will be clarifying difficult words or comments, providing pertinent historical facts, or distracting you with humorous nonsense. For example, the term "footnote" comes from the monks of medieval France who, while copying down manuscripts, would write notes on the soles of their feet. Often they were riddles or jokes for their monk buddies. They would extend their foot towards their friends and giggle endlessly while they were supposed to be working. This led to the introduction of sandals by irritated abbots (chief monks).

number, go to the bottom of the page and you'll find some useful bit of information.

I have tried to tell the tale exactly as it happened. I have tried to bring you the story in a way that makes you feel you are right there, in the action, in situ.[2] I've altered details only when they might be too gruesome or perhaps too greasy for anyone to enjoy. I've embellished only when necessary to make it interesting. Therefore, read on, oh reader! Turn the pages and learn the truth! Welcome to the first book in the saga of Hamish X: In Which Hamish X and His Companions Pit Themselves Against the Cheese Pirates of the Arctic Sea.

---

[2] "In situ" is just a high-browed way of saying "there." That's the beauty of words: there are so many ways to say exactly the same thing!

PROLOGUE

Fires blazed throughout the compound. Shouts and screams echoed in the corridors outside the little bald man's office. The little bald man bit back a cry of terror as he heard heavy, booted footsteps march towards the door. The elaborate brass doorknob rattled violently, but the door was locked. A shout was answered by several harsh voices. Something heavy slammed into the oak door, shaking its frame.

The little bald man was Francesco de Maldario, cheese master of the Parmesan factory at Parma. The door rattled again with a splintering sound that caused him to hug his knees closer to his chest and whimper in terror. He hid under his desk, knowing the door could not last much longer.

Usually Francesco loved being in his office. He sat behind his desk (not under it) every day, master of one of the oldest and most prestigious cheese-making houses in the world. The Maldario Parmesan Factory made the finest Parmesan cheese in the world and had done so since the eleventh century, supplying the sharp and slightly smelly cheese to popes, kings, and celebrities all over the globe. There wasn't a restaurant worth its salt[3] that didn't serve Maldario Parmesan on its pasta.

Francesco had never been brave. He was a good businessman, a good administrator. He was fearless at the negotiating table, but he doubted that the people who were breaking down the door were interested in negotiating.

After all, who attacks a cheese factory? thought Francesco. Nobody ever had, until tonight. Francesco had run at the first sound of trouble. He'd locked himself into his office and tried to call the police in Ravenna. But he discovered, to his dismay, that the lines had been cut. So he had ducked under his desk and prayed the invaders might overlook him.

No such luck. The door shook again. With a wrenching sound, it fell into the room and boomed on the floor. Francesco stifled the urge to cry out. He bit the inside of his cheek and tried to disappear.

An eerie silence gripped the room. No one spoke. Francesco had begun to wonder if they'd gone away when he heard footsteps on the polished wooden floor of his office. Clump. Clump. Clump. They came inexorably nearer. Finally, they stopped right in front of the desk. Francesco opened his eyes and saw a pair of high black boots in need of a good polish only a foot from his face. They smelled powerfully of rancid milk.

As quickly as a striking cobra, a huge hand darted under the desk, grabbing Francesco by the top of his head. He

---

[3] Restaurants in Ancient Rome were rewarded for their excellence by receiving a scale model of their owners carved out of rock salt. The sculpture would be proudly displayed in front of the establishment, and patrons were encouraged to lick it as they entered. The phrase remains to this day but, thankfully, the practice went out of favour because of a rash of tongue infections caused by the unsanitary nature of the licking.

was hauled out of his hiding place and held up in the air like a car in a scrap yard that's stuck to an electromagnet. His feet dangled above the floor as he kicked and writhed, trying to escape the vicelike grip that held him, but to no avail. Raucous laughter greeted his efforts.

Francesco quivered with terror. He tried to prepare himself for death but found it hard to imagine the world without him in it. He started to blubber uncontrollably. Big hot tears coursed down his face, through his moustache, and off his chin.

"Please! I beg you. Don' kill me!" he sobbed. "I giva you anything you wan'."

Uproarious laughter was his only answer. They guffawed as if it was the funniest thing they'd ever heard.

"Don' keeeel meee!" they mocked, and laughed some more.

"Silence!"

The command rang out and the hilarity stopped immediately. The voice was powerful, gravelly, and harsh. Francesco was so scared he stopped blubbering and hung limp.

Slowly, the hand that was clamped on his head turned him about until he was staring into the most terrifying eyes he'd ever seen. Bloodshot and huge, they loomed in his sight like blazing blue suns. He felt hypnotized by the glare, bathed in its evil radiance, burned by its cold fire.

"Who are you?" Francesco stammered.

"Who are we?" said the strange voice, dripping with threat. "We are the Cheese Pirates, of course."

A roar went up from the pirates, and Francesco thought that an excellent opportunity to pass out from sheer terror.

Part 1

WINDCITY

Chapter 1

On the afternoon that Hamish X arrived at the Windcity Orphanage and Cheese Factory, Viggo Schmatz sat in his office, a glass cube suspended above the factory floor, trying not to think about two things.

The first thing he was trying not to think about was cheese piracy. In his bony hands, Viggo held a newspaper. The headline on the front page announced the latest attack by the marauding Cheese Pirates on an Italian cheese factory. He crumpled the paper into a ball and flung it into a corner. He hadn't built up his magnificent cheese factory only to have it stolen from him by pirates. He would have to beef up security.

The second thing, which filled him with dread, was the arrival of a new child at his facility. He employed many children, but this boy was no ordinary orphan. He would require special attention, heightened vigilance, and intense scrutiny. Viggo wished he could refuse to take the child in, but you didn't say no to the Orphan Disposal Agency, not if you knew what was good for you.

From his perch, Viggo had a bird's-eye view of everything that happened below. Under the watchful eyes of the guards, the orphans laboured to produce the product that made Viggo rich: Caribou Blue cheese. Sitting in his comfortable chair, gazing down like a god from his lofty mountaintop as the children sweated and slaved, he felt important. Viggo decided to engage in his favourite pastime. He leaned back in his chair, laced his fingers behind his head, and daydreamed about himself.

In his favourite daydream he stood at the podium looking out over a sea of adoring faces. Years of tireless work had finally brought him to this moment. He was about to receive the highest honour of the cheese maker's profession: the Cheese Maker of the Year Award. In his mind he rehearsed what he would say as the chairman of the Cheese Board handed him the Golden Cheese Wedge, symbol of dairy excellence. A daydream still, but it would soon be a reality if Viggo stuck to his plan.

Viggo had invested his entire life in the pursuit of cheese mastery. The road had been long and arduous. After twelve years studying at the University of Trondheim School of the Milky Arts and then a four-year apprenticeship with Lars Porgengrister in the Bulgarian Highlands, Viggo was ready to go out on his own. His goal: to create the most beautiful, rare, and powerful of cheeses. It took him years of experimentation and failure, but he'd finally hit on "the" cheese: Caribou Blue.

He developed Caribou Blue from the milk of the caribou.[4] The caribou is a finicky animal, difficult to milk and completely impossible to train. To obtain the milk, Viggo had to approach them at night while they slept (they sleep standing up), attach high-speed milking machines, and get as much of the precious milk as possible before the creatures woke up. His body had been covered with hoof-shaped bruises during those early experiments until he finally perfected his technique.

The secret of Caribou Blue lies in the introduction of a very special, genetically engineered mould that produces

---

4 The caribou is the North American cousin of the reindeer of Lapland. The animal is more difficult to domesticate than the reindeer because of its wild nature and its intense dislike of Christmas.

a bluish-green marbling effect similar to Stilton or Roquefort.[5] Viggo created this mould himself by crossing several different strains in a laboratory. He'd used standard cheese moulds, moulds found only in Tibetan caves, and even moulds that he found under his own toenails until finally he had a strain of intense aquamarine colour and pungent odour. In its finished state, Caribou Blue could be consumed only in very small quantities. Eating too much of it or even spending a long time in close proximity could lead to blindness, paralysis or, in extreme cases, death.[6] Just one taste of the magnificent cheese, however, could yield a sense of wild euphoria or even induce hallucinogenic visions![7] No one had ever eaten more than three ounces of Caribou Blue and survived.

Having perfected his product, Viggo built a factory on the remote shores of Hudson's Bay with easy access to the migrating caribou herds and with water transport close at hand. Now all he had to find was a cheap, ready workforce. He solved his labour needs in an ingenious but heartless way: by turning part of the factory into a dormitory for orphaned children. Not only did he have a ready supply of children to labour in the dangerous cheese factory,

---

[5] Stilton and Roquefort are stinky blue cheeses from England and France, respectively. Both are left to grow mouldy for a while before they are eaten. Weird.

[6] One might ask oneself, Why eat something if it might kill you? Dangerous foods are not uncommon around the world. The Japanese eat a form of puffer fish that, if prepared improperly, can kill the eater. In Kazakhstan, some peasants eat hand grenades boiled in tomato sauce. Even a cow can be dangerous to eat if, for example, the cow is still alive. Ice cream can be dangerous, if fired out of a cannon or if very, very, very, very, very, very cold.

[7] This led to Caribou Blue being banned in the state of Wyoming.

children that no one cared about or wanted, but he also received tax incentives from the government for running a charitable organization. A vile, contemptible, heartless plan but one well suited to Viggo's vile, contemptible, heartless personality.

Viggo looked down at the children sweating below. Each one was delivered for his use by a shadowy organization called the Orphan Disposal Agency. Viggo had first contacted the ODA a few years before and they were only too happy to provide a number of fit orphans, gathered from around the world, perfect for Viggo's uses. The children ranged in age from three to fourteen. They were strong, healthy, and had the spirit already crushed out of them. Oh, there was the odd rebellious one, but Viggo found that the threat of an imaginative punishment was enough to keep even the most obstinate child in line. The sheer isolation of Viggo's operation also went a long way to ensure obedience and deter escape. The best part was that when a child grew to the difficult age of fourteen, the ODA took them away and provided a young replacement.

Viggo never questioned where the children went after the Orphan Disposal Agency removed them. He didn't want to know. Besides, the ODA wasn't the kind of organization one questioned. The children were terrified of the grey-suited agents with their goggles and gloved hands. Viggo had to admit that even he himself was a bit frightened of them.

Viggo located his factory on the border between the Canadian province of Manitoba and the Territory of Nunavut in a miserable little town called Windcity. Windcity got its name from the fact that it was officially the windiest town in the world. For a hundred and eighty-two and one-half days of the year a gale-force wind drove down from the Arctic Circle, causing every building in the town to lean southeast at a sixty-degree angle. On the other hundred and eighty-two and one-half days the gale-force wind shifted and blew northwest, causing the houses to change their slant to sixty-eight degrees in the opposite direction. The people adapted to the slant by wearing special clogs indoors that had one sole twice as thick as the other, allowing them to walk more or less naturally at an angle.[8]

Living in the windiest town in the world had other hazards. Walking through the streets could be perilous. Citizens who lost their footing could find themselves blown like tumbleweeds across the tundra, stopping only when they ran up against a building in Churchill sixteen hundred kilometres to the south.[9] Or, if they were less lucky and the wind was blowing northwest, they would never be seen again. The town council erected ropes throughout the streets linking all the buildings so that people could haul themselves along in relative safety. The wind was so powerful some days that it wasn't unusual to see people pulling themselves hand over hand to the supermarket, their bodies parallel to the earth. (One happy by-product of the activity was that Windcity had won the world Tug-o-War championships fourteen years running.[10]) Finally, as a safety precaution, two long nets

---

[8] The day the wind changed was called "Flip Day" and was celebrated twice a year by a change of clogs. Flip Day usually fell on the spring and autumn solstices.

[9] Sometimes they found themselves even farther from home. Homer Cudgeons, a Windcity resident, was discovered confused and wandering in downtown Minneapolis. When questioned, he said, "My nose was itchy. I only let go for a second."

[10] They were eventually banned from the competition.

were strung across the north and south sides of town to catch anyone whose hands slipped.

On top of the vicious winds, the terrain for hundreds of kilometres around the town was featureless, frozen tundra. Not so much as a single tree stood upright to break the monotonous landscape. Any child trying to escape the orphanage was sure to succumb to the desolate climate. The only possible hope for escape was to stow away on one of the cargo ships that docked infrequently in the harbour to bring supplies in and ship the cheese out. Ruthless, vicious dogs, part wolf and hungry for child flesh, patrolled the harbour. The dogs themselves were beaten and starved by the cruellest of Viggo's guards.

You might ask why a town would be situated in such an inhospitable place. The answer is simple: propellers! Windcity was founded to take advantage of the powerful winds for the burgeoning propeller industry. When airplanes were invented, a place was needed to experiment and produce the propellers required to keep planes flying. Entrepreneurs flocked to the site to make their fortune.[11] The jet plane eventually spelled the end for the propeller industry, however, and the people began to drift away.

By the time Viggo arrived looking for cheap space to house his cheese production business, the town was practically deserted. Only two people actually lived there any more: a widow named Mrs. Francis and an old man

---

[11] Dutch immigrants were among the most numerous of the new townsfolk. The Dutch were naturals when it came to building propellers. After all, they'd had centuries of experience building windmills. The invention of the airplane gave proof to the rumour that had persisted for many years: that Holland could fly. The whole country would lift off for short trips up and down the Baltic, until finally the authorities grounded her after a near collision with Latvia.

named Mr. Nieuwendyke who believed he was a cat. Viggo took possession of a huge brick building that had once been a propeller factory. He installed windmills (made from leftover propellers) to provide him with all the free electrical power he needed to run the operation. The wind also blew the cheesy fumes harmlessly away. Well, not exactly harmlessly: all the grass for half a mile turned black and died.

Everything Viggo needed to make his cheese was in place. He had a building. He had machinery. He had a steady supply of raw materials. And, thanks to the ODA, he had a workforce.

If the children arriving on the doorstep of the Windcity Orphanage and Cheese Factory had deluded themselves into thinking they might have a happy life, they were cured of their fantasies when they saw the place. The building was a huge, square, redbrick hulk. Viggo had spared all expense in making it homey. The front door was a vast steel affair that added to the overall prison atmosphere. All the dormitory windows were of the frosted variety, with wires meshed through the filthy glass for safety reasons. The windows on the factory floor were bricked up to prevent impurities from getting into the cheese and children from climbing out. As a result, the children never saw the sun in the entire time they lived in Windcity. The cafeteria had sun lamps installed to provide the children with vitamin D. They were effective but totally cheerless.

Sour-faced guards marched the new orphans off the boat and through the deserted town, clinging to the guide rope. It was an eerie trek through the empty streets and derelict buildings. The wind howled through the eaves, moaning sorrowfully. The factory loomed over the tilted town, lit up with searchlights and strung with razor wire.

An electrified fence surrounded the building, sparking ominously as bits of loose debris rolled against the chain links.

The new children marched through the front gate, through the service doors, and into the processing room. Each was given a breathing mask, a pair of overalls, a toothbrush, and a towel. Thus equipped, the miserable new conscripts trudged into the dormitory.

The children all slept in one huge room in row after row of lumpy cots. They all shared one bathtub, taking turns having baths once a week. The lights in the dormitory ran on a timer. They came on for two hours between shifts in the factory, while one crew was waking up and the other was going to bed. The lights were fluorescent, cold, and stark and throwing into relief the dormitory's dreary misery.

The hundred children were divided into two shifts of fifty. One shift worked from nine in the morning to seven at night. Then both shifts ate breakfast/supper, which consisted of oatmeal porridge and whey. The breakfast/supper lasted one hour, after which the first shift had an hour of free time and then went to bed while the second shift worked from eight in the evening to seven in the morning. Then came the meal of whey and oatmeal porridge and the working day started all over again, with the night shift sleeping and the day shift working. The day and night shift children hardly knew each other, and that was the way Viggo liked it. Friendships could only distract the children from their work.

To administer to the orphans' day-to-day needs, Viggo hired the aforementioned local widow, Mrs. Francis. Her husband had died many years before in a rabid owl attack,[12] leaving her to fend for herself. She was a shy, chubby woman who was often pink in the face from exertion. Viggo suspected she was too kind to her charges (Viggo believed in beatings and harsh discipline), but since the choices were limited in Windcity[13] he suffered her bouts of affection for the children and her requests for better food and warmer clothes.

Viggo's grand scheme seemed to be coming together just fine. He had installed the specialized equipment. He had trained the children. He had negotiated with the native people,[14] whom he trained in the milking technique, for a steady supply of the caribou milk essential to the cheese-making process. Finally, the operation was up and running.

Caribou Blue became an overnight critical success with cheese connoisseurs around the world. The *Sydney Herald* called it "a delightful assault on the nostrils and the palette." The *New York Times* food critic wrote, "Caribou Blue is a wake-up call. In his laboratory Viggo Schmatz has created the Frankenstein's monster of cheeses! Let it terrorize the village of your taste buds!" The *London Times* said simply, "Cariboova! What a cheese."

---

[12] Freakish indeed because birds do not carry rabies, but Mr. Francis was a very unlucky man. He once tripped over a stone and managed to swallow his own foot. What are the odds?

[13] Recall, the only other resident was a very old man named Mr. Nieuwendyke who believed he was a cat. He stayed in his house, meowing loudly and licking himself.

[14] The native people in the Arctic go by the name Inuit. They are commonly known as Eskimos. They don't like this name because it is a derogatory term in another aboriginal language and it means "eaters of raw fish." While it's true that they do eat raw fish, they'd rather be called by the name they give themselves, not a name someone else gives them. Which is fair, but Eskimo is fun to say.

Viggo was riding high. Orders were pouring in. He could charge what he wanted for his product and everyone would pay. And no one questioned his methods (apart from Mrs. Francis) as long as he continued to produce the fabulous cheese. He even had his picture on the cover of *Fortune* and *Cheesers Monthly*. The world was in the palm of his hand.

And so Viggo leaned back and imagined what the Golden Wedge might look like on the shelf above his desk. He could envision the cheering crowds as he accepted the award. He could see himself stepping to the podium, taking the shining prize from the hands of the chairman of the Cheese Board ...

A rap on the door of his office jarred him out of his daydream. Viggo started, almost falling over backwards in his chair. At the door, one of the guard foremen stood waiting. All the guards came from the same agency, and were chosen for the ugliness of their facial features.[15] The man at the door had a face that looked as if someone had dropped a bag of hammers onto it from a great height. Viggo stood up and stalked across to the door, flinging it open on the cringing guard. Immediately, the powerful smell of the cheesing floor wafted over him.

"Well?" barked Viggo.

"Uh, sorry, sir," Hammerface stammered. He held his stocking cap in his hands and wrung it nervously. "They're here."

---

[15] The agency is called "Mean and Ugly Security Options." Check out their website at meanandugly.com.

Chapter 2

"Follow me," Viggo demanded. He snatched a breathing mask from a hook on the wall by the door. Pulling it over his face, he started down the stairs to the factory floor with Hammerface trailing after him.

Everyone had to wear a mask on the factory floor. Without protection, the fumes generated by the maturing cheese could overwhelm a person in seconds. The masks sealed tight all around, with a window of clear plastic framing the wearer's face. Viggo tightened the straps on his mask as he descended.

Viggo was an extremely knobbly individual. When he walked, it seemed as if all the bones in his body were straining to leap out of his skin and escape. His hair was greasy. He never washed it, and so it stood up on end most of the time, like a ghastly albino hedgehog. His nose was long and pointy, almost touching the inside surface of the face mask he wore. His mouth was drawn in a perpetual scowl.

Hammerface was in every way the physical opposite of Viggo. He was loutish and large, a shambling, scruffy ogre of a man. At his belt hung a Ticklestick. Long and black with a bulging knob at the end, it delivered a powerful jolt of energy to the central nervous system, flooding the brain with a tickle reflex so profound that it reduced a person to a giggling, helpless blob in an instant.[16] The weapon slapped against Hammerface's wide buttocks as he shambled after Viggo.

As Viggo approached the factory floor the children avoided his watery grey eyes. One didn't look at Viggo directly for fear of bringing down some punishment.

Viggo reached the bottom of the stairs and looked with satisfaction at the cheesing floor. He felt a swell of pride at the grim efficiency displayed before him. For he had integrated all the children according to their ages and abilities into the cheese-making process. First, the caribou milk was fed into a large vat about the size of an above-ground swimming pool. In a sense, it was a swimming pool. For this first stage of the process, all the toddlers aged three to five were tossed into the milk vat wearing water wings. The toddlers would thrash and tread water, their water wings excreting rennet[17] and causing the milk to thicken until they could no longer move. When the milk was thick enough, the children were extracted by robotic crane arms attached to the ceiling, scraped off, and prepared for the next batch. The vat was then upended and the thickening milk poured into a pressing chamber.

The pressing chamber was the province of the children aged six to ten. First the mixture was trowelled out onto a large, flat, perforated floor. The children wore huge

---

[16] The Ticklestick is just one of the products available from Nonviolent Options Inc. of East Orange, New Jersey. They also offer a device that reproduces the sound of fingernails on a chalkboard and a hand-held projector that displays pictures of people getting paper cuts. All are extremely effective.

[17] Rennet is essential to cheese making. It is an enzyme found in a sheep's stomach that causes the milk to curdle. How anyone discovered this quality is uncertain. Perhaps a sheep had the flu and threw up in a milk pail. We may never know. And do we really want to?

paddles like snowshoes on their feet. Hour after hour they trudged 'round and 'round, pressing down with their foot paddles and forcing the liquid out of the thickening curds.[18] The liquid, whey, is a watery but nutritious by-product of the cheesing process. Viggo designed the floor with perforations so that the whey was channelled into a vat near the kitchen, where Mrs. Francis could use it in preparing her bland but nourishing meals for the orphans. Nothing was wasted in Viggo's operation. The children also carried baskets filled with salt and tossed handfuls of it over the curds to preserve the cheese.

When the cheese was pressed and free of liquid, the children aged eleven to fourteen came with picks and saws. They sawed the cheese into blocks a metre square and fifty centimetres deep. Using their picks, they flung the slabs onto a conveyor belt that ran along the wall of the factory. The work was back-breakingly difficult, and so the children took turns cutting and heaving.

The cheese chunks travelled along the conveyor belt to a hole in the floor where they fell into darkness. Below, the cheese was stacked in the dank, musty vault. The walls of the vault grew thick with a greenish-blue mould that impregnated the cheese and provided its distinctive marbling and aroma.

The finished cheese was then shipped throughout the world on freighters to markets hungry for the delicacy. An ounce of Caribou Blue sold for twenty-seven dollars. Viggo was quickly becoming a very rich man. Unfortunately,

[18] Curds, not Kurds. Curds are immature morsels of cheese that must be ripened and aged over time. Kurds are a people who inhabit a region that encompasses southern Turkey and northern Iraq. No one knows if Kurds ripen with age, but it is likely that if they were pressed, liquid would come out of them.

very little of the wealth trickled down to the orphan workers at the factory. They received the bare minimum necessary to keep them alive. Their clothes were bought second-hand by the pound. Viggo made sure the children were strong enough to work, but nothing more. Their diet consisted principally of oatmeal porridge and the whey recovered from the pressing process.

Viggo was very, very strict in his accounting practices. He always kept track of every ounce of cheese. No one could have pilfered and gotten away with it. Not that anyone really wanted to—the smell of the cheese factory floor was enough to put a child off cheese for life.

Viggo smiled as he surveyed the children at work. The grey and lifeless faces pinched behind the masks pleased him. They looked defeated, and a defeated child was a productive child.

Just as he turned towards the big doors that led to the cafeteria section of the complex, he felt a tug at his trouser leg. He turned and looked down to find a little brown face with large eyes blinking up at him. The face belonged to Parveen, an eight-year-old, feet laced into his curd-pressing shoes.

"What?" Viggo groaned. "Speak up!"

"Begging your pardon, sir," Parveen said in his flat, emotionless voice, "I was wondering if I could speak to you about possible improvements to the assembly line."

He was a small boy with brown skin that bespoke his South Asian origin. He wore spectacles that made his eyes owl-like and wide behind his breathing mask. Parveen was quiet and didn't really mix with the other kids, preferring to spend his off-duty time in the orphanage's meagre library reading anything he could get his hands on. He amused himself (though no one had ever seen him smile) by devising machines and gadgets and drawing blueprints and plans, even though he'd never had the opportunity to put his ideas into practice in the Spartan[19] world of the Windcity Orphanage and Cheese Factory. Still, at eight years old, he was clever enough to make most adults uncomfortable, and Viggo, who despised cleverness in anyone but himself, particularly so.

"Improvements?" Viggo said through gritted teeth. "Im*prove*ments?"

Parveen was unaware of the menace in Viggo's voice. He wasn't a very empathetic boy; that is to say, he couldn't read people's emotions. The other children moved away to distance themselves from the coming storm. Parveen rummaged in the pocket of his overalls, digging out a small pad of paper. From behind his right ear, he pulled a stub of a pencil.

"I've drawn up a couple of schematics that would definitely cut down on the number of hands on the floor at any given shift." Parveen pointed with his pencil at the figures on the paper. "According to my calculating, we could cut down the workday for each shift by three hours and still maintain the same level of production." He looked up at Viggo expectantly.

Viggo glared down at Parveen. Suddenly he grabbed him by the front of his overalls, lifting the boy up to eye

---

[19] The Spartans were a bunch of Ancient Greeks who lived in a town called Sparta. They were warriors who lived with very few personal comforts: no playing, no toys, no ice cream or video games. The video games weren't such a hardship because they hadn't been invented yet. Not even Donkey Kong or Pac Man. As a result, the Spartans excelled at fighting. Another example of misdirected energy. *Spartan* is now synonymous with frugal, harsh living conditions. If you read a holiday brochure and it says the hotels are wonderfully Spartan, don't go.

level. Viggo pressed his face into Parveen's until their masks clicked together. "Why would I want to shorten the shifts? Why should I make anything easier for you lazy little children?" he shrieked, spraying spittle onto the inside of his mask. "You orphans are lazy enough as it is without my giving you opportunities to slack off any further."

Parveen dangled in Viggo's grip, calm and emotionless, blinking mildly, foot paddles flapping. His passivity enraged Viggo even more. He shook Parveen, making the little boy's feet jig in the air.

"Don't waste my time with your stupid ideas. The only thing I want you to do is get back in that chamber and stamp those curds." With that, Viggo hurled Parveen into the pressing chamber, where he skidded across the greasy surface of the curds and bounced to a halt against the far side.

Two guards stepped towards the fallen boy, grinning foully and hefting their Ticklesticks. They advanced on Parveen, but before they could reach him one of the children stepped in to bar their way.

"Back off, ya big galoots!" The girl stood with her hands on her hips, defying the guards to make a move. She was one of the older orphans. Although tall and thin, she was strong and wiry, with a fierce light in her eyes that let the two men know she wasn't scared of anything. The guards faltered and looked to Viggo for guidance.

Viggo knew the girl only too well. Her name was Mimi and she was one of his rare failures. He had managed to completely destroy the spirit of all the children in the Windcity Orphanage and Cheese Factory, but in all the seven years Mimi had been there he'd never managed to break her completely. She got into fights, sassed back to the guards, and generally made a nuisance of herself. The Ticklesticks were useless against Mimi. She laughed when they used them on her. And somehow she managed to laugh defiantly rather than helplessly, which was the real point of the Ticklestick.

Mimi had adopted little Parveen as her personal project. Viggo often toyed with the idea of asking the ODA to take her back, but he didn't want the grey-suited agents to think he couldn't handle himself. In two years she'd be carted off anyway to wherever the grey agents took the fourteen-year-olds, so he tried to be patient and endure her annoying behaviour.

Right now, he didn't have time to deal with her antics. Viggo sneered and waved his arm dismissively. "Back to work!" he shouted at the children.

"Back to work!" the guards parroted.

All the other children instantly turned to their tasks. He watched for a moment to make sure they were doing as they were told. Viggo smiled in satisfaction, but when he remembered the waiting visitors, his happiness evaporated. He spun on his heel and stalked off through the big double doors.

Parveen slowly raised himself to the sitting position. He tucked away his little pad and stuck the pencil back behind his ear. Mimi hauled the little boy to his feet.

"You gotta keep yer mouth shut, bub!" she said. Her voice had a flat Texan drawl. "It'll only get ya into trouble around here."

"I merely wished to improve production quotas," Parveen answered, rubbing his sore shoulder.

"Whatever!" the girl said. "Just keep yer head down." Her green eyes narrowed as she glared at the doors Viggo had just exited. "He'll get his one day and I hope I'll be givin' him some of it."

A guard stepped up. In his hand he held a long black club with a bulb on the end: a Ticklestick. He menaced Mimi and Parveen.

"Stop talking!" he shouted. "Back to work!"

Mimi flexed her fists, glaring at the man. Finally, she turned back to her task of slicing up the cheese.

VIGGO STRODE BETWEEN THE TABLES of the cafeteria, empty at this time of day, and came to a locked metal door. He pulled a card out of his pocket and held it up to a small pad on the door's right side. A tiny light went from red to green. He pulled on the door and it opened easily, admitting him to the hall that led to the processing area.

He collided with Mrs. Francis, who was hurrying from a side corridor. Hammerface, right at Viggo's heels, then ran into Viggo.

"Watch where you're going!" Viggo snapped at the flustered woman.

Mrs. Francis was just about as wide as she was tall. Everything about her was round. She had a round white face and round little sausage fingers. A scarf over her head failed to deter strands of grey hair from escaping at all angles. She lived in a tiny apartment attached to the kitchens. Of course, Viggo deducted room and board from her minuscule salary, but she didn't complain, couldn't complain for fear of losing her job. Jobs were scarce in Windcity these days. Never mind that the only other person who actually still lived there was that crazy Mr. Nieuwendyke who thought he was a cat, Viggo wouldn't hesitate to hire him despite all his meowing and licking his hands. Ever since Mr. Francis had been attacked by that rabid owl twenty years before, Mrs. Francis had had to look out for herself. And since there wasn't a lot to spend money on in Windcity she bought the children little treats, careful to hide her philanthropy from Viggo.

"I-I-I'm sorry, Master Viggo. It's hard to keep track of everything, what with one hundred children to feed and clean up after every day. I'm run off my feet."

Viggo towered over her, leaning in like a rickety scaffold. "Are you suggesting that you can't handle the workload, Mrs. Francis?"

Mrs. Francis threw up her hands in dismay, "Never, Master Viggo! I can manage!"

"I hope so," Viggo smiled sweetly, "because I'm sure there are many who would be glad of the work should I advertise for a new Chief Domestic Supervisor!"

"Of course, Master Viggo. I appreciate that." The bell rang again, more insistently, and Mrs. Francis hurried off down the hall past the kitchens (her tiny domain). Satisfied that he'd struck fear into her heart, Viggo strolled after her through the hall that led to the processing room. Hammerface puffed after him.

The Orphan Processing Room (the OPR for short) was a large warehouse space where children fresh off the boat were processed. A huge door slid up on rails to admit fresh arrivals. When new children arrived, they stood in lines to be sprayed with delousing agent and receive their uniforms. Then they watched a video telling them about what they were expected to do and what punishments they could expect if they failed. Finally, they stepped through a metal detector to ensure they carried nothing dangerous into the factory. When all these processes had been executed, the thoroughly depressed children were marched off to their assigned cots in the dormitory to prepare for their lives as cheese factory workers.

The arrival today was highly irregular. To save money and time the ODA usually delivered orphans in groups, but today was different. ODA Headquarters in Providence, Rhode Island, had called to say they had a special child for Viggo to take on, and he had lain awake for the last five nights fretting over it. Everything was running so smoothly now. The last thing he needed was to have *that* boy to worry about. Again, he wished he'd refused to take him, but one didn't refuse the ODA. Bad things happened to people who did.

Viggo's worried thoughts were interrupted by a loud booping sound. An amber light began to flash high on the wall. The great door started to slide open, clanking loudly in the vast concrete room.

The wind roared through the opening, plucking at Viggo's clothing and chilling him instantly. Mrs. Francis clapped a hand on her head to hold her scarf in place.

Outside the door a glistening black helicopter settled on the concrete, the runners touching gently down amid a swirl of snow. It was an amazing piece of flying considering the constant prevailing winds that threatened to drive the aircraft into the side of the building. The helicopter was completely featureless, sleek and black like a giant flying beetle. Presently, doors popped open on either side of the cockpit and two grey figures stepped down to the ground. They wore wide-brimmed fedoras that stayed in place despite the breeze. A grey greatcoat flapped around each spare frame. Their faces were pale and long, their mouths a cruel horizontal slash. Their eyes were invisible behind black goggles that covered most of the upper half of their faces. They were, in short, typical agents of the ODA. One of them turned and pulled a boy out of the door, lowering the child roughly to the ground.

The boy's hands were cuffed in front of his body, held by a pair of white plastic bracelets that glowed faintly. His head lolled forward like a rag doll and he staggered ahead, falling to his knees in the swirling snow. The agents each clutched an elbow in grey, gloved hands, heaved the boy to his feet, and frog-marched him in through the OPR door. The boy's head may have lolled like a rag doll, but his steps were quick and sure. He wore a pair of large black boots on his feet that, though they seemed heavy and the boy seemed dazed, never missed a step.

The two agents and their charge came to a halt in front of Viggo. One kept a hand on the boy's shoulder and the other held a small rucksack in his gloved hand.

Viggo shivered, and not just from the frigid temperature. He found the agents unnerving. The men looked at him silently for an awkward moment. Viggo felt like a bug under a microscope.

"Welcome, Mr. ...?" Viggo finally broke the silence, stepping forward and holding out his hand. The ODA agent merely looked at the proffered hand as if he'd never seen such a bizarre gesture before. Viggo nervously dropped it back to his side.

"I am Agent Candy," the grey man said in a surprisingly lyrical voice. Viggo had met agents before and puzzled over the accent they all shared, but he never managed to nail it down.

"May I introduce my associate, Agent Sweet." Agent Candy gestured towards the other man dressed all in grey, identical in every way to Mr. Candy but perhaps an inch or two shorter.

Their prisoner stood, swaying slightly with his head down. He seemed barely able to stand upright. Mrs. Francis asked, "What's wrong with him? Is he sick?"

Both agents swung their goggled faces to scrutinize Mrs. Francis. She regretted having spoken, wishing they would stop staring at her with those glittering, goggled eyes.

"Not ill," Mr. Candy chirped.

"Merely under restraint." Mr. Sweet held out his hand. Mr. Candy reached into a pocket of his greatcoat and deposited a small, square piece of plastic into his colleague's palm. Mr. Sweet tapped the square against each of the boy's bracelets in turn and they immediately lost their glow, opening with a snap.

Instantly the boy looked up. For a moment his eyes met Mrs. Francis's, and she almost gasped. They were beautiful, a most extraordinary colour: pale gold rather than brown. And somehow, as they flicked away from her, she saw a strange reflective flash like a cat's eye when a headlight catches it in the darkness.

"Where am I?" The boy looked around him in confusion. His eyes fixed on Viggo. "Who are you?"

Viggo felt compelled to answer. "I'm Viggo Schmatz."

The boy grinned, showing all his teeth in a predatory glint that made Viggo's stomach lurch. "The pleasure's all yours, Viggo. I'm Hamish X!"

Chapter 3

Viggo looked into those strange golden eyes and felt vaguely uncomfortable. Covering his discomfort with disdain, he curled his lip into a sneer. "Well, what an honour," he said coldly. "The infamous Hamish X: scourge of orphanages the world over. In the flesh."

"What a treat for you, sir!" Hamish X smiled, gazing around the room as if taking an inventory. "Cheerful place you've got here, Viggo! Pity I won't be staying long." Hamish X looked down at his feet, lifting one boot and then the other. He smiled again.

"Impudent pup," snarled Hammerface, reaching for his baton, but Viggo raised a hand and the guard subsided.

"You will call me Mr. Schmatz," Viggo said.

Hamish X shrugged. "Whatever."

Mr. Candy ignored the boy. "He's a thorn in the side of our organization."

"A pebble in our shoe, as it were," added Mr. Sweet. "He's escaped from every one of our high-security orphan containment facilities—the Orphan Pens in Tasmania, our Undersea Algae farms in the Baltic, the Corn Mines of Central Bolivia ..."

"The Gobi Desert Synthetic Ice Cube Factories," chimed in Mr. Candy.

"Indeed, Mr. Candy, indeed," Mr. Sweet nodded, head ducking like a pigeon's. "He has managed to escape them all. Granted, we always manage to track him down again, but it's an embarrassment ..."

"A nuisance." This from Mr. Candy.

"A distraction." Mr. Sweet ducked his head again. "We are counting on you to put him in his place and keep him there. I hope our faith in you isn't misplaced, Mr. Schmatz."

"Schmatz?" Hamish X said suddenly, "That's a funny name."

"X?" Viggo snapped back. "That's a stupid name. What is it? A family name?"

Hamish X's brow wrinkled. "At least it's easy to spell."

A snort of laughter escaped from Mrs. Francis. Everyone turned to glare at her. She twisted her apron nervously. "He doesn't look dangerous."

The agents looked at each other briefly, then Mr. Sweet spoke. "He is dangerous. Very charming ..."

"But dangerous," Mr. Candy interjected. "He must be watched."

"But we have every confidence ..." Mr. Sweet began.

"That you will break him, Master Viggo," Mr. Candy finished.

"I assure you," Viggo simpered, "your confidence is not misplaced, gentlemen. I will do everything in my power to ensure that this ... delinquent," he jabbed a finger at Hamish X, "shall rue the day he arrived in my jurisdiction."

"Indeed," said Mr. Candy.

"Indeed," echoed Mr. Sweet.

"Now we must be off," Mr. Candy said. "Do not disappoint us, Mr. Schmatz."

The conversation was over. Mr. Sweet dropped the square piece of plastic into his pocket. Mr. Candy handed Hammerface the leather knapsack. "The boy's personal items," he explained. Without a backward glance, the two agents walked out of the OPR. Viggo felt a surge of relief as they disappeared into the helicopter and the craft lifted off. Hammerface pressed the button to lower the door. With a thud, the wind and swirling snow were cut off.

Viggo turned his attention to Hamish X. "Well, well, well!" He clasped his bony hands behind his back and slowly walked around the boy, looking him up and down with the intention of rattling him. But Hamish X just looked Viggo up and down, which rattled Viggo. Finally Viggo stopped, facing his new detainee directly. "So you're Hamish X. Not much to look at."

Hamish X shrugged. "Look who's talking."

The boy wasn't all that remarkable at first glance. He stood about four feet tall. It was impossible to tell if he was fat or thin because he wore a bulky flannel jacket. The jacket was woolly red plaid and looked as though it had seen a lot of hard days—the colours were faded and the elbows frayed, the buttons mismatched and the hem dangling loose threads. Hamish's hat was sheepskin, greasy and soiled. His rucksack was also made of some variety of animal skin. And his bag was so dirty and stained that an accurate identification of the animal of origin would require DNA analysis.

"And these are the famous boots?" Viggo bent slightly at the waist like a hinged stick. He looked at the boots with deep mistrust.

Apart from his unsettling eyes, the most intriguing thing about Hamish X were his boots. The boots were profound: black, heavy, large, and shiny. The soles were studded with rubbery knobs for traction. There were no laces. In fact, they had no fastening whatever, making one wonder how he put them on his feet, and once they were on his feet how they stayed there. The surface of the boots was completely seamless and black as midnight, but traces of iridescent colour shimmered in the light like oil in a puddle. Viggo could almost sense an aura of energy surrounding the boots, a glow just beyond the visual spectrum. He felt his dread of the boy deepen the more he studied his footwear.

Hamish X took the scrutiny without comment. While Viggo examined his boots, the boy turned his gaze on Mrs. Francis. He smiled at her and winked. She winked and smiled back.

Viggo tentatively laid a hand on the toe of the left boot. It was warm to the touch, almost as if it were a living creature.

"Nice, aren't they?" Hamish X said suddenly, startling Viggo so that he tipped over and fell on his bottom.

"Not really!" Viggo snarled. He jumped to his feet. "Well, well, well! I've heard of your exploits—your daring escapes, heroic rescues, blah, blah, and blah. Oh, yes. The famous Hamish X, King of the Orphans!"

"Whatever you say, Chief," was the simple reply. Hamish X continued to look at Viggo, one eyebrow cocked and a smirk of disdain on his lips. Viggo stood directly in front of the boy and looked down his nose at him.

"Compared to all the other places you've been locked up, I'm sure you think the Windcity Orphanage and Cheese Factory is a dawdle." Viggo stopped, staring down at Hamish X, who said nothing. "I hate to disappoint you ... What am I saying? I absolutely *adore* disappointing you! You're never going to escape from here. Do you understand? Never! No one ever has and no one ever will. The guards are vicious, ruthless, and stupid ..."

"Hey," Hammerface objected.

Viggo ignored him. "The fences are electrified. If you try to climb them, a million volts of electricity will fry you."

"I see." Hamish X shrugged.

Viggo was a bit disappointed in his new charge's reaction. "We have dogs, too! Large dogs. Half-starved and blood-mad dogs."

The boy frowned. "Why don't you feed the dogs twice as much? Then they wouldn't be half starved."

"I want them half starved! It makes them want to eat anyone who's escaping!"

"I get your point."

"Good for you! Here's another point, *Hamish X*," Viggo hissed, leaning into Hamish X's face. "Even if you managed to get past all the security measures and get out of the compound, there's nowhere to go. The nearest town is hundreds of kilometres away across barren tundra. If you aren't eaten by bears or wolves,[20] the cold will stop your heart and the wind will flay the flesh off your bones. No, my little friend, you will not be escaping from Windcity Orphanage and Cheese Factory, so put it out of your arrogant little head."

"You have nothing to worry about then," Hamish X said mildly, looking around the OPR with frank curiosity.

That mild response took the wind out of Viggo's sails. "Quite so," he said. Viggo looked down at the rucksack that Hammerface carried. "What's in there?"

"Oi! This weighs a ton, Master Viggo!" Hammerface said. He tipped out the contents on the floor: two pairs of underpants, a rather worn toothbrush, a ball of twine, and a large book bound in green leather with gold lettering

---

[20] Viggo omitted mentioning the carnivorous Arctic foxes that, though small, have been known to gently eat sleeping people without waking them. Also, hordes of lemmings might run over anyone caught unawares, but the likelihood is minuscule.

on the front. Hammerface squinted and tried to sound out the title. "Gree-at Plum-bers ..."

Hamish X suddenly lashed out and grabbed the book out of Hammerface's surprised hands. The boy clutched the book fiercely to his chest. Mrs. Francis could have sworn that the boots pulsed with a faint light when Hamish came in contact with the book, but perhaps her eyes were playing tricks.

"*Great Plumbers and Their Exploits*. It was a gift from my mother." He seemed utterly certain of the statement.

"Hoi! Give me that!" Hammerface tried to grab the book back, but Hamish X twisted away. Hammerface reached for his Ticklestick.

"Wait!" Mrs. Francis shouted. Everyone froze. Mrs. Francis, realizing she was the centre of attention, blushed and nervously twisted her apron. She went over and picked up the rucksack. Holding out her hand to the boy, she smiled reassuringly. "Let me hold the book and your rucksack. I'll take care of them for you. Don't worry."

Hamish X looked at her through slitted eyes, calculating. She smiled at him again and reached out her hand again. Finally, the boy held out the book. Mrs. Francis took it and carefully placed it in the rucksack.

"I'll keep it safe," Mrs. Francis said and stepped to one side.

"Thank you, Mrs. Francis."

Viggo's finger stabbed out at the boots on the boy's feet. "The boots," he snapped.

"Yes?" the boy smiled.

"Take them off," Viggo demanded.

"I can't."

"What do you mean, you can't?"

"I mean they won't come off."

Viggo snapped his fingers at Hammerface, who came to attention as best he could.

"Take his boots off," Viggo ordered.

"I wouldn't if I were you," Hamish X warned.

Hammerface leered at the boy and pushed him onto his back. He planted one foot on his chest and grabbed his right boot in both hands, heaving with all his might.

There was a flash and the smell of burning hair. The air crackled with static electricity. Hammerface cartwheeled across the floor, landing on his back, steaming softly. Hamish X hopped to his feet and shrugged. "I warned you. They don't come off."

Hammerface struggled to his feet. His hair stood out at all angles. "They don't come off," he mumbled stupidly.

Viggo crossed his arms and glared at the boy. *He's a born troublemaker,* he thought to himself. *But I have to keep the ODA happy if I want the cheap labour to keep coming. Orphans don't grow on trees.*[21] *I'll just have to keep a close eye on him.* To Hammerface he said, "Take him to the dormitory. He'll join the day shift."

Mrs. Francis stood to one side, completely unnoticed by Viggo, the rucksack behind her back. Her heart went out to this little boy. He seemed so strangely self-assured, but she could sense a loneliness in him that was common to all the children in Windcity: they were alone in the world without family to love them. She did her best to

---

[21] Viggo is correct that orphans don't grow on trees, but there are orphans who grow *in* trees. In the Turgwazi tribe of Central Africa, orphans live in tree houses because it is deemed unlucky if orphans touch the ground before they are sixteen years old. They grow to adulthood in the trees and then become members of society in full standing. So, technically, some orphans do grow, if not *on* trees, in them.

give them a little bit of that love they desperately needed, but there were so many of them and she could spare them so little time.

Hammerface laid a heavy hand on Hamish X's shoulder and marched him through the metal door that led to the dormitory. He looked so small. Mrs. Francis bit her lip and wrung her hands, a look of concern in her eyes. Suddenly, she realized Viggo was staring at her.

"Mrs. Francis. Don't you have somewhere to go?" the cheese master demanded.

"Oh. Dinner!" Flustered, Mrs. Francis turned her back on Viggo and hurried up the hall towards the kitchen, where the oatmeal porridge simmered in a vast steel cauldron.

Viggo stood for a moment in the OPR trying to identify a new feeling he was experiencing. When he'd looked into the face of the new boy he'd felt a shiver run up his spine. Finally he concluded that he was probably coming down with a cold. He couldn't possibly be feeling afraid of a boy who couldn't be more than ten years old. He barked a quick, uneasy laugh and stalked off to his personal quarters to get ready for dinner.

Mr. Candy and Mr. Sweet

High above the grey chop of Hudson's Bay, Mr. Candy and Mr. Sweet sped eastward through the night.

"Well Mr. Sweet, I wonder how long the subject will take to escape this time."

"Indeed, Mr. Candy. It should be very interesting to watch."

"Fascinating in fact, Mr. Sweet. We are so close. Shall we return to Providence HQ to monitor his progress?"

"Let's."

Chapter 4

Mrs. Francis hurried into the kitchen, her pudgy torso wrapped in a dingy brown apron stained with the memories of porridges past. She picked up the canoe paddle she used as a spurdle[22] and began to churn the oatmeal, trying to break up the slimiest of the lumps. Mrs. Francis knew the children hated the taste of the porridge passionately, so she did her best to keep it as smooth as possible. At least, she reasoned, the vile food would be easier to swallow.[23]

Feeding one hundred children is a big job, even if the only food you have to prepare is oatmeal. The cauldron Mrs. Francis used was more like a large bathtub than a cooking pot. A gas element burned underneath it, setting the greyish, lumpy mixture to a seething boil.

The cauldron doubled as a serving tureen. Mrs. Francis had only to swing open a pair of metal shutters on the wall above the cauldron to ladle the oatmeal into the bowls of the children who were lining up impatiently. She dipped

---

[22] A spurdle is a tool for stirring porridge. It is a long stick with a thistle-shaped knob at the end. Invented in 1436 by Ian Spurdle, a Scottish farmer, the spurdle was immediately voted the kitchen utensil with the silliest name of all time, easily beating out the spatula, the egg whisk, and the zester.

[23] One might wonder why, if they loathed it so much, the children were served porridge for every meal: all part of Viggo's master plan. Before he opened the orphanage he sponsored a study to find the food children hated most in the entire world. Porridge scored highest, followed closely by cauliflower and dirt. Since oatmeal was slightly cheaper than cauliflower and less expensive to transport than dirt, Viggo chose it as the staple of the children's diet. To put it simply, Viggo was mean.

and doled, dipped and doled the hot goop, all the while keeping an eye out for the new boy.

OUT ON THE FACTORY FLOOR, Mimi leaned her pick against the wall with all the other tools. She joined the mob of children shuffling to the change room. Parveen fell in beside her.

"Ya oughtta keep yer ideas to yerself, Parveen," she said. "Viggo isn't interested in makin' things easier fer us."

Parveen shrugged. "There is no logic to Mr. Viggo's attitude," he said in his softly lilting English. "Certainly, it is in his own interest to increase the levels of production."

"Logic don't enter into it," Mimi drawled. "He's just a mean fellar and mean fellars ain't interested in makin' things better fer anyone, even themselves. Heck, he already makes more money than he knows what to do with! He enjoys makin' us suffer."

They stripped off their face masks and grey overalls, hanging them on hooks that ran the length of the changing room. The stink of the cheese followed them into the room from the factory hall, clinging to their hair and coating their skin. In the hall the stench of the cheese reached dangerous levels, hence the face masks. Exposure to raw Caribou Blue fumes for an extended period was fatal. The smell clung to the children every moment of their waking lives, and even coloured their dreams. Their overalls were cleaned once a week and the masks boiled every other day, but they never lost that wretched stench of the factory.

The two meals they received each day were a respite for the orphans. While the food itself was barely palatable, they were allowed to sit down while they ate. To the children coming off shift who'd been on their feet all day, sitting down was like a holiday. They trudged into the cafeteria, picking up a bowl from the stack by the door and shuffling into line in front of the hole in the wall where Mrs. Francis ladled out the oatmeal gruel with a splash of whey that was their nightly ration.

The cafeteria[24] was a place to steal the last warmth out of any beleaguered soul. It was furnished with battered aluminum benches and tables, scuffed and gouged by continuous use. The walls were painted pink, but not a happy pink. No, this pink was not the pink of delicate wildflowers in a waving sea of prairie grass or the glorious pink of a summer sunset after a cool rain. No, the pink Viggo chose to coat the walls of the orphanage cafeteria was the pink of slimy creatures that live under rocks and never see sunlight, or the pink found on the inside of an ailing goat's intestine.[25] Guards stood in the four corners of the room to make sure none of the children made any trouble.

Mimi glared at the guard who stood by the door. Three more guards worked in the factory itself. She'd tangled with all of them, singly and in groups. Mimi had regular run-ins with the powers that be, but usually in reaction to some cruelty or other the guards perpetrated on the orphans. Parveen was a favourite target for humiliation. The guard answered her glare by shifting his gaze to his left shoe. Mimi wasn't worth provoking.

---

[24] *Cafeteria* is an ancient Greek word meaning "food cemetery." The Ancient Greeks had a special temple in each of their cities where horrible, bland, or disgusting food was taken to be buried. In later centuries, the Romans mistook these food cemeteries for restaurants, digging up the discarded food and helping themselves. The modern cafeteria has its origin in this Roman misunderstanding.

[25] The author was invited to tour a goat's intestine one weekend at the Goat Enthusiasts Convention, so he knows what he's talking about. One might question how a human might fit into a goat's intestine, but let the reader be assured that the goat in question was freakishly large and the author, extremely flexible.

Mimi's stomach rumbled as she picked up her bowl. She handed one to Parveen and they took their place in the line. She was so exhausted she almost didn't notice the boy in front of her in the queue. What drew her attention to him was the whistling. A happy sound like whistling was totally out of place in the Windcity Orphanage and Cheese Factory. He wore new overalls, meaning he was a new inductee.

"Hey!" Mimi poked the boy in the shoulder.

The boy stopped whistling but didn't turn.

"Who are you?" Mimi asked. "I ain't seen you around before."

"Mind your own business, lady."

"Who are you callin' lady?"

The boy turned around and looked at her, up and down. His eyes were strange, golden like no eyes she'd ever seen.

"My mistake," he said, frowning. "You aren't a lady. In fact, I'm not even sure you're a girl." He smiled at her sweetly.

Mimi planted her fists on her hips and stuck out her chin. "Are you tryin' to make fun of me?"

"I'm not trying," the boy said, squaring up to her even though she stood a few inches taller, "I *am* making fun of you."

All the children in line gasped. Quick as a wink, the boy and Mimi stood alone in the centre of a circle of empty floor. Every eye in the cafeteria was glued to them. Hamish X looked around at the crowd of children with their faded grey faces and faded grey overalls. Then he turned back to the tall, raw-boned girl standing in front of him. He cocked his head to one side, studying her.

Here's what he saw. Mimi was quite tall for a girl her age. She stood just over five feet and was thin as a fence post. And just like a fence post, one would certainly feel it if you ran up against her. Her skin was pale and her hair was black as coal, curly, and profuse, sticking out like a wiry cloud around her head. She had a sharp face with a hatchet for a nose that looked like it had been broken at least once. Not that she wasn't pretty ... Well, maybe she wasn't exactly pretty, but there was something handsome about her face: there was strength in her brilliant green eyes.

The tension in the room was as thick as the porridge in Mrs. Francis's cauldron. All four guards leered happily. They loved to watch a fight. Even more, they loved to punish those involved.

Mimi and the boy stared at each other for a few long seconds. Finally Mimi spoke.

"What's your name?" she asked in a dangerously soft voice. "So's I know who it is I'm beatin' on."

The boy stepped back and straightened his new overalls, ran his fingers through his hair, and smiled. "The French call me L'Orphan des Bottes. The Germans call me Der Wunderknabe mit die Grosse Schwartze Schuhwaren. The Chinese call me Golden-Eyed Booted Devil Child. The Russians, Rot Kid. In Spain, I'm known as El Niño con Grandes Botas Negras. In Australia, they call me Greg."[26] The boy stopped and looked straight at Mimi. "But my mother called me Hamish. Hamish X!"

The guards scowled and Mrs. Francis dropped her ladle into the porridge. A collective gasp went up from the children. "Hamish X?"

"He escaped from Orphan Island by building a raft out of inflated underpants," one child whispered.

"He defeated the Emperor of Mongolia in a two-day ankle-wrestling match," whispered another.

[26] The Australians have always been odd.

"He climbed Mount Everest and danced with the Yeti's mom!" squealed yet another.

Parveen cocked his head to one side and looked at the new boy with frank curiosity. "Hamish X? But ... how could that be?"

A flicker of uncertainty danced across Mimi's face, but she held her ground. "You're Hamish X?"

"Yes. You still want to fight me?"

Mimi sneered. "I ain't got nothin' better to do."

Parveen reached up and held her arm.

"It's not worth it," he said. "Let it go."

Mimi shook him off and glared at Hamish X.

"Now that the introductions is over," she snarled, "let's dance!" She launched herself at her opponent.

Though she lashed out as quickly as a viper, Hamish X ducked easily under her. He rolled neatly through her legs, stood up behind her, and gently tapped the back of her knee with his boot. Mimi's leg folded and she stumbled to her hands and knees.

Furious, Mimi leapt to her feet. She whirled around to find Hamish X standing, arms folded, looking smug. "Nice try! I've trained under some of the finest martial artists in the world. I've studied kung fu with the Xaing Xuo Monks of Ti Twa!"[27]

"I ain't been trained by monkeys," Mimi gritted, "but I kick like a mule."

Mimi kicked out at his belly. He caught her foot with his free hand and turned it, dumping her onto her face on the floor.

---

[27] The Xaing Xuo Monks of Ti Twa were famous throughout China for their technique of diving through the legs of their attackers and kicking their enemies in the buttocks. A gang of one-legged ninjas eventually defeated them.

The children were shouting and cheering now. They all wanted Mimi to teach the new boy who was boss.

"Oh dear!" Mrs. Francis was looking out through the serving hutch. She covered her hand with her mouth. While she didn't want to get the children into trouble, she also couldn't bear the thought of them hurting each other. She ran off to find Mr. Viggo.

Mimi was up again. She brushed the dirt off her overalls and glared at Hamish.

"Now tell me *your* name and we'll just call this a draw," Hamish said.

Mimi snarled and dove for Hamish's feet. He leapt forward, tucked into a ball and tumbled, landing easily on his feet as Mimi skidded across the floor on her belly. Scattered applause greeted Hamish's landing.

"I studied tumbling with the Flying Crimini Brothers in Italy,"[28] Hamish said to the crowd by way of explaining his last manoeuvre. "They asked me to join their troupe, but I got bored with the circus. Too many clowns."

He wheeled around and ducked a roundhouse kick from Mimi, who had crept up for another attempt. Mimi's momentum swung her around so that she faced away from Hamish. He grabbed a handful of her overalls and, falling backwards, flipped her over his feet so that she fell flat on her face again. Hamish bounced to his feet once more.

---

[28] The Flying Crimini Brothers toured the world with their amazing somersault show. The act broke up after Tony, the experimentalist in the group, attempted to do a somersault with his body formed into a triangle rather than a circle. He ended up stabbing two of his brothers so badly they were forced to leave show business.

"Judo—I picked it up from a guy in Mexico.[29] Not really appropriate culturally, I know, but there you are!"

Mimi pushed herself up onto her hands and sucked at the air. She'd had the wind knocked out of her. Raising her head slowly, she looked at Hamish.

"So," Hamish said sweetly, "will you just tell me your name and we can put all this nastiness behind us?"

Mimi gritted her teeth and staggered to her feet. She was about to launch herself at Hamish again when a voice piped up.

"Mimi!"

Mimi froze and turned to glare at someone in the crowd. Hamish followed her gaze to find Parveen. "Her name is Mimi." Parveen pushed his thick glasses back up his nose.

"What's going on here?" Viggo's voice barked out. Hamish and all the other children turned their heads to see Viggo marching through the swinging doors at the end of the cafeteria. Mrs. Francis trailed after him, a worried expression on her face.

"Ah, Mr. Viggo!" Hamish X said brightly. "We were just demonstrating some new calisthenics for the rest of the kids. Right, Mi—oof!"

Mimi took advantage of the distraction provided by Viggo's arrival to plant a haymaker into the side of Hamish's head. The blow struck him directly on the temple. His eyes rolled back and his entire body stiffened. Then he fell like a tree under a lumberjack's axe, slamming full-length to the floor at Mimi's feet.

"Yeah," she huffed. "What he said."

---

[29] Hamish's reference to a Mexican judo master is puzzling. Perhaps he is referring to Taco Takana, a half-Mexican, half-Japanese martial artist rumoured to wrestle under the stage name "Spicy Tuna" in the Mexican Wrestling Federation.

Chapter 5

Hamish awoke to find himself spinning in the wind. A harness similar to one a skydiver might wear was hooked to a rope which was in turn fastened to the edge of the factory roof.

"Enjoy the view," a harsh voice called. The voice belonged to one of two guards standing on the roof, pointing and laughing. One of the guards was Pianoface. His face looked as though someone had dropped a piano on it. He was only marginally uglier than his companion, however, whose face looked as though it had merely been beaten with a tuba. He was affectionately known as Tubaface.

"You and your girlfriend have a pleasant evening," Tubaface shouted.

"He ain't my boyfriend!" Hamish X focused as best he could and saw that he was not alone. Mimi was dangling in the wind beside him. "When I git down from here, y'all are gonna be sorry!"

The two guards howled with laughter. "In't that a fine pair of kites!" crowed Pianoface.

"Fine indeed," cackled Tubaface, slapping his knee. "Grand night for a kite flight."

Pianoface stopped laughing, a sudden look of wonder coming over his ugly visage. "Tubaface! That's poetry," he said. The two guards looked at each other for a moment then turned and went through the door, closing it behind them.

Hamish X and Mimi whirled on the end of their tethers at the mercy of the gusts.

"There ain't nuthin' worse than bein' dangled. Nothing!" Mimi cursed.

Windcity, as pointed out earlier, is windy. Extremely so. There is no place on earth that is more reliably consistent in its windiness. On any given day, at any given moment, one could say, "I bet it's windy in Windcity." No one

would take the bet.[30] Therefore, it's only natural that Viggo would devise a punishment that took advantage of this fact.

Hamish X and Mimi spun at the end of their tethers, whirling at the mercy of the blasting gale. The effect was quite disorienting. Hamish clenched his teeth and stifled the nausea he felt rising in his stomach. He stuck out his arms and discovered that he could influence his spin by angling his appendages. After experimenting for a few moments, he found that he could stop his spinning altogether. In fact, he could remain upright. He hung, spread-eagled, at the end of his rope. Beneath his feet the earth was fifteen metres down, dusted in drifting snow. He looked to his right and saw Mimi in the identical posture looking back at him.

"Well, ain't this a treat," Mimi declared. "It would be quite a view. Too bad there ain't nothin' to see!"

Hamish X agreed. The town of Windcity looked miserable from ground level. From the sky, it looked more desolate still. The houses, empty and dark, teetered in the wind on the verge of collapse. Hudson's Bay, grey and ice-strewn, stretched out to the eastern horizon.The sun hung low in the west, painting the sky red, but it wasn't a warm, comforting red. Rather, the sky looked inflamed

---

[30] The exception always proves the rule, however. The wind actually stopped for twelve minutes and fifty-eight seconds on June 3, 1963. The results were devastating. Everyone in town fell over due to the lack of wind resistance. For twelve minutes, there was no wind at all. People suddenly realized they'd been yelling at the top of their lungs their whole lives up to that point. People also became aware of how curly their hair was now that it wasn't being blown straight out behind them. Several people rushed to the hairdressers but cancelled their appointments when the wind started blowing again.

and sore, like a dirty wound. Lights shone from the guard shack on the wharf. A cargo boat bobbed and heaved at anchor in the harbour. To the north and west, flat, barren tundra spread out as far as the eye could see.

"Well, I guess I owe ya an apology," Mimi said.

"Why?"

"It's my fault we's stuck up here."

"Not at all. Anyway, I had no other plans for this evening."

Mimi laughed. She looked at her companion and shivered in the cold and at the memory of his strange reaction to the punch. "I never thought I'd meet the great Hamish X."

Hamish X laughed. "I never thought you would either. You're just lucky I guess."

"You think pretty highly of yerself."

"If I don't, who will?" he grinned. "I never thought I'd meet you either, but I'm glad I did."

They hung quietly for a while. Hamish X broke the silence. "How long are we going to be up here?"

"Couple hours," Mimi said. "Maybe till mornin'. Depends on how mean Viggo's feelin', which is usually pretty darn mean."

Again they hung quietly for a while, listening to the wind whistle through the lines. Again, Hamish X broke the silence.

"How about we start again as if we never met?"

"Sounds good."

"My name is Hamish X."

"Mimi Catastrophe Jones."

"Catastrophe?" Hamish laughed. "Your parents named you Catastrophe?"

"Yeah," Mimi said sheepishly. "They just liked the

sound of it is all."

"It's a Greek word."

"How do ya know that?"

"I don't know. I guess I learned it somewhere. Hmm. Catastrophe ... It suits you," Hamish nodded. "Anyone with a left hook like that ought to be called Catastrophe."

Mimi tried to hide her delight. "That's the nicest thing anybody ever said to me. Apart from my daddy, that is." She frowned.

"You remember your dad?" Hamish asked. His strange eyes stared at her with a yearning, hungry look. "I don't remember my mother at all. I know I have one and that she loved me, but I don't have a clear memory of what she looks like. I envy you. I just know I have to find her."

"Sometimes I wish I didn't remember nothin', y'know? I wish I didn't have that sore place in my heart all the time. It might be a sight easier to stand livin' here if I never knew nothin' better existed."

"Never say that," Hamish X said gently. "Tell me about your dad."

Mimi went quiet for a while. Then she looked over at Hamish X. His eyes were focused so intensely on her, so strange. They seemed almost luminous in the darkness. "I never told nobody my story before," Mimi said, "'ceptin' Parveen. And he don't count."

"I'll make you a deal. You tell yours and I'll tell mine as best I can." Hamish shivered in the frigid wind. "It'll take our minds off the cold."

Mimi was quiet for a moment longer. Then, as the sun went down, she told Hamish X her story.

Chapter 6

MIMI'S STORY

I was born in a little town called Cross Plains, Texas. Cross Plains is barely a bump in the road. You'd hardly slow down if yah drove through. There ain't a stoplight or stop sign and if there were you'd be tempted to run right through it. That's how miserable the town o' Cross Plains is. Tornados loved it though on account of all the trailer parks in the vicinity. Trailers seem ta draw tornados like honey draws ants. My daddy swore we'd never live in a trailer. We'd be sittin' on the front porch after a dinner of boiled water and ketchup and he'd say, "No matter how lowly our house may be, at least we ain't livin' in no trailer. 'Cause if you're livin' in a trailer, you're neither here nor there. It ain't a house and it ain't a home."

We lived in a little house, a bit run down but Momma made it pretty. My daddy were a proud man. He worked ever' day to make sure me and Momma had sumthin' ta eat, even if it were only ketchup and boiled water. He could tell stories and they would make ya laugh so hard that you'd ferget about any problem you had or the rumble in yer stomach.

He did odd jobs as a handyman, tryin' to make ends meet. When he was younger, he played baseball in the minor leagues. He was a pitcher. He'd take me out after he came home from workin' and we'd throw the ball in the field out back the house. He taught me how to make the ball dance and swerve like it was on a string. He said I was a natural. That was just the best time, throwin' the ball until it were too dark to see it no more.

My momma was a very beautiful woman and smart as a whip. She went to college and everything. She knew lots o' stuff. She got a degree and she learnt to be a teacher. That's how she met my daddy. He was workin' at the school fixin' a leaky sink and they got to talkin'. Before long, he'd charmed her so much she agreed to go out for a date with him. A year later they was married. Then I come along. With Momma's teachin' and Daddy's handyman work we made it okay. I don't remember her face too well. I were only young when she died. But I remember her smile and the feel of her hands when she put me to bed.

Things started to go bad after my fourth birthday. Momma lost her job. She was teachin' at the local school until it was stolen one night. I ain't kiddin'! The school was one o' them portables, and durin' one dark night some jokers hooked it to a truck and hauled 'er off. That's how desperate poor people were.

So, my momma had no place to teach. That meant we had to make do on just the money my daddy could make. Daddy knew he needed to find a way to make more money so's we could live a good life. He hit upon an idea. He'd breed tapirs.

He mortgaged our little house and bought a little farm to breed these animals. Now tapirs is a strange little animal that comes from South America.[31] My daddy thought they was cute and I suppose they was. They had little hoofs like

---

[31] Tapirs are indeed an endangered species. They inhabit wet, swampy areas in South America. Tapirs are not lovable to look at. In fact, they were voted least lovable of all endangered mammals in an independently conducted poll in 2002.

a mini-aycher horse but they's got a silly long nose that they dig in the ground for roots and things. They's an endangered species from the jungle and their only natural predator is the jaguar.

My daddy thought they'd be worth a load o' money on account o' them bein' so rare. He took every last cent we had and bought four breedin' pairs. He flooded most of our farmland so they could frolic around in the swampy ground, which were their natural habitat.

The one problem with the plan my daddy had was that he had no idea who we was gonna sell the tapirs to. They just kept breedin' and breedin', growin' and growin' until there was hundreds of the gosh darn things. We couldn't afford to feed the blamed things any more. Without jaguars to keep the numbers down they were reproducin' like mad. It was only a matter of time before somethin' bad happened.

One day, there was a thunderstorm and the lightnin' was blastin' somethin' awful. We were huddled in the kitchen lookin' out at the storm. I remember it real clear. The sky just seemed to turn all purple with clouds and then it happened: a tornado come to Cross Plains. My daddy said that tornados is a long finger of the devil stirrin' and scrapin' at God's creation. The funnel walked through the farm suckin' up anything in its path and flingin' it hither and yon. And as it moved across our farm, headin' straight for our little house, it picked up hundreds of the poor little tapirs.

My momma told us all to go down into the storm cellar. She went to get some candles in the kitchen drawer but she never made it. The papers called it the strangest fatality on record. Hundreds of tapirs rained down, squealin' like demons, crashin' through the windows and ceiling. She never even saw it comin' and I don't think she felt any pain.[32]

O' course my father blamed hisself for the tragedy. He spent most of his days drinkin' beer and cursin' tapirs. He was kind to me though. The bank repossessed the farm and we was forced to live with my dad's sister, my Aunt Jean. She were mean. It weren't very imaginative but I called her Mean Jean. Mainly 'cause it rhymed. Worse than that ... she lived in a trailer. A brown one, too. Brown as a cow pat.

Aunt Jean weren't too fond of me. Said I was too boyish a girl by half. Tried to make me wear dresses but I tore 'em up. They smelled funny anyway. She made me wear clothes she got from her work. She worked in the local funeral parlour and she got to keep all the clothes the dead people were wearin' when they come in. Mostly they was old ladies' clothes and they didn't fit worth a darn. All the other kids at the school would laugh at me and I was forced to make 'em stop with my fists. I got pretty good, I reckon.

I tried to tell my daddy how mean Aunt Jean were but it was like he weren't really there any more. My father tried his best to get work where he could, sweepin' out barrooms and washin' the toilets and such. I could tell he was real sad about Momma.

---

[32] The Day of Raining Tapirs is documented in several sources, including the *Austin Telegraph*. Tapirs fell as far away as Clearwater and one even fell through the roof of the Holiday Inn in Tucson, Arizona, hundreds of kilometres away. Fortunately, that lucky tapir broke through the ceiling of the swimming pool and the water broke his fall. He was adopted by the hotel as its mascot and was given the appropriate name "Lucky."

Money was very short and things were gettin' very dire when my father come to me one day to tell me he had the offer of a job. I'd just come home from school and I'd had a fight. My lip was bleedin' and I had a black eye but I gave better 'n I got, truth be told. My daddy sat me down at the kitchen table to tell me he'd been accepted to work on an oil rig in the Caspian Sea. That's somewheres in Russia. The money was good but he'd be gone fer a while. He'd send money home and when he had a place he'd send fer me, but until that time Aunt Jean would be takin' care o' me. I cried all night, I don't mind admittin' that. He left the next day. He told me to be good and work on my slider.

I did my best to get along with Aunt Jean, but she were an ornery cuss of a woman. I was certain she was takin' all the money my daddy sent home and keepin' it fer herself but she swore she never got a cent from my "good fer nuthin" daddy. She never let me get the mail from the mailbox at the end of the lane so I couldn't be shore if she was lyin' or not.

To make a long story short, a letter came one day with bad news. It were from the oil company my daddy got hired on with. The letter said he'd been lost in a storm, swept off the rig in the darkest part o' the night. There was nothing left of him. Just like that, I were all alone in the world. All I have to remember him is a picture of me and my momma and him, smilin' on the back porch in the sunshine. And his baseball mitt. I keep 'em under my bunk.

As soon as Mean Jean found out I was orphaned, she couldn't get me outta her life quick enough. The very next day she called a number and the ODA come and carted me off. I ended up here. And that's just about the whole sorry tale.

Chapter 7

Mimi finished her story as the sun finally plunged behind the rim of the tundra. It seemed that the sun itself had decided that the story was too sad to bear and hid its face behind the earth.

"How long have you been here?" Hamish X asked.

"Seven long years," Mimi said.

"Have you tried to escape?"

"Escape to where? There ain't nowhere to go. The nearest town is nine hunnert kilometres away over barren wastes. If the cold don't get ya, the giant polar bears will. Or the wolves.[33] I imagine some orphan meat would make a fine change from the seal they're used to."

Hamish was silent as he thought for a moment. "What about a boat? The harbour?"

"Ya ain't gonna have any joy there. There's savage dogs and the guard at the dock is the meanest of 'em all. Got a face that looks like somebody dropped a forklift truck on it. We call 'im—"

"Forkliftface?"

"How'd ya guess? Anyhoo, he carries the key in his pocket all the time." Mimi shook her shaggy head. "Might as well resign yerself to a long stay in Windcity Orphanage makin' cheese fer Viggo. I only hope I can hold out two more years till I turn fourteen. Then I hope I can go back to Cross Plains and whup old Mean Jean." Mimi smiled

[33] Or the Arctic foxes, as mentioned earlier.

fiercely at that thought, her features barely visible in the fading light.

"What if you can't stick it out that long?"

"Oh, I will. There ain't no other choice. Some kids crack and they get taken away by the grey agents, them ODA folks. They's never heard of agin. I don't know what happens to 'em but I bet they just dump 'em on the street somewheres to fend fer themselves. I'll make it two more years. I shore will."

They hung in silence for a moment, thinking about years and how long they could be. "What about you?" Mimi asked suddenly. "You gotta tell your story now. Only fair."

"I'd really like to tell you my story but ..."

"But nothin'," Mimi said. "You gotta tell!"

"It's not that I don't want to. I wish I had a story to tell," Hamish X said. "I don't know where I come from or where I've been. I know one thing though ... I have to find Mother. I have to find her. I know she's out there waiting for me."

"Yeah, ya said that before." Mimi shook her head. "Yer like a broken record."

"I'm sorry. I don't mean to ..."

He faltered when he saw a light down below him. In the darkness it bobbed along the flat roof, coming closer to where the lines holding the kites were moored. As the source of the light approached Hamish and Mimi could make out Parveen's face in the glow cast by a lamp strapped to his head. He was carrying a bucket. When he reached the mooring lines he looked up at Mimi and Hamish, his round glasses glinting in the glare of his headlamp.

"Hello," he waved. "My name is Parveen."

"I'm Hamish X," Hamish X answered with a wave.

"Right. So you say." Parveen raised a critical eyebrow. Then he raised his hand to show a steaming bucket. "I have brought you some dinner."

"How did ya manage to get up here?" Mimi asked.

"Mrs. Francis was worried, so she sneaked out some food for you." Parveen set the bucket down. And pulled two bowls out of his baggy overalls pocket. Two spoons followed the bowls. "The guards were asleep, so getting up here was no problem. Mrs. Francis used her keycard on the locks. She says to tell you she's sorry for reporting you to Master Viggo, but she was most concerned that you might injure each other."

"I appreciate your effort Parveen, and the kindness of Mrs. Francis," said Hamish, tugging at his tether, "but we're a bit tied up."

"Leave it to me," Parveen called. He set the bowls down and rummaged in his pockets again. From several pockets, small and large, he produced little bits of metal, hooks, and pieces of wood.

"What's he doing?" Hamish asked Mimi.

"He does this sorta thing all the time," she answered. "He's good with his hands."

A few minutes later, Parveen stood up. In each hand he held a strange object: a boxlike frame of sticks with a hook sticking out of the top. Each one had a little sail made out of knotted handkerchiefs. He took the bowls and laid each one into a frame where it fit snugly. That done, he tipped the bucket of steaming porridge, filling first one bowl, then the other. He stuck a spoon into each bowl, lifted them by the hooks, and placed the hooks over the tethers holding Mimi and Hamish in place.

Immediately, the handkerchief billowed out like a sail in the wind and the frame carrying the bowl shot up the tether into Mimi's and Hamish X's waiting hands.

"Would you look at that," Hamish X exclaimed.

"Like I told ya," Mimi said. "He's good with his hands."

"Thanks!" she called and hungrily tucked into the porridge.

"Thanks," Hamish called.

Parveen pushed his glasses up on his nose with his index finger and looked at Hamish X. Suddenly, he asked, "How old are you?"

Hamish X shrugged, almost spinning out of control. "I ... don't really know."

Parveen stared at Hamish X for a little longer. At last, he picked up the bucket and headed for the door.

"Wait," shouted Mimi. "What should we do with the bowls when we're done?"

Parveen flapped his hand dismissively. "Just let go of them and the wind will do the rest." Then he disappeared through the doorway.

Hamish and Mimi ate their porridge as they dangled in the howling wind, warmer and happier than they'd expected to be. When the porridge was gone, they tossed the bowls with their ingenious frames into the wind. The wind whisked the bowls up and out of sight in an instant.

"Clever," said Hamish.

"Too right," said Mimi.

Hamish watched the bowls disappear into the darkness. "I wonder ..." he mused.

"Wonder what?" Mimi demanded.

"Oh, nothing," he smiled at her.

"It's your turn," Mimi said.

"My turn?" Hamish was confused.

"What's your story?"

Hamish X shook his head. "Aw, you don't wanna hear about me. It isn't that interesting."

"Are you kiddin' me? You've been everywhere! Done everythin'!"

"I guess. It doesn't seem so big a deal to me. I'll tell you one thing for sure, though."

"What's that?"

"There isn't an orphanage that can hold me. I always escape."

"Always?"

"Always."

The door to the roof opened, interrupting their conversation. Light from electric lanterns played across them. Pianoface and Tubaface shambled to the edge of the roof. They looked as if they'd just woken up.

"Cold enough fer ya?" Pianoface yawned and they both laughed.

"It's exactly cold enough, thanks," Hamish X called.

"You're a weirdo," Pianoface answered.

"A weirdo with big boots," Tubaface chimed in. They grabbed a line each and started hauling the danglers in.

Prodded by the guards, they staggered down the steps back towards the dormitory. Hamish and Mimi were cold and miserable, but at least they hadn't missed their dinner. Mimi was looking forward to flopping onto her cot and sleeping. She looked at her companion. He had been awake and alert up on the roof but now he seemed exhausted, his eyes half-closed under heavy lids. He was having trouble keeping up with Mimi and kept lagging behind. Every few steps he staggered and the guard had to haul him to his feet again.

They came to the door that led to the cafeteria and dormitory: the secure section of the complex that housed the children. The door was made of dull grey metal, thick and heavy. Pianoface pushed it open easily.

"Get in!" Pianoface barked. With one meaty hand, he shoved Mimi so hard that she sprawled on her face on the cafeteria's linoleum floor.

Hamish X didn't look good. He swayed on his feet. His mouth hung open, loose and slack. His eyes were barely open.

"You, too!" The guard reached for Hamish X.

Suddenly, Hamish X vomited a gout of porridge all over Pianoface's front and slumped against Tubaface, clutching at his uniform.

"Aaaaggh," Pianoface squawked. "He's puked on me."

"Get off me!" shouted Tubaface. He pushed Hamish so that he fell headlong into the cafeteria, lifeless and limp. Then he hauled out his Ticklestick and advanced on Hamish X. Mimi leapt to her feet. Fists clenched, she stepped into the guard's path, standing over Hamish's prone body.

"Leave him alone," she snarled.

"Gad!" Pianoface interjected, holding his vomit-soaked shirt away from his skin in disgust. "Let's just get back to barracks so I can get cleaned up."

Tubaface faltered. He held Mimi's gaze a moment longer, then tucked the weapon back into his belt. To tell the truth, he was glad of an excuse to avoid a tussle with the terrifying girl in front of him.

"Let's get outta here. There's a poker game tonight."

"Let's go then." They stepped back through the door and pulled it closed.

"Do you think he has rabies or something?" Mimi heard as the door slammed.

Mimi squatted down beside Hamish X lying motionless

on the floor. She gently turned him over. His eyes were closed. She laid a hand on his forehead, just as she remembered her mother doing when she was sick in her bed in Cross Plains.

"Are they gone?" Hamish X asked.

Mimi jerked her hand back. Hamish X opened one eye.

"Are they gone?" he asked again.

"Yeah." Mimi watched in astonishment as the boy vaulted nimbly to his feet, his illness seemingly vanished as suddenly as it had come.

"You were fakin'?" She was awestruck.

"Of course," he laughed. "Puking on command can come in handy. Fakirs[34] do it in Nepalese markets. I remember I saw it once."

"You can puke on command?" Mimi asked.

Hamish nodded. "It's not that difficult. I can teach you how if you like."

"But ..." Mimi grabbed Hamish X's arm. "Why?"

"I needed a distraction," he said, "so I could grab this."

As if by magic, a plastic security keycard appeared in his hand. Mimi stared in disbelief. "That card opens all the doors. We can escape!" She clapped her hands in delight. "We're as good as out of here." Her delight turned to dismay. "They'll miss the card though. Pianoface will report it lost and they'll change the locks."

Hamish X shook his head. "You underestimate the stupidity of the guards and their fear of Viggo. Would you like to report to your boss that you've lost the key

---

[34] Fakirs are performers after a fashion. They do things that are seemingly impossible, like lying on beds of nails, swallowing swords, or enjoying spinach. There is usually some sort of trick, some sleight of hand. The word "fake" finds its origin in the work of fakirs.

to the prison? These men are big, strong, and ugly too, but they're cowards. I think we can assume they won't report the missing card." He tucked it into the top of his right boot.

"This way." Mimi jerked her head towards the far end of the cafeteria. In one wall a swinging metal door led to the factory floor where the sounds of the night shift drifted through. Mimi led Hamish X to another door on the opposite wall that led to the dormitory.

They walked through the quiet common room, a tiny, cramped space with some rickety chairs and a wobbly table, and into the sleeping quarters. Rows of dark shadows marked the cots holding the sleeping day-shift children. They passed Parveen snoring softly in his narrow bed, his glasses still on, a pencil behind his ear. A little mound of news magazines rose and fell on his chest in time with his breathing. Hamish X watched as Mimi stopped and gently lifted the glasses off, folding them and tucking them under Parveen's pillow. The little boy stirred and mumbled then went back to sleep.

"G'night, Hamish X." Mimi lay down on the next cot. Hamish X dropped down onto his stiff mattress, boots and all. He was asleep almost as soon as his head hit the pillow.

Piratical Interlude

The Roquefort Castle stood in a picturesque valley in the heart of the French Alps. For centuries, the castle was the centre of production for one of the world's most treasured cheeses: Roquefort. The pale white cheese, marbled with veins of mould found only in the caves that dotted the mountainsides, had long been a source of wealth for the Countess de Roquefort and her family. The castle represented the living history of the family and its fortunes. And now the castle was in flames.

The Comptesse[35] de Roquefort, her expensive nightgown from a fashion atelier in Milan spattered with mud and soot, knelt in the rain watching her home burn brightly despite the cold drizzle falling from the night sky. All the work she and her family had accomplished gone in one night. She covered her face with her hands and wept.

---

[35] *Comptesse* is the French word for Countess. The French tend to have a different word for almost everything. The title of Count/Countess originates in the ancient past when their largely uneducated neighbours held people who had learned to count in high esteem. "Counters" were given positions of responsibility in the community, eventually forming a powerful ruling class or aristocracy. The title was shortened over the years from "Counter/Counteress" to "Count/Countess." Counting became less and less important as a qualifying skill for becoming a Count. Many Counts and Countesses today are unable to count at all.

All around, pirates roared with laughter at her misery.

"Quiet!" The command brought instant silence.

"Are you animals?" growled a menacing voice. "That's no way to treat a lady."

"Sorry," some in the group muttered sheepishly. "Got carried away."

The Comptesse raised her face from her hands and saw the owner of the commanding voice.

He was tall and broad in the shoulders, outlined against the firelight in silhouette. She couldn't make out his facial features, but a broad-brimmed hat framed his head with a bedraggled ostrich feather sticking out of it. He exuded menace and the rank stench of rancid dairy products. The source of the stench was the thick, matted beard that hung stiffly from his chin, covering his chest completely. The beard was solid with melted cheese, glistening and greasy.

The Comptesse screamed, "Who are you? Why are you here? What do you want of me?" She began to weep again.

The shadowy man cocked his head towards her.

"To answer your questions in the order they were presented," he began. He held up a finger. "One: we are Cheese Pirates." He held up a second finger. "Two: we are here for your cheese." He held up a third finger that was missing its tip, ending in a scarred knob at the first knuckle. "Three," he said, "we want you to come with us."

Hoots of laughter went up from all the pirates. The Comptesse screamed herself hoarse. A shadow blocked out the stars. She stopped screaming long enough to see that something huge obscured the moon and the few stars peeking through the clouds. She heard the thrum of engines.

Chapter 8

The next morning, the klaxon sounded at seven. The lights came on, long racks of heartless fluorescent tubes flickering to life. The light of a fluorescent bulb is specially designed to discourage optimism and dampen the spirits of children,[36] and these lights excelled at their allotted task.

When Mimi woke up she found that Hamish was already dressed. He wore his new pair of overalls but still had the same huge boots on. The cuffs of the overalls had been cut along the seams to accommodate the boots. He sat on his cot, rucksack plunked down on the floor at his feet. A huge book rested on his knees. He was poring through the pages with intense concentration, his golden eyes flicking back and forth.

Mimi was feeling a bit tired from all the dangling the night before. She propped herself up on one elbow and looked at Hamish X's boots. They were marvellously smooth and shiny. Hamish X sensed Mimi looking at him.

"Good morning, Mimi." Hamish X smiled.

---

[36] Fluorescent lights were invented by a crabby elementary school vice-principal in Yugoslavia. The children in his school were rambunctious, joyous, and lively; a combination that inspires envy and jealousy in all elementary school vice-principals. The lights were so effective in dulling the minds and spirits of the children that they were soon installed in gymnasiums, classrooms, and public buildings all around the world. The crabby vice-principal from Yugoslavia became incredibly wealthy on the royalties from the sale of his invention and now lives in a giant fluorescent tube outside Sarajevo.

"Nothin' particularly good about it," Mimi grumbled sleepily. "Just don't puke on me."

Parveen returned from the common room. He spent a lot of time there studying whatever reading material he could get. Mrs. Francis saw that he got all of Viggo's discarded magazines and newspapers as well as whatever used books she could find. She also made sure scraps of paper and pencils found their way into Parveen's hands. He currently carried a wad of scrap paper. Seeing Mimi and Hamish X awake, he tucked his pencil back behind his right ear. "Hello," Parveen said. "Did the bowl kites function as I intended?"

"Perfectly." Hamish X slapped Parveen on the back heartily. The little boy winced.

"The porridge was a bit of a waste though," Mimi laughed.

She described the scene at the door to the cafeteria in detail. Parveen listened in silence to the tale. When it was finished, he turned to Hamish X.

"Voluntary projectile reverse peristalsis," he said. "Fascinating."

"Messy, too," Mimi laughed again.

"You stole a keycard," Parveen said, his brow creased in a serious expression much too old for his little brown face. "Such actions are extremely dangerous. They can lead to a lot of trouble."

"Borrowed," Hamish X corrected. "Dangerous but necessary."

Parveen immediately stepped closer to examine the book on Hamish X's lap, leaning closer to read the title.

"*Great Plumbers and Their Exploits?*"[37]

"My mother left it with me," Hamish explained. "I read from it every day. I'm sure my mother hid a message for me in it somewhere. If I can just figure it out, I'll be able to find her one day."

"Your mother?" Mimi said. "I thought you was an orphan."

"Only for the purpose of official classification," Hamish said breezily. "She was forced to leave me at an

---

[37] Don't bother trying to find this book. It has been out of print for over fifty years and with good reason: it is the most boring book of all time. Not to disparage the work of plumbers. Indeed, plumbing is a noble profession practised by noble folk. Regardless, *Great Plumbers and Their Exploits* is a giant, thick tome that has little charm unless you are a plumber, and even then the book is written in such a laborious, dull, mind-numbing style as to challenge even the most dedicated reader to stay awake for more than a chapter. The book is best used to hold open large doors or to open walnuts. Some of the pictures are nice, though. It was published in Providence, Rhode Island, and had a print run of exactly twenty-three. Strangely, the ODA's headquarters are located in Providence, Rhode Island, and some might point out a possible connection between the two. Some might.

orphanage but she left me the book as a clue to where I would find her."

"Well, I don't mean to be the squirrel in the peanut butter, but if she's still out there somewheres, why doesn't *she* come and find *you*?" Mimi asked.

Hamish X's face darkened and his strange eyes flashed. "Because she can't. I have to find her! That's the way it has to be!" he snapped.

Mimi flinched. "Whatever you say! Don't get yerself in a lather!"

As quickly as his anger came, it went away again. Hamish X smiled sheepishly. "I'm sorry. I'm a little sensitive about Mother."

"Well, how come you haven't managed to crack the code? In all these years?"

"If it was easy to crack, it would hardly be a secret code, would it?"

Mimi had no answer to that.

Parveen bent over the book, examining it minutely through his thick glasses. He looked at Hamish.

"May I?" he asked.

Hamish X narrowed his eyes and clutched the book tightly. Parveen held out his open hands. "I promise I'll give it right back." Hamish X hesitated a moment longer, then handed the book to Parveen.

Parveen ran his hands over the cover. The book was bound in leather and inlaid with gold leaf. It would have been very valuable had its subject not been so obviously boring. Parveen carefully opened the cover and flipped through the pages. There were diagrams and black ink illustrations throughout. The print was fine and dense. Parveen studied the book silently for a moment. "I would very much like to examine this at leisure, Hamish X.

Perhaps I could help you decipher something, given time."

Hamish X shook his head, snatching the book back. "Only I can crack the code. I have to do it alone." He placed the book on his cot. Then he picked up the rucksack and dumped the rest of his belongings onto the scratchy grey flannel blanket that covered the bed.

"Not a lot to show for myself," he said, looking at the meagre bundle of possessions. "Just these things and, of course, my boots." He plunked them on the floor: one, two.

"May I?" Parveen asked again, pulling a magnifying glass out of the pocket of his overalls.

Hamish X smiled. "Be my guest."

Parveen spent the next five minutes examining the strange boots in detail. He tapped them. He stroked them. He lifted each one and looked at the knobby soles. Finally, he sat back on his heels. "Where did you get them?" he asked.

"I don't remember exactly," Hamish said. "It sounds weird but … I've always had them. I can't remember a time when they weren't on my feet." He laughed.

"C'mon," Mimi scoffed. "You tryin' to tell us those boots grow with ya?"

"That's exactly what I'm trying to tell you, Mimi. And what's even weirder is, I've never, ever taken them off."

"You've never seen your own feet?" Parveen's eyes were wide behind his glasses, which made him look even more owlish. "That is truly disturbing!"

"How is it even possible?" Mimi said. "How can boots grow?"

Hamish X shrugged. "I only know what I've seen with my own eyes. They're my best friends, these boots!" He slapped the shiny black footwear. "They've been with me through thick and thin. I like to think maybe a wizard put them on me. That they're magic or something."

"Whatever!" Mimi rolled her eyes. "Got any other surprises?"

He looked around him to check that they weren't being watched. All the children were in the cafeteria and the one guard, Hammerface, was dozing in a chair by the wall.

"Just this," he whispered.

Hamish stuffed the fingers of his right hand down the side of his right boot. With a flourish like a magician in a stage show, he produced a bulky Swiss Army pocketknife.

The knife looked like most Swiss Army knives; red on the sides with an inlaid Swiss Cross, utensils neatly folded into the centre. The only difference was in the number of utensils: there were too many to count. The knife practically bristled with them. The strange thing was that the knife didn't seem to weigh as much as it should considering all the bits folded into it.

"Nice knife," Parveen whispered, awestruck. He loved tools and gadgets of any description, but this knife was a thing of beauty.

"How did you git that past the metal detector?" Mimi asked incredulously.

"It must be made of a non-metallic alloy that the detectors can't pick up," Parveen said. Hamish X tossed it to him. The smaller boy held the knife cradled in his brown hands like a priceless treasure.

"It was given to me by the King of Switzerland," Hamish X said, a strange look coming over his face. "I'm supposed to give it back to him one day."

"Switzerland is a republic," Parveen said. "They don't have a king."

"Yeah, they do. He gave me this." Hamish X took the knife back and held it up so that it sparkled in the fluorescent lights of the dormitory. "There's a corkscrew, a screwdriver, a boning knife, a saw, a magnifying glass, a pair of scissors, a spatula for flipping tiny pancakes, a spoon, a fork, three different knives ... There are lots more but I haven't had the time to look for them yet."

He stuffed the knife back into his boot and sat on the edge of his cot.

"Why didn't you use it last night?" Mimi demanded. "You could have cut us loose!"

"Sure," Hamish X shrugged. "Then what? We'd have been blown like leaves across the freezing tundra. No, I needed that time to sound out whom I could trust in this dump. I know I can trust you, Mimi. You pack a punch but you're honest and true."

Mimi blushed. Hamish X turned to Parveen.

"You were willing to risk getting into trouble to bring us that food. And those little bowl kites have inspired me. I think I'll take you with me, too."

"What do you mean?" Parveen asked. "Where are you going?"

"Isn't it obvious?" Hamish smiled. "I'm going to escape and you're both coming with me."

Parveen and Mimi sat in stunned silence. Finally, Mimi shook her head.

"It's impossible," she whispered. "There are too many guards."

"Stupid guards," Hamish pointed out.

"And dogs," Parveen added.

"I have a way with animals."

"And even if you get past them," Mimi insisted, "there's the electric fence. You'll be fried for sure."

"It is very, very electrical," Parveen said simply. "Probably a million volts."

"Electrical fences are a personal favourite of mine," Hamish X said airily.

"And even if ya did get out," Mimi reasoned, "where would ya go? The nearest town is nine hunnert kilometres away across a frozen wasteland. If the bears don't eat ya,[38] you'll freeze to death."

"Now that's the most fun part of the whole plan." Hamish smiled and patted Parveen on the back, not so hard this time. "And I have Parveen to thank for that."

"Me?" Parveen said nervously.

"You," Hamish X confirmed. "Just be ready when the time comes."

Mimi couldn't help herself. "Is it gonna be soon?"

"As soon as possible," Hamish X nodded.

Parveen shook his head. "I find it very hard to believe that there is any possible escape from this place. I am resigned to wait out the years until I am fourteen and then I will be removed from here to live a productive life perhaps working for an electronics firm."

"How do ya know they'll let ya go after ya turn fourteen, huh? The ODA come and pick ya up and then yer never seen again!" Mimi realized she was talking loudly. She looked around and continued in a whisper. "I fer one don't wanna wait. Hamish X, are you shore we can git out?"

"Trust me," Hamish said. "Can you?"

Mimi and Parveen exchanged a look. "I won't go without ya, Parv."

---

[38] Also remember wolves and foxes.

Parveen sat looking at Hamish X for a long moment. When he finally spoke, he asked a strange question. "You're quite certain you don't know how old you are?"

Hamish X thought about it. "I think I'm about ten years old. Why?"

Parveen looked hard at Hamish X for a few seconds before he put away his magnifying glass. "You don't seem to know very much about yourself at all," he said. "Yet you expect me to trust you?"

Hamish X hung his head. "I know. You're right." He raised his golden eyes to Parveen and then to Mimi. "There are holes in my memory. It scares me a bit. People tell me about the things I've done and the places I've been ... And I don't really remember them clearly. It's like they happened to somebody else. There are things I can't explain. My boots, for example. Things I'm able to do that I don't remember learning. It's all kind of weird." Hamish X reached out and grabbed Mimi and Parveen by the hand. He looked up into their faces with an intensity that was almost frightening. "But I promise you, I can get us out of here. I'd like to take everyone with us, but Windcity is too remote ... too dangerous. I can only take you two. Do you trust me?"

Parveen and Mimi looked at each other for a moment then made their decision.

"We're in," Parveen said softly.

"What have we got to lose?" Mimi added.

"Exactly." Hamish X clapped his hands and stood up. "Now, let's get some of that delectable porridge. It's time for me to learn the ropes and become the model worker."

He turned and led the way through the common room to the cafeteria. Mimi and Parveen followed him.

VIGGO ASSIGNED HAMISH X to cutting detail. Mimi showed him what to do and he mastered the job quickly. He was surprisingly strong for his size. He could shovel and cut and heave as much cheese as anyone and he did it cheerfully, even finding time to help others if they fell behind.

Viggo watched Hamish X from his glass box of an office, high above the factory floor. He was surprised at how the new boy fit in so seamlessly, but he couldn't help but be suspicious. Every time the boy caught Viggo looking at him, he would wave and smile in an infuriatingly impudent way. Hamish X was a troublemaker and he would have to be watched. Viggo would have to leave that in the hands of the guards, however. Other important events consumed his attention.

Chapter 9

As the days passed, Hamish X seemed so at home in the factory that Mimi began to wonder if he'd forgotten all about escaping. He never mentioned anything about breaking out. Only by studying him closely could she see anything but the perfect little cheese worker. But there was something going on behind the facade. She sensed that he was watching and learning, taking everything in.

Hamish X worked all day slicing and heaving. He didn't complain. He whistled cheerfully, and kept up a running chatter with whoever was close by. Frankly, his workmates didn't know what to make of him. They were used to keeping their heads down and working in silence. But Hamish X asked the children questions about themselves, about their time in the orphanage, about their work in the factory. Innocent enough questions, but Mimi watched how carefully Hamish listened to the answers, as if he were storing up the information for use at a later date.

Hamish X even took time to learn about the other aspects of production. He played with the young children as they paddled in the milk tank. He tried his hand at pressing, too, trudging around and around singing strange songs in strange languages to keep up the rhythm. When asked, he said he didn't know what the words meant, couldn't remember where he'd heard the songs before. His good humour was infectious. Hamish X was strange, but the children grew to like him.

Thus the time passed. Hamish X settled into life at the Windcity Orphanage and Cheese Factory. On the surface it was still the same crushing grind of boredom and hard work, but somehow there was a difference. Mrs. Francis noticed it as she ladled out the porridge and poured out the whey. Every once in a while, she saw a smile on a child's face. Not a big smile, certainly. Not an outright, coast-to-coast, face-splitting, blue-ribbon grin. Just a little smile from time to time, but it warmed Mrs. Francis's heart nonetheless.

What did Viggo think of the change in atmosphere? He didn't notice. Normally he would have pounced on any little glimmer of good feeling and crushed it underfoot, but he was preoccupied. Over the weeks since Hamish X's arrival he had been under a lot of stress. Reports about the marauding Cheese Pirates were coming in daily.[39]

Therefore, he paid less attention to Hamish X than he should have. He let the guards take care of disciplining the boy.

The undercurrent of good feeling that Hamish X inspired was disturbing to the guards. Furthermore, they noticed a discrepancy in the cheese count. Several ounces were missing. Someone had been pilfering small amounts of cheese. Only a few dozen ounces were unaccounted for, but Viggo was extremely possessive of Caribou Blue. Even a small amount of wayward cheese could add up to a large financial loss over time.

---

[39] Cheese piracy is as old as cheese itself. Gangs of marauders terrorized the cheese makers of Poland during the Middle Ages. A group of Cheese Pirates calling themselves "The Brothers of the Curd" took control of the Greek island of Feta in 1645, demanding a toll of cheese from all who passed through their domain. Though cheese was never invented in China, Tofu Pirates have been a scourge and a plague since the time of the Han Emperors.

Pianoface, Tubaface, and Hammerface (following an elaborate game of paper, rock, scissors) decided that Hammerface should take the bad news to the boss. The unfortunate guard reluctantly climbed the stairs like a man climbing the gallows. He arrived at the glass door of Viggo's inner sanctum and hesitated, looking back to his friends at the bottom of the stairs for encouragement. But they had already scattered in anticipation of the coming storm. So Hammerface gulped, screwed up his courage, and rapped tentatively on the door.

"What is it?" the voice barked.

"Master Viggo, sir," Hammerface stammered. "May I speak with you for a moment?"

The door flew open to reveal Viggo, his hair a greasy corona around his head, his eyes sunken and hollow. "What could you possibly want to talk about?"

"Uh …" Hammerface was so terrified that his entire body was clenched—which was fortunate because if it hadn't been, he might have wet himself. The strange thing was that Hammerface could have snapped Viggo in half had he chosen to, and then snapped someone else in half without feeling the slightest bit tired. But Viggo was a master of cowing people with his intense displeasure. Lion tamers are puny compared to the fierce animals they control. Will is all that stands between them and the snap of the lion's jaws.[40]

Hammerface recovered his voice. "It's just that the children … since this new kid arrived … We're worried that they might start enjoying themselves … and that won't be no good."

---

[40] Needless to say, lion tamers are no fun to go on holiday with because they constantly get their own way—and they carry a whip and chair everywhere they go.

"Is that it? *That's* why you've disturbed me?" Viggo's eyebrows rose like a thundercloud.

"That ... and some cheese is missing," Hammerface blurted out.

He waited under Viggo's terrible glare to be verbally flayed. When Viggo finally broke the silence, however, he didn't shout. In fact, he seemed almost reasonable.

"Perhaps I have been neglecting the mental state of the children in my charge," he said. He sat down in his swivel chair. "I've had a lot on my mind lately. I have many responsibilities. Inspiring fear and loathing in one hundred and one children is a challenge. It requires dedication, imagination, and creativity."

"You're a constant source of inspiration for us all," said Hammerface.

"I appreciate that. It's a lonely job, being hated, but someone has to do it. I haven't managed to accumulate great wealth and prestige in the world of dairy science by being a nice guy."

"You certainly haven't, Master Viggo."

Viggo glared at him.

"But you aren't without your nice qualities, Master Viggo," Hammerface backtracked and was rewarded with a softening of the glare.

"Indeed," Viggo said suddenly, "I will address the problem of morale at the evening meal. And the issue of the missing cheese. Now, go back to your duties."

Hammerface gratefully backed out of the room, bowing and wringing his hat in his scarred hands. Unfortunately, backing out of Viggo's office is ill-advised, situated as it is at the top of a steep staircase. He stepped backwards, missed his footing, and bounced end over end down the seventy-two steps to the factory floor.[41] Pianoface and Tubaface hurried to help their fallen comrade.

Viggo closed the door and gazed out the window over the leaning rooftops of Windcity. Somewhere out there, a gang of Cheese Pirates waited to pounce. He shivered in his cozily heated office then turned his gaze to the factory floor below, seeking out Hamish X. The boy was carving the flabby curds, a bright smile on his face. While Viggo watched, the lad turned and looked up at him and winked.

"Everything was going fine until you came along, Hamish X." Viggo smiled a nasty smile. "I think it's time I put you in your place."

---

[41] Grovelling backwards down the stairs is an exceedingly dangerous proposition. As a result, most palace architects build throne rooms on the ground floor to avoid unnecessary injury to grovellers. The one exception is the palace at Gerfink-Holgestein in Southern Germany where the throne room was on the top floor, but after losing three trusted advisers, the Grand Duke of Gerfink-Holgestein thoughtfully built a waterslide at the end of his audience chamber.

Chapter 10

The children stood waiting in the cafeteria, shuffling their feet nervously. In hushed voices they discussed the reason for the assembly. No one could remember a meeting where both work details were present at the same time. "What's goin' on?" Mimi asked as they joined the crowd. The shift had just ended when the guards had come through the dormitory demanding that everyone from both shifts assemble.

"I'm completely baffled, I assure you," Parveen shrugged.

"Who knows?" Hamish X said. "Maybe we're going to get a day off?"

"In your dreams," Mimi scoffed. They took their place in the back row.

And there they stood for almost half an hour before Viggo appeared. He stalked in from the factory floor through the big double doors, elbowed his way through the waiting children, and climbed onto a chair, held steady by Pianoface and Tubaface. (Hammerface was in bed recovering from several fractures.) Viggo turned and faced his orphan workforce.

"I'm sure you're all wondering why I've called this meeting," he began, running a hand absently through his hair and making it stand up on end even more strangely than usual. "It certainly isn't to praise your work habits, which are slovenly and inefficient. Rather, it is a matter of security. Not that I think any of you could ever escape ..." He glared meaningfully at Hamish X. "Escape is impossible. Escape is IMPOSSIBLE. Let me reiterate that phrase: ESCAPE IS IMPOSSIBLE!"

Hamish X raised his hand.

"What is it?" Viggo barked.

"I was just wondering … Is escape possible?"

"NO!" Viggo shrieked at Hamish X. Hamish X smiled back. Viggo regained his composure with effort.

"Over the past few months, the world cheese community has been the subject of an ongoing campaign of terror perpetrated by a dastardly group of lawless brigands. According to eyewitness accounts, these 'Cheese Pirates,' as they style themselves, have attacked cheese-making facilities all over the world. They strike in the dead of night! They steal and burn and loot. They take all the valuable cheese and disappear before the authorities can arrive to deal with them.

"The World Dairy Organization has instructed me to be on high alert for the appearance of these marauders. I have assured the Organization that I will be vigilant. If these criminals arrive at our doorstep they will be dealt with in the harshest manner."

Viggo paused for effect, looking at the little faces all around him.

"How does this affect you? Obviously, anything that threatens this facility threatens your continued health and welfare. Although I make all the profits from the cheese factory, you receive food and shelter, and so the continued well-being of the factory is essential to your continued well-being. On a very real level, I don't care about you as children or human beings but I do care about the cheese your labour produces. Therefore, I have taken measures to ensure the safety of the facility. This would be an excellent time for grateful applause …"

The children dutifully slapped their hands together. For sheer lethargy, the sound rivalled an exhausted golf crowd on the Sahara in August at noon. Viggo stood, head bowed, receiving his false praise. He raised a hand for silence.

"I have undertaken to double the contingent of guards. New recruits will arrive within three days. A second electric fence is to be constructed around the one that already exists and a radar warning system installed. These changes will occur over the next few weeks.

"Also, to ensure your safety, all exercise in the yard shall be suspended indefinitely."

A little girl put up her hand. "There is no yard," she said.

"Then you won't miss it, will you? Work details will be increased in duration by one hour per day. It's easier to protect you while you are asleep or at work. Sadly, the money for these measures has to come from somewhere. I'm afraid I am forced to cut your food ration in half to raise the money for the increased security."

A groan went up from the children. The guards laughed cruelly. Mrs. Francis, who stood watching in her kitchen window, gasped in disbelief. Eventually, the children fell silent.

"Believe me, it breaks my heart," Viggo sighed with feigned anguish. "I know you will do your best under these new circumstances because … you have no choice.

"Finally, it has come to my attention that someone has been pilfering cheese from the vault." He paused and glared right at Hamish X. The boy didn't flinch. Viggo gestured to Pianoface. "I'm sure no one would own up to such a dastardly deed, so I have decided that random punishment would be the most cruel and the most satisfying." Pianoface handed Viggo a book. Hamish X's eyes went wide. It was *Great Plumbers*.

"I am confiscating this book until the perpetrator of the deed is willing to own up."

"That's my property!" Hamish X shouted. Mimi held his arm to prevent him from lunging through the crowd at Viggo.

"Tut! Tut!" Viggo tucked the large book under his arm. "I'm merely holding it for safekeeping until someone owns up to the crime. It will be safe in my office for the time being. Maybe if some people respected my authority and stopped cheering people up around here these measures wouldn't be necessary. That is all. You may applaud now."

Viggo hopped down from his perch and strode across the room amid desultory clapping. Then, escorted by Pianoface and Tubaface, he swiped his keycard and left through the security door as the clapping turned into ominous grumbling. Pianoface and Tubaface stayed behind to disperse the children.

"Half rations," Mimi spat. "We're barely survivin' as it is!"

"He stole my book." Hamish X's face was ghostly pale. The whites of his eyes were visible all around his golden irises. He looked as though he might faint. "I've got to have my book."

Mimi handed him a food bowl. "Are y'all right, Hamish X? It's just a book, after all."

Hamish X spun and glared at her with desperate eyes. "I have to have that book. My mother gave it to me. I have to have it."

"What can we do? Viggo has it," Parveen shrugged. He grabbed a bowl and made to join the food line. Hamish X grabbed his arm and Mimi's, pulling them to one side out of earshot of the nearest guard.

"I'll tell you what I'm going to do," he whispered. "I'm getting it back. Tonight. Then we'll escape. Tonight."

Hamish X turned and joined the porridge line. Mimi and Parveen nervously followed.

Chapter 11

Mimi must have dozed off because Hamish X's face was directly over hers as he shook her.

"Wake up, Mimi," he hissed.

"I'm up," she hissed back. His face disappeared. She heard the soft click of his boots as he padded away.

She sat up and looked around her. The dorm room was in darkness. Soft snoring sounds emanated from the cots all around. As her eyes adjusted to the dark, she saw Hamish X standing in the doorway to the common room, his rucksack slung over his back. He raised a hand and beckoned to her. Behind him a faint light glowed.

Mimi rolled out of bed as silent as a cat. She threaded her way through the cots of the sleeping children, their pale faces glowing in the darkness. When she reached the doorway, Hamish X ushered her through and closed it. Parveen was squatting on the floor. He had disassembled all the chairs and the table, laying them in a pile around him. In his hand, Hamish X's pocketknife was open to a chisel tool. Parveen was drilling holes in a table leg, working by the light of a small flashlight taped to his head. When Mimi entered he paused and turned his head so that the light shone briefly into her eyes.

"So," he said, "you're finally up."

"Why didn't anyone wake me?" Mimi whispered angrily.

"You weren't needed," Hamish X said softly. "So we let you sleep. No need to be angry."

"I can't believe ya kept all this a secret from me, Parv. What ya makin', anyway?"

Hamish X grinned. "Well, remember when we were up on the roof? His ingenious little kite bowls? I thought, what if we made some big enough to carry us out over the electric fence, or maybe even farther? That would be one way of escaping from this place."

Mimi thought for a moment.

"But then what?" she asked. "We'd be flung all the heck and gone over the tundra. We'd probly freeze to death before the wind saw fit to let us land anywheres."

"Great minds think alike," Hamish X smiled. "But Viggo might think we were desperate enough to escape that way. Help me with these."

He pointed to a stack of rags piled beside some old overalls. He took one of the overalls and started stuffing the rags into it. Mimi watched, her excitement growing.

"Decoys," she said.

"I knew you were more than just a pretty face," Hamish X said. She blushed and punched him in the arm. He winced theatrically and pointed at the next set of overalls. Mimi picked them up and started stuffing. Soon, all three were filled with rags.

Parveen finished his preparations at roughly the same time. He had made the dismantled chairs into kite frames that folded up into a long narrow bundle. He wrapped the three folded frames in some bed sheets, then strapped the three rag dummies to the bundle of poles. When everything was ready he gestured to Mimi. The two of them hoisted the bundle on their shoulders and turned expectantly to Hamish X.

He pressed his ear to the cafeteria door, then gently pushed it open a crack. He peered into the darkened room beyond.

"Stay close," he whispered.

He held the door open to allow Parveen and Mimi through. The cafeteria was dark, and for once the three children were glad of Viggo's stinginess. They padded across the linoleum floor between the empty tables to the security door. There, Hamish X reached into his coat pocket, pulled out the security card, and swiped it. The lock clicked. He pushed the door open and stepped through, Parveen and Mimi right behind.

They were in a dimly lit hallway. Mimi and Hamish knew from the day of their dangling that the stairs to the roof were on the left. The passage on the right led towards the kitchen, Viggo's apartments, Mrs. Francis's room, and, the front door. Muffled voices drifted from the direction of the roof stairs. The way they had to go.

The trio walked stealthily down the corridor until they came to an open door on one wall. The voices were louder. Hamish raised a hand to signal a stop and peered around the doorframe. Three guards sat watching a hockey game on a huge television. Pianoface and Tubaface were drinking cans of beer. Hammerface was lying on a gurney in a body cast. The commentator's voice was a steady drone …

"Fedetenkorenko rifles it into the corner and they go after it! Salmingborgensteen comes up with the puck and rips it off the glass but not out …"

The guards were sitting on a couch with their backs to the doorway. Hamish watched them for a moment to make sure they were concentrating on the game, then turned to Mimi and Parveen. He mimed pulling on a guard's peaked cap, raised three fingers to indicate the number of opposition, and raised a finger to his lips. Mimi and Parveen nodded.

The commentator's voice rose to a frenzied pitch.

"Krushnick beats the defender and steps out from the corner. He passes it back to the blueline ..." The guards were leaning forward in their seats, riveted to the screen as Hamish silently nipped across the open space. Mimi and Parveen started across after him. "Magnusson winds up and drives a shot ... HE SCORES!"

"YEAH!" the guards shouted, leaping to their feet. Hammerface swayed gently from side to side.

Parveen jerked in surprise and his end of the bundle slipped from his grasp, falling towards the floor. In that split second they were almost undone, but Hamish X dropped to the floor and caught the bundle on his chest before it hit the ground. He quickly wriggled out of the doorway, Parveen scrambling after him and Mimi, lugging her end of the bundle, bringing up the rear.

They scurried around the corner and found themselves at the foot of the stairs that led to the roof. There they paused for a moment to let their racing hearts slow down.

"That was close," Mimi whispered.

"A little excitement adds to the fun," Hamish X answered. Parveen rolled his eyes.

After a moment, they picked up the bundle and carried it up the stairs. Hamish X opened the metal door at the top and they stepped out onto the roof.

Mimi and Parveen bumped into Hamish, who had stopped dead just outside the door. Standing in front of him, a cigarette dangling from his open mouth, a guard stared at them in shock. Hamish X had never seen him before, but it had to be Forkliftface—for, indeed, his face looked as though someone had driven into it with a forklift.[42] He must have come up from the harbour to watch the hockey game.

His sudden chuckle sounded like rocks turning over in a tumble dryer. "What have we here?" he said. Hamish X wasted no time. He leapt at the man and kicked him hard in the belly with one big black boot. Forkliftface doubled over, the cigarette casting a shower of sparks on the wind as it flew from his mouth. Mimi dropped her end of the bundle and drove her fist into his temple. He fell on his side like a sack of potatoes and lay still.

Hamish X pointed at the door, and Parveen closed it. Hamish X reached down and laid two fingers on the exposed flesh of the Forkliftface's neck.

"He's out," Hamish X pronounced.

"He saw us!" Mimi groaned. She was flapping her hand in pain. "He's got a hard head."

"That's fantastic," Hamish smiled. "It only helps the plan."

"I can't see how," Mimi grumbled.

"You will. Let's get these kites up."

Parveen took over. In the lee of the doorway, out of the wind, they assembled the three kites, screwing the frames together according to Parveen's instructions. The hardest part was stretching the bed sheets over the frames in the

---

[42] As Hamish X guessed, this truly was Forkliftface, but unlike the other guards he wasn't called Forkliftface because his face looked like it had been hit by a forklift. He had actually been born with the name Dave Forkliftface, and by a happy accident his face was hit by a forklift later in life, allowing him to find security work at the Hit-in-the-Face Security Firm (eventually renamed Mean and Ugly Security Options).

swirling gusts. Finally, the rag-filled overalls were strapped into the harnesses.

When the work was done, the three children hauled the kites to the edge of the roof.

"On three," Hamish X shouted. "One. Two ..." Just then Parveen, by far the lightest of the three, began to rise off the surface of the roof.

"Parveen!" Mimi shouted, letting go of her kite and grabbing one of Parveen's dangling feet before the wind ripped him out and away. "Let go!"

Parveen did as he was told and loosed his kite.

"I said to wait for three," Hamish X laughed and let his own kite fly. Parveen and Mimi fell in a heap on the roof.

"Thank you," Parveen said.

"Don't mention it," Mimi said, pulling him to his feet.

"Look!" They followed Hamish X's pointed finger and saw that the kites had already soared high into the night. "Perfect," he shouted, clapping his hands. "Phase one is complete. On to phase two! Let's go." They ran to the door and headed back down the stairs.

IN THE NORTH WATCHTOWER, at the far end of the factory grounds, two guards were playing Fish. Cards were the only defence against the incredible boredom of the night watch.

"Do you have any ... Jacks?" Bowlingballface asked Fridgeface hopefully.

"Go fish," Fridgeface answered. Grumbling, Bowlingballface reached to take a card off the deck when a shape whipped by the window. The astonished man stood up suddenly, overturning the card table and spilling cards onto the floor of the glass booth.

"What's the big idea?" Fridgeface shouted. "I was winning that hand!"

"Shut up and look." His friend pointed. Three large kites were wafting over the electric fence towards the tundra beyond. They stared in disbelief.

"What was that?" asked Bowlingballface.

"An escape!" Fridgeface bellowed. He reached behind him and slapped the red button on the wall. Throughout the Windcity Orphanage and Cheese Factory, alarm bells began to ring.

Piratical Interlude

The wind moaned through the rigging and buffeted the ship, but they made good headway. They were riding with the breeze, so the helmsman had merely to hold his course and the wind would do the rest.

The Captain stood at the helmsman's shoulder. Ahead was only darkness and swirling snow.

"How much longer?"

The helmsman consulted the chart. "If zis English pigdog isn't lyink, about an hour."

From the corner of the bridge a fearful voice stammered, "I assure you, I am being absolutely truthful! I swear on the good name of the Cheddar family!" The Captain stalked over and looked down at the pitiful creature chained to the bulkhead. Lord Cheddar cringed back, trying to make himself as tiny as possible. His dark pinstriped suit was torn and filthy. For three nights he'd been chained to the bulkhead–ever since the pirates had swept down on his cheese factory in Cheddar Hole just outside of Sheffield, England.

The Captain loomed over the quaking cheese master. "You'd better be telling the truth." Pulling a long, glittering sabre from his belt, he held it before the terrified Lord Cheddar's eyes. "Or I'll slice you from niblets to gubblits."

Though Lord Cheddar didn't know which parts of him were niblets and which gubblits, he hastened to reassure the Captain. "I swear. According to the latest issue of The Cheesemakers Directory, the directions I gave you are accurate."

The Captain grunted. He grabbed the funnel-shaped speaking tube that functioned as a communications system in the ship. He blew once on the mouthpiece, creating a whistling sound.

"Kipling," he shouted into the mouthpiece.

"Aye, sir," came the tinny response.

"Prepare the landing party!"

"Aye, sir!"

Chapter 12

Viggo stormed into the security centre. "What's going on?" he demanded. The cheese master was wrapped in a grey flannel bathrobe. His hair lay flat on one side of his head and stuck straight out on the other as if he'd just rolled out of bed, which, of course, he had. His pyjamas, visible underneath the robe, were baby blue with little horsies prancing on them. He pulled his robe tighter in a vain attempt to cover the horsies. Forkliftface slumped on a stool holding a bag of ice against his head. Bowlingballface sat manning the radar screen and Fridgeface was replaying the feed from the closed-circuit television cameras that kept watch on the perimeter of the factory. All three guards turned and stared at Viggo.

"WELL?" he demanded. The guards jumped to attention.

"Three children have escaped. They flew out on some kind of kitey things about ten minutes ago," Fridgeface explained.

"They've headed due south on the prevailing wind." This from Bowlingballface.

"They kicked me in the groin," Forkliftface moaned.

"I'll kick you in the groin too if you don't quit whining." Viggo stepped closer to look at the television screen over the guard's shoulder. "Who was it? Don't tell me! Hamish X!"

"And the crazy girl," Tubaface puffed into the room. Pianoface came in right on his heels, adding, "And the little Indian boy with the glasses."

Viggo watched as a screen showed a video playback of the three kites rising into the night. "I knew it! I knew it! That little troublemaker thinks he can make a fool out of me, but he won't. Oh no! We'll catch him. Assemble the guards at the front gate. Shut down the factory and lock all the children in the dormitory. Arm the guards and get the dogs!" Viggo ran his fingers in his hair with no appreciable effect. "Tonight we will hunt the great Hamish X down like the rat he is!" He laughed cruelly. The guards joined in after a moment. He raised his hand and the laughter stopped. "Let's go!"

Mrs. Francis stepped out into corridor. She'd heard the alarm and had gone immediately to check on the children. She was on her way to find Viggo when he burst out of the security room followed by the guards in full security gear: helmets, truncheons, and armoured vests. Viggo strode purposefully by on the way to the cafeteria.

"What's happened?" she asked him.

"That loathsome Hamish X and his two confederates have escaped. We're off to hunt them down." He continued past her and disappeared around the corner.

Mrs. Francis clutched her pink fuzzy dressing gown over her heart, trying to drive out the chill she felt. *I knew they were leaving*, she thought, *I just knew it! Oh please, Lord, keep them safe*.

She shook her head and stepped back into the kitchen and shut the door. It was past midnight and the morning meal was hours away. The kitchen was dark, but the metal utensils and hanging pots on the overhead racks gleamed faintly in the light that spilled from the door of her tiny adjoining apartment. She knew she'd get no more sleep tonight, so she walked across the tile floor towards her room to get dressed.

Just as she reached the bedroom door she heard a dull clang behind her. She stopped and listened, wondering if she had imagined it. The alarm was ringing still, making it hard to hear anything but its insistent clatter. She turned and looked back into the dim kitchen.

Nothing seemed out of place. Sacks of oatmeal leaned against the wall in the corner. The ladles hung from their rack by the serving hatch. The refrigerator hummed and clanked. The serving hatch was closed ...

Wait. The hatch wasn't quite closed. A sliver of light from the cafeteria shone through a crack in the barely open shutters. Mrs. Francis thought hard. *I'm sure I closed and latched that after dinner*, she thought.

Slowly she crossed the floor and pushed the shutters completely closed, flipping the latch to lock them tight. She was standing right beside the large porridge vat when she heard the clanging sound again, followed quickly by stifled whispers. She looked down at the vat.

It's coming from in there. She reached for her largest ladle, taking it from its hook with a care not to cause any noise. Then, her heart in her mouth, she reached for the handle of the vat cover and suddenly flipped it up.

She gasped at what she saw. Hamish X, Parveen, and Mimi sat huddled in the vat looking up at her, their eyes wide. "What are you doing in there?" she gasped.

"I think it's obvious, dear Mrs. Francis. We're hiding," Hamish X whispered.

"Everyone thinks you've escaped."

"We've sent them on a bit of a wild goose chase," Parveen explained. "When they've all gone, we'll make our way out the front door to the harbour, steal a boat, and sail away."

"After I get my book back from Viggo's office," Hamish X said.

"Of course," Parveen corrected.

"Why not just run?" Mimi rolled her eyes. "Who cares about the book?"

"I do. I told you: It's all I have left of my mother," he hissed.

"No need to get all shirty," Mimi sulked.

"Sorry." Hamish X laid a hand on her shoulder. He looked up at Mrs. Francis. "Just put the lid back on and pretend you've not seen us."

Mrs. Francis stood holding the lid up, dumbfounded.

"Good idea, Mrs. Francis!" Viggo's voice made her drop the lid with a clang and spin around. Viggo stood in the doorway, with his parka on over his pyjamas and dressing gown. He strode into the room. Mrs. Francis stepped between him and the vat.

"You should have some porridge on the boil for the search party. We should be back shortly. They can't have gotten far!"

"I'll start right away." She stepped to the sacks of porridge and grabbed one. "Any idea where they're headed?"

"South, of course," Viggo said. "The wind only blows one way."

"Of course," Mrs. Francis stammered. "What a silly I am." She didn't bother to remind Viggo of Flip Day, when the wind changed direction. "Oh yes. Silly! Silly! Silly!" She tried to pick up her spurdle but dropped it clattering to the floor.

Viggo's eyes narrowed. He stepped closer. "You seem a little nervous, Mrs. Francis. Why?"

"Me? Nervous? I'm not nervous. No, just a little flushed with all the excitement. You know. Ha!" She fanned her face with her hand and avoided Viggo's look. He reached out and turned her head so that she stared into his eyes.

"You didn't know anything about this escape attempt, did you Mrs. Francis?" he purred softly, dangerously. "I'd hate to think I couldn't trust you."

"N-n-n-no. Never! I didn't know a thing." It was so hard not to look at the porridge vat. She managed to hold Viggo's gaze with her own.

"Master Viggo, sir!" A guard appeared in the doorway.

"What?" Viggo snapped.

"We're all waiting at the front gate."

Viggo held Mrs. Francis for one more agonizing moment, then let his hand drop. "Let's not keep them waiting then," he said finally as they left the room.

Mrs. Francis practically fainted with relief. She sagged against the porridge sacks, wiping her brow with the back of her hand. The lid of the vat opened and the three children peered out.

"Is the coast clear?" Hamish X asked.

"Coast? Oh, yes. The coast is clear," Mrs. Francis squeaked.

"While you're up," Hamish X smiled with all the charm he could muster, which was a formidable amount, "could you throw some food into a bag for us? We've a long journey ahead."

Mrs. Francis smiled, grabbed an empty porridge sack, and reached for the keys to Viggo's private larder.

Chapter 13

Outside in the night, snow had begun to fall. Fall is perhaps the wrong word. Rain and snow always moved sideways in Windcity. But regardless of its orientation, precipitation in the form of frozen water came from the sky. The guards shuffled from foot to foot in the courtyard waiting for Master Viggo to appear. Snowmobiles idled, the roar of the motors merging with the din of the gale. Snow swirled through the columns of light cast by the lamps around the perimeter of the factory.

Presently, Master Viggo burst through the steel front door and stomped down to the assembled guards. He cast an appraising eye over their ugly faces and spoke.

"All right gentlemen, we have a job to do. At approximately 01:30 tonight, three children made an escape. Our job is to find them and bring them back. Every minute the factory is down, I lose two thousand, seven hundred and thirty-eight dollars and forty-seven cents. Therefore, we must find them and find them fast. They were last seen heading south by southwest in three makeshift kites. We'll head in that direction, fanning out and using our heat sensors to track them. Any questions?"

Tubaface raised his hand.

"Yes?"

"Where do babies come from?"

"That question is wholly inappropriate to our present situation. Someone slap him." Pianoface obliged.

"Ow!"

"Any other questions? No? Let's move out!"

THERE COMES A TIME in every story when one thinks one has everything figured out. The plot is advancing nicely. The reader can guess what's going to happen. Everything is neat and tidy: Viggo heads off with his guards on a wild goose chase, the three children escape into the night, steal a ship, and so on. Yes, it's all there for you, mapped out in your mind. All that's left is the actual telling.

Then, things suddenly change.

That's the point we have reached in this story.

SUDDENLY, OUT OF THE NIGHT SKY, a huge metal spike plummeted down, driving itself into the frozen ground and trailing a chain that snaked up into the sky. Forkliftface, who'd been standing in exactly the same spot, disappeared completely.

Viggo looked at the spike in confusion.

"What the ..."

That's when the first explosion rocked the factory. Viggo was thrown to the pavement as the ground shook. He pushed himself to his hands and knees and looked at the factory. The heavy steel front door had been completely blown in.

A whistling sound grew louder and louder. One of the snowmobiles exploded, casting Bowlingballface and Fridgeface into the air. They fell in crumpled heaps and lay still.

"We're being attacked!" Viggo shouted as more whistles announced a new volley of missiles. He looked up into the sky and saw flashes from above. A massive shape loomed, blocking out the few stars that were in the sky. Ropes snaked out of it, falling in heaps amid the guards.

Soon, wild-eyed men slid down the ropes, screaming and waving swords.

"The Cheese Pirates!" Viggo gibbered. He leapt to his feet and dashed for the smoking hole that had once been the factory's front door. "Slow them down!" Pianoface and Tubaface, the only guards left, looked at each other and instantly dropped their weapons. "We surrender!"

"WHAT WAS THAT?" Mimi asked as the first explosion shook the building.

"It sounded like an explosion," Parveen said.

"An explosion?" Mrs. Francis gasped.

Another concussion rattled the pots and pans. Bits of dust sifted down from above. Mrs. Francis went to the doorway and looked down the hall towards the front gate. Snow was swirling through the hole where the door had been. Shouts, screams, and clashes of metal echoed down the corridor. As she watched, Viggo staggered into the hallway followed by a horde of shrieking, ragged men brandishing curved swords and pistols.

Viggo spotted her in the doorway. "Mrs. Francis! Help!" That was all he had time to shout before being overwhelmed by his pursuers.

"Oh dear!" cried out Mrs. Francis involuntarily. "Stop that!"

All eyes turned towards her. For a moment, the men just stared at her in silence.

A more motley, unsavoury group of men would be hard to assemble. Some wore big black boots. Some were barefoot. Some had earrings and nose rings. Some had no ears or noses. There were tall ones, short ones, fat ones, and thin ones. Most had scars in abundance, and dental hygiene did not seem to be high on their list of priorities. Their outlandish clothes looked to be a mishmash of anything that took their fancy as long as it was colourful.

All of them were armed to the teeth and all of them were looking at Mrs. Francis.

"A lady," said one, a short man with an extra eyebrow and a broken nose. The invaders grinned and headed towards her. Mrs. Francis shrieked and ran back into the kitchen, slamming the door and sliding the bolt. She had only a few seconds.

"What's happening?" Hamish X asked. The three children strained to see past the round body of Mrs. Francis.

"Pirates!" Mrs. Francis hissed. The pirates began pounding on the door. "Get down and keep quiet," Mrs. Francis ordered, lifting the lid and slamming it down just as the pirates smashed the door open and swarmed into the kitchen. They stopped short in amazement when confronted with Mrs. Francis standing defiantly in the middle of her kitchen with a porridge-stirring paddle in her hands. "Stop right where you are," she shouted.

The pirates laughed and whistled. One of them, a man with a missing ear, pointed a sword at her. "Look at this, boys. She's gonna paddle us!" General laughter greeted this witty gem. A man with a hook for a hand took a step towards the frightened cook with his hook extended. "Hand me the paddle, love. Before you hurt yerself."

Mrs. Francis brought the flat of the paddle down over his head. The man crumpled to the ground. Mrs. Francis seemed as surprised as the pirates. She raised the paddle above her head once more.

"Who's next?"

The pirates hesitated. For a few seconds, no one moved. Finally, One-Ear laughed harshly.

"It's a lady with a stick. Are we pirates or what?" They pondered that fact for a moment.

"It's a big stick," observed one of his fellows.

"She can't whack us all. On three! One! Two …"

Mrs. Francis knew she couldn't withstand a concerted attack. But she had to lure the pirates away from the children hiding in the vat. So before One-Ear could finish counting, she screamed and rushed the pirates in a pre-emptive strike.

Nothing is more terrifying to a man than an angry woman. Add a long wooden implement to the equation and the effect is profoundly unnerving. Mrs. Francis's charge bowled over the front row of pirates and a powerful sweep of the paddle downed two more, opening a pathway to the kitchen door. Momentum carried her out into the hallway. She set off as fast as her short legs could carry her.

The stunned pirates recovered their composure and in seconds they were after her, led by the one-eyed pirate called One-Eye.

"Get 'er boys!"

The children were safe for the moment. Now, Mrs. Francis could only hope she could find a way out of the factory. Her hopes were dashed when she turned the corner that led to the main gate only to run into another gang of cutthroats blocking her escape. She turned to run back the way she came but her pursuers scrambled around the bend, blocking her way. Cornered, she brandished her paddle.

"Stand back!" she shouted, not feeling as brave as she sounded. "I'm not afraid to use this!"

One-Ear grinned and held up his sabre. "I'm not afraid to use this, either." He spun the sword in a rather show-offy display, accidentally slicing off one of his comrades' pinky fingers.

"Ow."

"Sorry. Give me a bit of space when I'm showing off."

"My mistake."

One-Ear smiled at Mrs. Francis, baring yellowed teeth. "Time for some fun, sweetheart." He was about to lunge when a sharp voice stopped him.

"Hold!"

Mrs. Francis turned to see a tall, slim man step through the ranks. He wore a sailing captain's hat at a rakish angle and a tattered peacoat. In his hand was a pistol aimed at One-Ear. His clothes were old but well kempt. He had a gentlemanly bearing, as if he were used to a better sort of company. "We have rules, One-Ear." The man smiled faintly at Mrs. Francis. "Ladies are not to be hacked apart with swords. It reflects badly on pirates in general and on our outfit in particular."

"C'mon Mr. Kipling! She brained Hookie with that paddle," One-Ear said petulantly.

"I'm sure she was provoked," the man called Mr. Kipling said. He turned to Mrs. Francis. "Madam, I beg you, please relinquish your paddle and you will be treated with the respect and decorum befitting such a lovely lady." He bowed, sweeping off his hat to reveal a shiny bald spot on the back of his head.

The gesture left him open to a paddle attack to the skull. Mrs. Francis felt tempted to whack him, but looking around at the assembled pirates she knew it was a foolhardy gesture. She dropped the paddle.

Immediately, One-Ear lunged at her. He made only two steps before a shot rang out. "OW!" he shouted, grabbing the side of his head where his single ear had been before Mr. Kipling's bullet had removed it. "That's not fair! I have to change my name to No-Ears now."

"Forgive me." The gentleman pirate shook his head sadly. "At least your hats will fit snugly." He turned to Mrs. Francis. "Now, my lady, allow me to introduce myself. I am Mr. Kipling, first mate and second in command of the airship *Vulture*. We are unfortunately here to plunder and pillage this facility. If you'll allow me to escort you, I will introduce you to the Captain. I'm sure he'd love to make your acquaintance."

He offered her an arm. At a loss for some other course of action, she took it and they made their way, escorted by the gang of pirates, into the cafeteria.

On their arrival, they found Viggo in dire straits. A huge, brawny pirate held the skinny cheese maker by the throat like a butcher holding a chicken. Viggo's feet dangled above the floor as he kicked and writhed, trying to escape the vicelike grip that held him. Raucous laughter abounded.

"Look at him kickin'!" a pirate crowed.

"Like that Irish show with all the dancin'. What was it called?"

"Riverdance?" one of the men suggested.

"That's the one. Magnificent show! Bubbling with irrepressible energy," pronounced the man holding Viggo. He was missing an eye and several teeth.

"A celebration of the human spirit," enthused a short man whose arm had been sloppily amputated below the elbow and replaced with a spiked club. "The audience left the theatre completely energized."

Viggo listened to the commentary in disbelief, shaking with terror. "Please! I beg you. Don't kill me!" he sobbed. "I'll give you anything you want."

More uproarious laughter. The men elbowed each other in the ribs and pointed at Viggo as if he were the funniest thing they'd ever seen.

"Don' kill meee!" they mocked and leaned on each other as they laughed some more.

"Put him down, you brute!" Mrs. Francis shouted and stamped her slippered foot. She had no love for Viggo, but she couldn't stand cruelty. The pirates turned and looked at her in surprise.

"Oi! Who you calling a brute?" The man holding Viggo dropped him in a heap. "I oughtta teach you a lesson in manners." He took a step towards Mrs. Francis. The pirates hooted with glee.

"Stop!"

The command rang out and the hilarity ceased immediately. The voice was powerful, gravelly, and harsh. A huge man stood silhouetted in the light of factory doorway.

Mr. Kipling guided his captive a step closer. "Captain, this is ...?" Mr. Kipling left the question hanging.

"Mrs. Francis," she offered.

"Excellent." Mr. Kipling nodded. "Mrs. Francis, may I introduce the Scourge of the Skies, the Terror of Dairy Farmers, the Lord of Lactose, Master of the Cheese Pirates of Snow Monkey Island, Captain Cheesebeard."

The man turned and looked at Mrs. Francis, smiling in a most unsavoury way. "The pleasure is all mine."

Chapter 14

He was taller than any of the others by a head and a half. His shoulders were broad and powerful, his chest deep. He wore an old-fashioned three-cornered hat like a pirate in a storybook. His long black leather coat brushed the floor, covering the hilt of a sabre that hung from a red sash at his waist. Certainly, he looked every inch a pirate Captain. All the trappings aside, the most striking feature about him was his beard.

Oh! The beard. There are many kinds of beard, from the tiny chin triangle of the musketeer to the astute goatee of the psychiatrist to the grand rug-sweeping beards of the famous Beardlords of Denmark.[43] None of those beards, however, could hold a candle to the beard of the man standing before Viggo in the cafeteria.

Oh, the beardiness of this beard. A quintessence of facial hairiness, it hung from his chin to his belt, completely covering his chest. It was so broad that it stuck out on either side of his body. It was a beard that could

---

[43] Perhaps the Beardlords of Denmark are not as famous as they once were. These men ruled Danish society in the latter years of the nineteenth century. They grew beards of such prodigious length that they eventually dispensed with clothing altogether, weaving dense body sheaths from their whiskers. The beards were so dense that they rendered the wearers immune to blades and bullets. The Beardlords ruled with an iron fist, brutally oppressing the Danish people. (When I say Danish people, I mean the people of Denmark, not people made of Danish pastries.) The Beardlords were overthrown finally by a coalition of barbers who sprayed them with depilatory cream. Beards are still frowned upon in polite Danish society.

clear a path through an angry mob. Powerful, stupendous, and beardy.

What was the colour of this beard? I hear you ask yourselves. Not a colour you've seen before. No one knew what the colour of the hair beneath actually was because that colour was lost under a crusty encasement of cheese.

The three children had climbed out of the vat and were now watching through a small crack in the kitchen shutters. They got a good look at the pirate Captain as he walked into the cafeteria and stood over Viggo.

"Yes, I am Captain Cheesebeard," the man intoned.

Sometimes a name doesn't mean anything. There are

plenty of people named Smith who have no knowledge of blacksmithing. There are loads of people named Green who aren't green at all. Captain Cheesebeard was a man whose name described him perfectly. His beard, as mentioned above, was thick with cheese.

"Indeed, my beard is a map of my conquests, a tapestry of my glorious history as a pillager of the finest cheese repositories in the world." As he spoke, he ambled around the circle of his compatriots who leered and shook their weapons. "My hearty crew and I have gathered all the rarest and finest cheeses for ourselves, and now the final jewel will adorn my crown."

"Is that all you want?" Viggo whimpered. "Take it. Take all the cheese and go."

"Oh I will take the cheese, Master Viggo Schmatz," Captain Cheesebeard smiled grimly. "I will take it. But that's not all I want." The pirates giggled and hooted until Cheesebeard raised a hand asking for silence. "I want the cheese, but that is only the beginning. I have bigger plans than simple thievery. I believe one has to look to the future and secure a position of power to ensure one's ultimate survival and prosperity. That is why you are coming with me."

"Me? Why me?"

"I am assembling a brain trust of the finest cheese makers from around the world. You are the last and the best, Master Viggo. From my headquarters on Snow Monkey Island, in the Arctic Ocean, I shall create a new and magnificent cheese the likes of which humankind can't even to begin imagine. Soon, I will dominate the cheese market and then the world." A great roar of approval went up from the pirates.

"What about the children?" Mrs. Francis asked. Silence

fell. All the pirates turned and looked at her. Cheesebeard spun and walked until his face was inches from hers. Mrs. Francis tried to resist the urge to gag. The smell of the beard was utterly rancid.

"Of course, we'll be taking them with us. They will fulfill the same duties for me as they do for master Viggo here. Only, they will find that I'm not such a soft touch. Round them up."

Pirates leapt to do his bidding. Mrs. Francis struggled against the grip of Kipling but remained held fast. She turned her gaze to the shutters of the serving hatch and, for a moment, locked eyes with Hamish X. Her eyes went wide. Her surprise was cut short, however, when one of the pirates came into the room holding a cloth sack in his filthy hands.

"Captain, I cleaned out the office. Nothing of interest besides some papers, and this." The man reached into the sack and pulled out Hamish X's book.

At the sight of the book, Hamish X made to launch himself through the shutters into the cafeteria. Mimi and Parveen had to wrestle him back with all their strength.

Cheesebeard leaned over, reading the cover. "*Great Plumbers and Their Exploits*," he sniffed. "Sounds boring. But it might be worth something. Hang on." He reached out and plucked the scrap of paper from its position between the pages. His voice dripped with hatred as he read. "Hamish X!"

All the pirates gasped. Cheesebeard lunged forward and grabbed Viggo by the collar, thrusting his cheesy beard into the cheese master's face. "Hamish X. Is he here?"

"Was! Was here! He's escaped this very night," Viggo stammered. "We were about to go hunt him down when you attacked us."

Cheesebeard glared hard at Viggo. At last, he threw him to the floor. Turning to Mr. Kipling, he shouted, "Take him to the ship. Load the cheese and the children."

"He's just a boy with big boots," Viggo muttered. "I don't see what you're scared of."

A gasp went up from all the pirates, followed by hushed silence. Cheesebeard glared at Viggo again.

"Scared?" the pirate Captain rumbled. "Scared? I'm not scared of Hamish X! I have a score to settle with that boy. I want to kill him!"

Cheesebeard's booted foot connected with Viggo's bum, sending him sprawling.

"Ow," Viggo yelped. "That was my bum!"

"Say I'm scared again and you'll be wearing my boot on your bum permanently," Cheesebeard growled. "Take him away!"

The pirates hurried to follow their leader's orders, dragging Viggo out of the cafeteria and marching Mrs. Francis after him. She cast one worried look over her shoulder towards the serving hatch before she disappeared through the door in the clutches of two unsavoury-looking men.

In the kitchen, Parveen and Mimi fought to keep Hamish X from leaping out of the vat and through the shutters. They finally managed to keep him still by Mimi sitting on him while Parveen clamped both his hands over Hamish X's mouth.

Kipling and Cheesebeard stood talking in the cafeteria as the other pirates herded the children past.

"Hamish X. I didn't think he really existed," Kipling said.

"Oh he's real enough," snarled Cheesebeard, his hands clutching the heavy leather book as if he imagined it were Hamish X himself. "He killed my brother Soybeard in the

South China Sea two years ago. Soybeard and his crew had just raided a bean-curd factory on the Pearl River and were headed home with their spoils when they ran up against Hamish X in the delta. After a pitched battle, Soybeard and the cursed Hamish X fought hand to hand. My brother was about to land the killing stroke when that wretched boy kicked a hole in the ship with those ridiculous boots and sent my dear Soybeard and his crew to a watery grave."

Inside the kitchen, Mimi nudged Hamish X and whispered, "Is that true?"

Hamish X shrugged. "He deserved it."

Parveen shushed them. Kipling was speaking.

"Shall I organize a search party? He can't have gone far."

"No point. In this wind, he could have reached Saskatoon[44] by now." Cheesebeard grinned evilly and caressed the book's cover. "No. I have something the boy wants. With any luck he'll seek me out and then I'll have my revenge. Oh, and it will be sweet. Sweet like fresh ricotta! Get the children on board. We must get back to Snow Monkey Island as soon as possible."

The Captain tucked the book under his arm and strode out of the cafeteria. Kipling extracted a handkerchief from his sleeve and blew his nose. Wiping his nose daintily, he

---

[44] Although its name sounds whimsical, Saskatoon is not particularly so. It is a largish city in the Canadian province of Saskatchewan. It was named for its founder, a Ukrainian circus strongman named Saskia the Invincible who went west to seek his fortune. He walked the whole way from Montreal with a prefabricated town on his back. He had just crossed the Saskatchewan River when he stumbled on a rock and dropped the prefab town, which opened up upon impact. Saskia was forced to settle on the site and named the town Saskia's Town, which was later mispronounced by Scottish settlers as Saskia's Toon. Eventually, it was shortened to Saskatoon.

stuffed the handkerchief back up his sleeve.

"My book!" Hamish X hissed, heaving suddenly and causing Parveen's head to bang against the lid of the vat. The muffled clang sounded painfully loud in the enclosed kitchen. Mimi clapped a hand over Parveen's mouth before he could make a noise. Then she drove her fist into Hamish X's stomach, knocking the wind out of him.

Kipling froze. He cocked his head to one side and slowly turned to look at the shutters. Parveen and Mimi shrank back, willing him not to see them. The pirate laid a hand on the hilt of the elegant sword that hung from his left hip. With a slithering hiss, he drew the sword from its sheath and stood, listening.

Mimi's heart thudded in her chest. Parveen blinked in terror and Hamish X, sensing their fear, lay as still as he could, gasping for breath. Kipling's eyes narrowed and he took a step towards the shutters.

Mimi almost jumped out of her skin when the refrigerator suddenly started up with a clanging whir.

Kipling visibly relaxed. "A refrigerator," he chuckled. "Kipling, you're getting old." He slid the sword back into its sheath, spun on his heel, and walked out of the cafeteria without a backward glance.

In the kitchen, the three children huddled down.

"Sorry I punched ya but I had to do it."

"I've got to get my book back," Hamish X said.

"There are too many," Parveen insisted. "And there are only three of us. They would cut us to pieces."

"He's right. We cain't just march out there and git it. Besides, it's just a book."

"It's not just a book!" Hamish cried. "It's all I have left of my mother. I can't lose it. I can't. It's a special book. She meant for me to have it and it's the only way I can ever hope to find her."

They sat for a moment, thinking about that. Finally, Mimi shrugged.

"All right. I guess that makes as much sense as anythin'. Parveen?"

"I agree, although it's against my better judgment."

They went together to the kitchen door and peered down the hall.

No one was there. The loading had been completed. Outside the building, above the howl of the wind, huge engines coughed then grew in strength to a full-throated drone.

Hamish X, Mimi, and Parveen hurried along the hall. Cautiously they peered out into the courtyard. Above them, the huge cigar shape of the pirate airship slowly turned into the wind. Its anchor cable dangled as it was hauled up into a trap door in the bottom of the vessel. Even before the door closed, the airship swung its mighty nose around and the propellers roared, driving the ship north across the night sky. The three children watched it dwindle in the distance.

"What now?" Mimi asked.

"We go after them," Hamish X announced. He turned and went back into the factory. "We save Mrs. Francis. We free the children. We defeat the pirates. We save the day."

"I was afraid you'd say that," Parveen said.

"Come on, Parveen." Hamish X slapped the smaller boy on the back, making him wince. "Anything else would make for a very dull story."

Part 2

THE JOURNEY NORTH

Another Note from the Narrator

Having fun? The story is really taking off at this point. Daring escapes! Pirates! Zeppelins! Just the sort of elements that cracking good stories require. Not to mention engaging and delightful narration, I think you'll agree.

The ability to narrate is unique to humans in the animal kingdom. Animals are notoriously unaware of the beauty of narration. They tend to think of everything in the present tense, leading to very poor storytelling. The following is an example of a cat recounting her morning meal, obtained by computer simulation at the Animal Narration Laboratory at Yale University.

> **I am a cat. I have four paws. Oh! There's the thing with food in it. I am eating food. It is food. There's a bird at the window. I can't eat it. I'll eat this stuff instead. I am eating food. It is soft. It smells like fish. Oooh! There's a crunchy bit. I am a cat. I am licking my paws. Etc.**

You get the idea. Terrible! What a difference with a human narrating the same action:

The cat stood patiently on the tiled floor of the kitchen, its whiskers twitching in anticipation. Her owner lowered the bowl, brimming with moist, delicious tuna delight in front of her eager face. The moment the bowl struck the floor, the cat happily dug in. Nothing could distract the cat from its delectable repast. Nothing, that is, save a meadowlark alighting delicately on the window ledge. The cat raised its muzzle briefly to consider the possibility of capturing the saucy bird but realized the window was closed. With a rueful flick of the ears, she tucked back into the tuna delight, pausing only to savour a small fish bone before licking the bowl and her paws clean.

See what I'm getting at? Although the cat's version has a certain sense of immediacy, animals just can't infuse a situation with emotion and intention the way a human narrator can. Humans are the best narrators.

Many great stories have been lost to the human race over the years due to poor narration. Just think about it! Have you ever heard The Thrilling Tale of the Invention of the Shoe? The Story of Glunk, the First Girl to Discover Water Was Wet? Or even The Sweeping Epic of the Lost Keys of Dave? No, you haven't. Why? They didn't have a narrator who was up to the task. How fortunate Hamish X is. How fortunate you are! I have been assigned this tale by the Universal Narrators' Guild and I promise to exert myself to the very limit of my storytelling powers to provide you with an accurate yet thrilling narration of the story. Enough said.

We're about to enter the second part of the story. It involves a long journey during which our heroes will be tested to their limits and discover their true inner strength. Sadly, in our lives we're rarely offered such opportunities. Seldom do pirates invade our homes, stealing our loved ones and requiring us to perform a daring rescue. In fact, we hardly ever have any chance to show the heroic side of our character. I once saved a horse from drowning, but the incident really didn't carry the kind of epic grandeur one might hope for. Certainly, the horse was grateful, but he couldn't exactly tell anyone about my exploits. And even if he could, his narration would have been awful. Horses are scarcely better than cats at telling stories. They spend a lot of time talking about hay and don't use a lot of adjectives.[45]

One must make do with reading about heroic acts and selfless sacrifice and hope that will be enough to feed the soul. On that note, let's return to the story.

---

[45] The exception was Jenny, the circus pony who wrote a wonderful ten-part epic poem about the fall of Atlantis entitled "Uh-oh! Earthquake!" Sadly, it is now out of print.

Chapter 15

First, they went back to the kitchen and loaded their knapsacks with the food Mrs. Francis had poached from Viggo's private larder. Soon they had all the supplies they could carry.

Next they went to the security centre. There, Parveen did his best to plot the course of the pirate's airship on the radar screen. The airship was still visible as a blip.

"They're headed north and west, up towards the Arctic Ocean." Parveen tore a laminated map of North America off the wall, laying it flat on the card table. "They will try to save time by going in as straight a line as possible." He plucked the stub of pencil from behind his ear and drew a line on the map. "If they continue on this course they will be heading for this group of islands here. But please understand that it is only a guess."

"He said Snow Monkey Island," Mimi said. "Ever heard of it?"

"No." Parveen pursed his lips, thinking. "I have never heard of monkeys inhabiting an Arctic region before. macaque monkeys live in snowy climates, but they are native to Japan. My guess is that Snow Monkey Island is one of this cluster of volcanic cones here." His small brown finger stabbed down at the map, indicating a scattering of small black dots off the coast of Victoria Island in the Amundsen Gulf.

"We have no time to lose," Hamish X said. "Quick! Grab whatever you can use and we'll start after them immediately."

Parveen rolled the map into a tight cylinder. He found a compass, a fancy one with Global Positioning Satellite capability. It linked up to a satellite to tell one exactly where one was on the globe. While he was doing this, Hamish X outlined the plan.

"We'll take the boat that's down at the docks. The fastest way is to sail up through Hudson's Bay and then strike west. We'll have to assume they're heading for that island group. There's no reason to think Cheesebeard was lying. He didn't know we were listening. Let's just hope the weather's good."

"But what's the plan? What'll we do when we git there?" Mimi asked. "Just walk right in and ask 'em fer the book?"

"And the children, too," Hamish X pointed out. "We can't leave them in the hands of those nasty pirates."

"And Mrs. Francis," Parveen said, polishing his glasses on his sleeve. "She's a lovely, nice lady. They can keep Viggo for all I care. He's a big poo."

"Agreed," Hamish said.

"Let's review." Mimi counted on her fingers. "We trail them pirates, find ther hideout, and make 'em give back the book, the kids, and Mrs. Francis."

"That's it in a nutshell," Hamish X smiled.

"We ain't got a doughnut's chance at a police station," Mimi declared.

"You have to start at the beginning and take things as they come. First, we need transport."

Ten minutes later, after a slog through the wind, hand over hand through the deserted city, they stood on the docks. The guardhouse was a smoking ruin and, happily, no vicious dogs were in sight. One could only assume the animals had run off or succumbed during the pirate attack. On the downside, the boat that served as a supply ship for the factory rolled gently back and forth in the breakers. Keeled over on its side, a gaping hole in its hull, it wouldn't be taking them anywhere.

"Well, that just stinks," Mimi announced.

"Indeed," Parveen agreed.

"What now?"

"We find alternative transport." Hamish X turned and started back towards the factory. Parveen and Mimi followed suit.

They checked the snowmobiles, but every one had been smashed beyond repair to foil any pursuit. With the snow swirling about them, they watched Parveen poking at the engines. "I might be able to cobble together one working machine out of the parts, but we'll lose a lot of time. Besides, we have to cover a lot of distance fast and a snowmobile won't do."

This depressed the three would-be rescuers to no end. They slogged back to the cafeteria, where Hamish X used the lockpick tool on his knife to break into Viggo's larder. He liberated some milk, cocoa, and sugar and made hot chocolate to lift their spirits. While they sipped the delicious drink, Hamish X sat lost in thought.

Suddenly, he snapped his fingers and leapt to his feet. "What fools we are," he laughed. "We already have a way of going after them."

"What?" Parveen and Mimi looked at each other.

"The kites. They worked fine, didn't they? So we make more kites! Or, better yet, one big one! That's it. We have all the sheets we need. We can use the maintenance shop and all the guards' tools. It's perfect."

Parveen took out a pencil and dropped to his hands and knees, sketching on the floor of the cafeteria. He drew feverishly, pressing hard with his pencil. The tip broke. "Bother!' Parveen shouted. "Hamish, may I use your knife, please. I must sharpen this."

"I think I saw a pen in the kitchen. I'll go get it ..." Hamish X stood. Parveen shook his head. "NO PENS!"

Mimi and Hamish X were shocked by the little boy's vehemence. "What's the matter, Parv?" Mimi asked gently.

Parveen shook his head. "My name is not Parv." He held out his hand to Hamish X. "Please, your knife." Hamish X nodded and dipped his fingers into his boot, extracting the pocketknife. He handed it to Parveen, who folded out a short, sharp blade and whittled his stub of pencil to a point. He handed the knife back and bent over his drawing again. Mimi and Hamish X exchanged a questioning look and watched as he finished his plan.

Five minutes later he looked up, pushing his glasses back up on his nose.

"We will need a lot of sheets," he said, "but I believe it is possible." Mimi and Hamish X wasted no time and ran to the dormitory.

They worked through the night, making the cafeteria their workroom. Parveen was in charge. He told them what to do, with what and where. Beds were stripped and the sheets gathered in a heap. Hamish X found aluminum poles and rope in a storage shed. Following Parveen's instructions, he assembled a light but strong frame for the kite.

Mimi discovered an ancient sewing machine in Mrs. Francis's room. It was the kind of sewing machine that had a table attached, the kind you could imagine someone being chained to day in and day out, sewing pants for wealthy bank officials. She hauled it out into the cafeteria and set to work sewing the sheets into a large square sail. She wasn't a natural sewer, and spent a lot of time kicking the machine, threatening it, and complaining to the others. "Why do I have to do the sewin'? 'Cause I'm the girl? Is that it? It ain't fair, I tell ya!"

Parveen was deaf to her complaints. He was too busy with his welding tools. He scavenged bits and pieces from all kinds of different machines—cogs, belts, tubes, chains. When he had assembled enough junk, he lit an acetylene torch and began welding it all together. Sparks cascaded on the linoleum floor, scorching the yellowed surface and causing minor fires that Hamish X quickly extinguished with buckets of water. Parveen never noticed the danger. His focus on the task at hand was phenomenal. He drank only when Hamish stuck a straw between his lips, gulping absently like a machine drawing fuel from a hose.

When the larger pieces of the frame were assembled, Hamish and Mimi carried them into the Orphan Processing Room. Next, they brought in the kite sail rolled like a carpet. It was heavy, but they managed to drag and unroll it. They assembled the frame and stretched the sail over it, securing it to the poles with pieces of stout rope. When they were done they stood back and surveyed their handiwork.

The sail was the shape of a flattened triangle, about ten metres from wingtip to wingtip and three metres from nose to tail. When the large door opened the sail would fit through it, but barely.

"Nice sewing," Hamish X said.

"Ha! Ha!" Mimi bit her lip. "I hope it holds together."

A clatter of metal drew their attention to the doorway. Parveen was pushing a strange object into the room. It was metallic and bathtub-shaped. It took a moment for him to recognize it but when he did, Hamish X laughed out loud.

"Ha! The porridge vat!" He clapped his hands.

"Command gondola," Parveen corrected. He rolled the vat on its metal casters over to the middle of the floor. Mimi and Hamish X gathered around to look at the thing.

The vat had undergone some changes. First of all, a number of instruments were mounted at one end. Parveen pointed at them and listed their functions. "Radar. I stole it from the security centre. It has a range of fifty kilometres. Farther in good weather. Geosynchronous Compass. Radio transmitter. Steering controls. And a little stove. It will be cold in the upper air." Parveen didn't smile, but he looked very proud of himself. "Help me attach the gondola to the frame."

Hamish X grabbed him by the arm and looked into his eyes. "Great work, Parv."

Parveen blinked once and sniffed. "My name is Parveen. Not Parv. The gondola attaches to the frame via these chains."

They set to work. While Hamish X and Mimi fastened the frame to the gondola, Parveen disappeared again. He returned a few minutes later towing a small cart. On it were two small engines.

"Snowmobile engines," he explained. "They will help us navigate if we must fly against the direction of the wind. We won't be able to carry much fuel, so we must use them only in great emergencies." He took a wrench out of his tool belt and bolted the first engine to a plate mounted halfway up one wing.

Soon the entire vehicle was assembled, loaded, and fuelled. The bizarre creation rested on three small wheels, one in front and two in back. A discarded propeller (of which Windcity had plenty) was mounted on the front of the gondola. Parveen had rigged it to a generator that could supply electricity for the onboard instruments.

Finally, after twenty-six hours of hard work, they were ready to set off after the pirates. On the bright side, the snow had ceased to fall. On the dark side, they didn't know if the thing they'd built would fly.

Parveen climbed into the gondola and manned the controls. Hamish X pushed the button and the big door began to rise. Instantly, the wind began to churn through the open door. Tiny bits of ice and snow scoured their faces.

Hamish X shook his head. "I just realized," he said ruefully. "We want to go northwest to get to Snow Monkey Island."

"Yeah? So?" Mimi demanded.

"Well, that wind is blowing southeast. We can't steer into the wind."

Parveen looked at his watch. "Correct. That would be a problem on most days of the year, but not today."

"Why not today?" Hamish X asked.

Parveen continued to stare at his watch for a few more seconds, then held up his hand. As if by magic, the wind died, suddenly and completely.

"Today," Parveen announced to his astonished friends, "is Flip Day."

Mimi and Hamish X looked at each other and smiled. "Flip Day!" they crowed.

"Enough of that," Parveen said crossly. "We have to get this thing out in the right position when the wind picks up again."

Mimi and Hamish X each got behind a wing and quickly pushed the strange vessel out into the early morning light. Without any wind, the day was eerily quiet. All around them houses popped and creaked in their release from the constant pressure, as if a great weight had been lifted. The

sun shone down, faint and watery yellow. The oddest sight of all was the clouds drifting to a halt. The three children marvelled at the sky and the clouds and the silence, revelling in the wonder of being outside in the morning light. Parveen called them back to business.

"We have to align the vehicle on the right trajectory to take advantage of the wind when it comes. Hurry."

Mimi and Hamish X got behind the wings and pushed the little flyer until it aimed more or less down the road towards the docks. They had barely managed to get the craft out onto the concrete apron in front of the factory when the wind began to stir.

"Look!" Mimi shouted, pointing up at the sky. The clouds were now streaming to the northwest. And from the southeast a sound began to grow, a rumbling, howling whoosh that filled the horizon.

"Get ready," Parveen shouted just as the wind picked up.

The little vessel began lifting in short hops that left Mimi and Hamish X suspended in the air, their feet churning. They heaved as hard as they could, trying to keep the wings level. "I'm starting the engines!" Parveen shouted. First one, then the other sputtered, coughed, and finally caught. The forward push of the motors drove the aircraft forward with growing speed. Soon, Hamish X and Mimi were holding on for dear life, dragging behind the wings.

With a chorus of ear-splitting creaks, pops, and moans, all the houses in Windcity slowly tilted from one side to the other in the new prevailing wind. It was an awesome spectacle to see the entire town shift steadily in the opposite direction.

The children didn't have the leisure to appreciate the sight. Their craft picked up speed as it headed down the wide main street that led to the docks. The slanted houses whirred by as the dock approached alarmingly fast. Hamish X clutched the metal frame, pulling himself up and clinging like a monkey under the wing. He looked over to see how Mimi was doing.

She was having trouble holding on. She couldn't manage to pull her long legs up high enough to hook them over the wing strut. As he watched, one of her hands ripped free.

"I'm gonna fall!" she shouted, desperately trying to swing her free hand up to catch the frame.

Parveen had enough to worry about. He was hauling back on the stick, trying to get the craft off the ground. They were running out of road: the dock was only a couple of hundred metres away. It was up to Hamish X to help Mimi.

He started pulling himself hand over hand down the wing until he got to the gondola. He dropped easily in behind Parveen.

"I don't know if we're going to make it," Parveen called.

Hamish X thumped him on the back. "I know you can do it." He scanned the floor of the gondola and found what he was looking for: a length of rope. Quickly, he tied one end of it to the handle of the gondola and knotted the other end as tightly as he could around his waist.

The machine was bouncing along the dock now. Parveen gritted his teeth and hauled back on the stick for all he was worth.

"Help!" Mimi shouted. She still dangled from one hand, but now she was barely hanging on. Hamish X stepped up on the edge of the gondola and tensed to spring.

Mimi's fingers finally gave out. She let go just as the kite lifted into the air off the end of the dock, rising up over the cold grey water of the bay like a gull. Hamish X launched himself into space, extending his arms as far as they would reach. He managed to grab a fistful of Mimi's parka hood as she fell past him. Holding on for dear life, he braced himself as he reached the end of the rope. But despite its wicked snap when it went taut, Hamish X didn't lose his grip. The kite rose gently on the stiff wind with Hamish X dangling beneath it and Mimi dangling below Hamish X.

They swung, the rope creaking gently and the wind rushing past. Hamish X grinned down at Mimi and Mimi grinned up at him.

"It's the only way to fly," he said and began to haul her up.

Mr. Candy and Mr. Sweet

Thousands of kilometres away, in a small white clapboard[46] house in East Providence, Rhode Island, Mr. Sweet and Mr. Candy sat drinking tea. East Providence is the oldest neighbourhood in a very old city. The tiny house stood on a quiet, leafy street, cupped in the hand of pleasantness and normality.

Mr. Sweet and Mr. Candy sat in an old-fashioned kitchen with chintz curtains and Formica countertops and gleaming chrome appliances: a toaster, a blender, an automatic mixer. They faced each other at a black and white kitchen table on black and chrome chairs, sipping tea that was thick and black from white china cups. The only things that looked out of place were Mr. Candy and Mr. Sweet, who were dressed in long grey coats, gloves, fedoras, and goggles despite the warmth of an early spring day.

---

[46] *Clapboard* comes from the Dutch "claphout" which means "clapping house." This was a structure in ancient Dutch towns where people would go to clap vigorously as a form of exercise. The Dutch believed that good circulation in the hands was essential to good mental health. Visitors to Holland believed exactly the opposite when they saw the Dutch stream into little houses and clap vigorously for no reason at all. Clapboard houses have overlaying boards that help dampen sound, and so we call any house with wooden siding "clapboard," though we rarely use them for the intended purpose.

A chime sounded, causing the two agents to lower their cups and cock their heads. A lovely female voice filled the kitchen.

"Subject Hamish X is moving north on vector 718. Speed 257 kilometres per hour." The voice was rich and beautiful, feminine and kind.

"Give us a visual please," said Mr. Candy.

A three-dimensional map of the northern hemisphere flickered into existence on the tabletop, resting like an overturned bowl on the Formica surface. The image rotated slightly, mimicking the rotation of the Earth. The map, for such it was, held every possible feature of the Earth's surface–cities, rivers, mountains. All were picked out in perfect detail. A tiny amber dot blinked and crawled northward from the tiny dot that represented Windcity.

The two agents leaned in like hungry children around a birthday cake.

"Mr. Candy, it has begun again."

"Indeed. For the last time."

"Shall we go?"

"Let's!"

They put down their cups of tea and walked out the back door.

Moments later, a black helicopter rose above East Providence, sweeping out to sea and then heading north.

Chapter 16

The kite sped northwest, driven by the powerful tailwind. The small engines were switched off to conserve fuel. Parveen stood at the controls, angling the rudder so that they sped at a forty-five degree angle to the gust due north. He kept one eye on the radar screen, the other on a bank of black clouds lowering in the distance.

"That storm front is keeping its distance so far, but heaven help us if it decides to move across our path." He tapped the face of a dial on the console. "According to the GPS, we are now a thousand kilometres to the northwest of Windcity."

Hamish X and Mimi huddled near the stove. Hamish X had fallen asleep, his head lolling gently with the swaying of the gondola. Mimi watched his face for a moment. He mumbled something that sounded like "Mother," frowned, and shifted slightly. He didn't wake up.

Mimi stood up carefully to avoid waking him and moved to Parveen's side. She stretched and looked around at the darkness below. There were no signs of habitation below them, no lights. She wore a touque[47] on her head, forcing her frizzy hair down around her ears into a fluttering halo.

---

[47] *Touque* is the French Canadian word for a knitted woollen cap. It was invented in 1734 by Gerard Touque, a native of Quebec City, as a primitive form of hair replacement therapy. Touques became a favourite of trappers because in a pinch, you could use them as a bag to carry musket balls, coins, or salted nuts.

"Any sign o' them pirates?" she asked.

"No sign," Parveen assured her. "All we can do is stay on their last known course and see if we can catch up to them." He cast a glance back at their sleeping companion. "He's a very strange person. Not bad, but certainly there are a lot of odd things about him."

"He shore is strange. I don't know what to make of 'im."

"I've been doing some reading," Parveen said. "Granted, my access to research materials is limited, but from what I could gather, the first time Hamish X appeared in the newspapers was twelve years ago."

"Twelve years," Mimi echoed. "That's impossible! He cain't be more than twelve years old now."

"My thoughts exactly," Parveen agreed. "That means either he isn't who he says he is or ..."

"Or what?"

"There's something weird going on. With the ODA involved, anything is possible. There may be more to him than meets the eye."

"More to who?" Hamish X pushed himself to his feet, stretching. He smiled at them and pulled his woolly jacket closer as the cold air whistling past began to freeze his exposed face.

"Uh, Cheesebeard. That pirate! What's with the beard?"

Mimi elbowed Parveen subtly but painfully. "Yes," he added, "how can he stand the smell of it, I wonder?"

"People can get used to any number of odd things about themselves," Hamish X said meaningfully, looking at his friends each in turn. "Sometimes you have no choice. He's a bad guy though. Luckily, we all trust each other and we accept our differences. They make us stronger. We have to trust each other or else we'll fail."

Parveen and Mimi exchanged a pointed[48] look.

No one spoke for a moment as they looked out over the tundra below, a vast flat expanse of dirty white stretching to the horizon in every direction. No trees grew: they were above the treeline.[49] "Makes a body feel small, don't it," Mimi said finally. "I'm gonna get some more sleep." She sat down next to the stove and closed her eyes. Before long, she was snoring softly.

"Want me to take over?" asked Hamish X, breaking the silence.[50] Parveen thought about the offer for a moment. He shrugged and moved aside, holding the stick until Hamish X could step in and take it in his gloved hand. Immediately, Hamish X had to brace himself to hold the craft steady. He marvelled at the strength Parveen hid in his tiny body.

Parveen pointed to the compass. "Keep the needle steady at NNW. That's the last course we know they were taking." He dug in his pocket and pulled out a heel of crusty bread, tearing off a corner daintily and chewing.

Hamish X concentrated on steering for a few minutes until he thought he had the hang of it. The clouds in the

---

48 *Pointed* in this sense means "full of meaning," not pointy. Exchanging truly pointy looks can lead to someone losing an eye.

49 The treeline marks the most northerly point that trees may grow in the world. Many believe the treeline is a function of climate, but it's actually the result of a treaty negotiated in 1852 between the British and the Inuit. The Inuit like to be able to see anyone coming for a good distance before they arrive, and so they keep the trees cut back. Also, it makes it easier to drive a dogsled on the flat ground, although the stumps can be a hazard.

50 To be honest, there was no silence to be broken: chains rattled, fabric flapped, air whistled, tools jangled, etc.

east looked to be coming closer. He stole a quick glance at Parveen. The boy's small dark face, framed in the fur hood of his parka, was emotionless and still. He chewed the bread mechanically, without pleasure, as if it were merely fuel to keep the machine that was his body and mind running.

"Parveen?"

"Uh huh?"

"I've never seen you smile about anything the whole time I've been here."

Parveen stopped chewing. He turned and looked at Hamish X, blinked once, twice behind his glasses. Hamish X persisted.

"What's your story? How did you end up here?"

"It is no interesting tale."

"I'd like to hear it anyway. We have time to kill. Mimi told me her story. I've told you all of mine."

Parveen thought for a moment. He shrugged and stuffed the bread back into his pocket. After he checked the instruments one last time, he started to talk.

Chapter 17
PARVEEN'S STORY

I come from India. It is a hot place, as hot as this place is cold. I lived in a house in the centre of a fairly big town with my twelve brothers and sisters, my father, and my beautiful mother.

We were very happy, though we were never very rich. We had enough to eat and clothes to wear. All the children slept in one large room. My six brothers and I slept against one wall and my six sisters against the other, all of us stacked in bunk beds that climbed to the ceiling. We would whisper to each other in the darkness, laughing and giggling until Mother called for us to go to sleep. I was the youngest child, and all my siblings teased me that I was my mother's favourite.

My mother was a beautiful woman with long, lustrous black hair and sparkling eyes. And that's not me saying that because she was my mother. Everyone in the village thought so. She was a musician: she played the sitar, a sort of Indian guitar but with many more strings. She sang in the movies sometimes, although you wouldn't have seen her. She sang the songs and pretty actresses mouthed the words. It made me angry sometimes that they could steal her voice. She was prettier than any of those actresses. She always tucked me into my bed at night. Before she turned off the light she would say to us, "Smile for me, my children. You are home now."

My father worked in a factory that made ballpoint pens.

He came home every night smelling of ink, but I thought his job was wonderful. I imagined that people all over the world took the pens and wrote all manner of amazing things: letters of love, notes to the milkman (in such places where milkmen existed),[51] poems about fishes in the sea, plans for brilliant inventions, scientific reports! Oh, how important and powerful a man was my father, who made sure every person in the wide world could write what he or she needed to write.

Our neighbours all thought my father and mother were a strange match. Often I would overhear them talking, saying that my father was nothing compared to my beautiful mother. They could never understand how important my father was. One man in particular was very jealous of my father. His name was Ndur Nath and he owned much property in the town. Ndur owned the pen factory where my father worked. He watched my mother whenever she went out of the house. He dogged her steps. It bothered me to see the way he looked at her, but he couldn't darken our happy home. We were all so happy together. Every night we would come home and my mother would say "Smile, children. You are home now."

Our happiness couldn't last. One day, my father began to feel poorly. He coughed and his hands shook. He took a day off work and then another, but he didn't improve. My mother was terribly worried. A doctor came and studied Father, looked under his eyelids, took his pulse. He spoke to my mother in the kitchen, and when he left Mother had tears in her eyes.

---

[51] Milk is not widely consumed in India. Cows are sacred and milk comes from cows, so it is also sacred. Butter is also thought very highly of and left alone. Yogourt is eaten but only after lengthy apologies.

"Father is very sick. The fumes in the factory have poisoned his blood," she explained. "We must take care of him now, because he has taken care of us."

I couldn't believe it. The very ink that I found so wonderful had made my father sick. We did our best to take care of him while my mother worked harder than ever to bring in money. Father didn't improve. He died in the night with us all around him.

The next day, Ndur Nath arrived at the door to tell us how sorry he was. Was there anything he could do to help my mother? My mother assured him she needed nothing and he went away—but not for long. He came the next day and the day after that. He hounded my mother to marry him. He promised he would take care of all the children as if they were his very own. She refused his offers, but as time went on and our bills began to mount, Mother started to soften. I could tell she didn't like him, but she needed some way to pay for food and rent. She wasn't able to get any work singing. I suspected it was because Ndur threatened anyone who wanted to hire her.

Finally, she agreed to be Ndur's wife. They were married and he took us into his big house in the centre of town.

As soon as we arrived, Ndur Nath's true nature was revealed. All of us were given separate rooms. We weren't allowed to speak to each other in the halls or at dinner. We were forced to go to bed at eight o'clock and our bedroom doors were always locked. We were virtually prisoners.

My mother did her best to spend time with us, but Ndur demanded she spend all her time with him. She still managed to see us at bedtime, but she wasn't the same. The light was gone out of her eyes. Ndur forbade her to sing in the house. Then he started complaining about us.

"These children are lazy and good for nothing!" he would shout. "They need to learn discipline!" One by one, my older brothers and sisters were sent away to schools far from each other. It broke my mother's heart. Soon, I was the only one left. My mother grew sick and weak. I remember the last night she came to my room. She was pale and trembled uncontrollably. She sat down on my bed.

"Little Parveen," she smiled, a ghost of her former smile, "I am afraid for you. I miss your father very much and I fear I may join him soon." I wept and hugged her close. She was so frail. She took my face in her hands. "I love you, little Parveen, and wherever we are together that is home. Smile. You are home now."

I smiled as best as I could. She kissed me on the cheek and turned out the light. The door was closed. The lock was turned. I never saw her again ... she passed in the night. I think it was from a broken heart.

The rest of the story is quickly told. Ndur called the ODA. The next day, the grey agents came and took me away. I was sent off to Windcity. I have been there ever since.

Chapter 18

"That's why no pens," Hamish X said, pointing to the pencil behind Parveen's ear.

Parveen nodded. "And no smiles."

"She loved you very much," Hamish X went on. "And you're lucky you remember her so well."

"Indeed," Parveen said. "I do not envy you having no remembrance of your mother or father."

They were silent for a while. The sheets fluttered. Mimi snored.

"You know, Parveen, I think your mother wouldn't have wanted you to go through your whole life never smiling again. She would have wanted you to be happy."

"Perhaps." Parveen shrugged. "Perhaps I will smile again … when I feel I have a home again."

They fell silent once more. Parveen checked the compass. He was about to check the reading against the stars when a green blip appeared on the very edge of the radar screen. The blip flickered and then grew stronger.

"It seems that we have found our quarry," Parveen said.

Hamish grinned, showing all his teeth. "I'll wake Mimi."

THE SUN ROSE in the east off the starboard side of the airship, casting a feeble light across the white plain of ice below. Mrs. Francis stood on the bridge of the *Vulture*. Around her, the crew manned the various machines that kept the airship aloft. Mr. Kipling loosely held her elbow, giving her a guided tour. "These levers here control our altitude," he said, indicating a series of sticks with rubber handles pointing out of a large cabinet. Cables ran out of the top of the cabinet and disappeared through a slot in the ceiling. The handles were manned by a toothless gentleman. "And this wheel controls the rudder that steers the ship." He pointed to a large brass wheel mounted on a post that faced the broad front window. The helmsman, a narrow-chested man with greasy hair, leered at Mrs. Francis.

"Hallo, darlink," the helmsman winked, licking his lips. "My name's Schmidt. You can call me Karl. You fanzy a little … Ow!" Mr. Kipling's gloved fingers pinched the helmsman's right ear, twisting the tender flesh painfully. He would have pinched the left ear, but the helmsman didn't have one.

"Keep a civil tongue in your head, Helmsman Schmidt. Mrs. Francis is a lady and therefore deserves your respect."

"Sorry, Herr Kiplink," Schmidt whimpered. "Forgiff me! I am a pirate after all."

"Duly noted." Kipling looked down his nose at the snivelling helmsman, "However, pirate or no, there is no excuse for bad manners. Any more indelicate comments out of you and I will cut off your arm and beat you to death with it. Understood?"

"Ja!"

"You've taken quite a shine to our guest, Mr. Kipling!" The Captain's booming voice was jarring in the enclosed space. He stood at the door of the bridge, his crusty beard swaying in time with the ship. Mr. Kipling released the helmsman's ear. Schmidt sneered at Kipling's back and turned to his work.

"I was just giving Mrs. Francis a tour of the ship, Captain." Kipling extracted his hankie from his sleeve and began to clean his fingers fastidiously.

"Just don't get too fond of her," the Captain growled. "She's a prisoner, a piece of property. I don't want you getting all bent out of shape if I decide we have to kill her."

Mr. Kipling became very still. He stopped fussing with his hankie and looked lazily at the Captain. Then he shrugged and stuffed the hankie up his sleeve. "Indeed," he said simply.

A klaxon sounded. Red lights flashed.

"Captain," the radar operator called, "I've picked up a contact. It's directly behind us." The Captain and Mr. Kipling rushed to the radar station. They bent over the screen, its green light casting a ghoulish glow over their faces. The radar operator pointed to a small dot flickering at the bottom of the screen. "It's small, sir," he said, "but it's moving very fast."

As they watched, the tiny dot moved closer to the centre of the screen.

"They're gaining," Mr. Kipling said. "They've closed to just under five thousand metres."

"How many feet is that?" Cheesebeard asked.

"I'm not sure." Kipling scratched his chin. "One point six kilometres to the mile, so …"

"Oh never mind," the Captain spat. "Bloody metric!"

"About sree miles, give or take?" the helmsman offered.

The Captain slapped him on the back of the head.

"Ow." The helmsman sulkily rubbed his skull.

"Who are they, Kipling?" Cheesebeard demanded. "Where did they come from?"

"It would appear from a reverse plotting of their course, Captain, that they followed us from Windcity." Mr. Kipling traced a line on the screen. "As for who they are, well, I'm sure I don't know."

Momentarily forgotten, Mrs. Francis felt her heart leap

in her breast. *Hamish X is coming*, she thought, feeling a first glimmer of hope since the pirate attack. *And Mimi and Parveen*. She allowed herself the briefest smile.

"How can they move so fast? We had over a day's head start."

"They are much lighter than we are, Captain."

"Annoying!" Cheesebeard picked a lump of Emmenthal from his whiskers and chewed on it furiously. He slapped the helmsman sharply on the back of the head again.

"Ow!" said the helmsman again. "Vot vas zhat for?"

"Bring us about," Cheesebeard ordered.

"Aye, Captain."

The helmsman spun the wheel. The nose of the ship began to turn slowly as its engines laboured to alter course. Cheesebeard glared out into the night, straining to pick out the pursuers. He raised a pair of field glasses to his eyes and scanned the sky. "Could it be ...?" he muttered into his cheesy beard. Aloud he said, "We'll take care of them and then head back to the island. No loose threads!"

"Indeed, sir." Kipling frowned.

"THEY'RE TURNIN' 'ROUND!" Mimi shouted.

"Four and a half kilometres and closing." Parveen hunched over the controls. "They'll be on us in less than three minutes."

"Can we turn away?" Hamish X asked.

"We are at the mercy of the wind," Parveen pointed out, "while they have powerful engines. We cannot hope to outmanouevre them."

"So what do we do?" Mimi turned to Hamish X. "Don't you have a plan?"

"My plan was perfectly formulated up to the point

where we caught up to them," Hamish X shrugged. "Now I have to come up with another plan."

"Range: three kilometres and closing," Parveen announced.

"We've gotta do something!" Mimi shouted.

Hamish X frantically looked around the interior of the gondola, searching for inspiration. There wasn't much. They had no weapons. There were three backpacks, some blankets, and a coil of rope attached to a makeshift anchor made of strips of iron welded together. Hamish X smiled. He grabbed the rope and handed it to Mimi.

"Attach this to the gondola. Tie it to something secure!" he shouted. Then he picked up the anchor. It wasn't particularly heavy, being intended as a grapple that would hook onto a stationary object and moor the little aircraft. He turned and watched for the approaching ship. Mimi searched around and finally decided on one of the handles on the side of the vat. She looped the cable through and tied it as securely as she could. She held the rest of the rope coiled loosely in her hands.

"One kilometre and closing," Parveen called out, keeping his eyes on the radar screen.

"What are ya gonna do?" Mimi demanded.

"When I tell you, let go of the rope," Hamish X said.

Mimi scowled and turned to watch the approaching pirate ship.

"CAPTAIN, THEY'RE COMING right for us," the radar man announced. "Should we change course again?" Captain Cheesebeard stood at the front of the bridge, looking through the broad window. He lowered his binoculars and sneered.

"No. Stay the course. If they ram us it'll be like a mosquito butting a rhinoceros. They'll be crushed." Mrs. Francis let out a little gasp, her hand flying to her mouth. The Captain turned his head and grinned at her.

"We'll have to scrape them off the windscreen like so much melted Monterey Jack, but otherwise it'll be a minor inconvenience." Cheesebeard laughed at Mrs. Francis's horrified expression. He raised his glasses and turned his attention back to the approaching vessel.

"Perhaps you would like to go to your cabin, Madam," offered Mr. Kipling gently, placing a delicate hand on her elbow.

"She stays and watches!" Cheesebeard barked.

"Aye, Captain." A flash of annoyance darted across Kipling's bland face. He stepped back.

"Five hundred metres and closing," the radar operator intoned.

ON THE LITTLE FLYER they could easily see the pirate ship coming closer. In the thin sunlight, its black skin was like a hole in the sky. The bridge was visible now and they could hear the thrum of her propellers over the rush of the wind.

"Parveen," Hamish X said, "here's what I want you to do. Take us straight in as if we're going to ram her, but at the last instant I want you to take us down so that we pass right under. I want to get a shot at the big propellers on the back end."

"Our flyer isn't very manoeuvrable, but I think I can manage that," Parveen answered, adjusting his glasses. He took a firmer grip on the steering stick.

"I think I see where yer goin' with this," Mimi said.

"Just be sure and let the rope go once I've thrown the anchor." Hamish leaned over the edge of the gondola, letting the anchor dangle out into space.

"One hundred metres," Parveen declared.

Hamish X grinned a savage grin, his hair flying in the wind. "It's good to be alive!" he shouted.

CAPTAIN CHEESEBEARD lowered his glasses in shock. "I knew it! It *is* him! It's Hamish X! I've heard he's brave, but this is suicidal."

"He's not afraid of anything," Mrs. Francis blurted.

"It doesn't matter. He'll be dead soon. They can't hope to survive an impact," Cheesebeard smiled. "My brother Soybeard will be avenged!"

Mr. Kipling stepped to the Captain's side. "Sir, I know they won't survive, but we might not survive either."

"What are you talking about, Kipling?"

"If they pierce the hydrogen bags, a tiny spark could cause an explosion. The result could be catastrophic."

Cheesebeard pondered this news. Tension showed in the faces of all the crew on the bridge. The Captain picked up a microphone attached to the

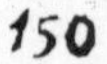

command console and spoke into it. "Forward gunners prepare to fire. Knock them out of the sky."

"No!" Mrs. Francis cried. "They're just children!"

Cheesebeard laughed. The crew laughed with him.

All except Mr. Kipling. Mrs. Francis glared at the tall man. "They'll die."

Mr. Kipling met her gaze and said softly, "But the hundred children in the cargo hold won't." Mrs. Francis opened her mouth to answer but couldn't think of anything to say. He was right. She had a duty to look after the orphans on the ship, and could only hope that the three children would survive the attack. So she turned and looked out the great window at the front of the bridge, biting her lip and wringing the belt of her pink bathrobe in her chubby hands.

"Impact in ten seconds," the radar operator's voice cracked nervously.

Cheesebeard turned and watched the flyer approach. He spoke one word into the microphone.

"Fire!"

Pirates in two gun pods on the underside of the ship opened fire simultaneously. Streams of bullets lanced out, seeking the fragile flyer as it raced forward.

"THEY'RE SHOOTIN' AT US!" Mimi shouted.

"Duck!" Hamish X grabbed her arm, pulling her down below the lip of the metal vat. Parveen hunched over, following their lead.

Bullets rang off the steel surface, denting but not piercing the thick metal. The wings, however, were not impervious to damage. The bullets stitched lines of ragged holes across the surface of the fabric. "We're hit!" Parveen shouted. He clung to the steering stick, trying to compensate as the flyer lurched.

The shooting continued, ringing the gondola like a fire bell, deafening the three children inside its enclosed space. A dark shadow passed over them. They looked up to see the bulk of the pirate airship. The shooting stopped.

"We're out of their firing arc," Parveen called out, wrestling with the stick. The flyer shimmied erratically despite his efforts.

Hamish X leapt to his feet, picking up the anchor. "Get ready. We'll only have one chance."

Mimi struggled to her feet. Hamish frowned in deep concentration as the airship sped by above. They were so close they could see the individual bolts on the cabins and the seams of metal plating on the hull. The thrum of the propellers grew louder. Hamish swung the anchor gently, biding his time.

"I cannot hold us much longer," Parveen called. "The flyer is too badly damaged."

"Just a little longer!" Hamish X cried. Finally, the thrum of the two propellers became deafening. They spun like huge pinwheels on either side, blindingly fast, driving the airship forward. Hamish tensed, whirled the anchor around his head once, and flung it upwards. With a clang, it crashed into the port propeller, snagged onto one of its blades, and began to whip around.

"Let go, Mimi!" Hamish X shouted. Mimi dropped the spool of rope and immediately it began to slither after the anchor, wrapping itself around the axle of the propeller and snarling it until it ground to a halt. The airship, driven now by only one propeller, began to veer off on an angle.

"Yes!" Hamish X pumped his fist in the air. "Now we climb up the cable and storm the ship."

"Are you nuts? There are only two of us!"

"Don't worry, Mimi," Hamish laughed wildly, "I'll leave some for you!" He reached for the cable to begin his ascent, but at that instant the rope came to its end. With a loud snap, the line broke. The deck lurched beneath them, throwing them to the floor of the gondola. Hamish X's face fell. "They're free! We failed!"

"The flyer has lost structural integrity. We are going down!" Parveen shouted.

"Grab hold of something!" Hamish cried.

The vessel began to dive steeply. Parveen hauled back on the stick, trying to avoid a nosedive. Hamish and Mimi clung to the edge of the gondola, watching as the snowy earth rushed up towards them. It was almost impossible to tell how far they were from impact because the ground was universally white and featureless.[52]

"Brace yourselves!" Parveen shouted.

They were thrown from their feet as the flyer skipped across the ice and snow like a stone. Once. Twice. Then the wing plowed into the ground, spraying up a sheet of ice and snow, spinning and sliding to a stop against a wall of ice. The flyer came to rest, creaking and popping in the frigid air. Nothing stirred.

---

[52] The white featurelessness of the Arctic is an age-old complaint of aerial navigators. Many plans have been proposed to combat the problem, including one that would have millions of gallons of orange food dye dropped onto the ice cap to improve visibility. Fortunately, the idea was rejected.

Chapter 19

The *Vulture* laboured in a wide turn, black smoke trailing from its crippled port propeller. The vast shadow of the airship passed over the crash site like a bad dream.

Cheesebeard surveyed the broken craft through his binoculars. Still nothing stirred.

"Status," he barked.

"Von of ze props is jammed!" shouted Schmidt. "I'll have to compenzate."

"Engineering reports that the axle is burnt out on the port propeller shaft," Kipling announced. "Our top speed is cut in half, but no major damage otherwise."

"Excellent," Cheesebeard said, lowering his binoculars. "Keep us on course for Snow Monkey Island. I'm going to my cabin." On his way out of the bridge he stopped beside Mrs. Francis. Tears streamed down her face. Her red eyes glared at him with pure hatred.

"You murderer!" she sobbed.

"Why thank you." Cheesebeard gave a little bow. "I'm also a cutthroat, a scoundrel, and I've defaulted on my taxes." He laughed heartily. The crew joined in, mocking poor Mrs. Francis and her tears. They all thought it the most hilarious fun. "I've done it! I've killed Hamish X! My brother is avenged!" The crew cheered.

All save Mr. Kipling, who looked decidedly uncomfortable. He fished out his handkerchief and offered it to Mrs. Francis. She scowled at him. "Keep it," she spat. "Don't pretend you're any better than these ruffians just because you're polite."

"Please, Madam …"

She cut him off. "I wish to go now."

Mr. Kipling frowned. He flicked his wrist at a guard.

"Take our guest to her cabin," he ordered.

"You can keep your cabin, sir. I want to go to the children. They'll be frightened. I should be there to comfort them."

"Mrs. Francis, I …"

"Take me to the children immediately!" Mrs. Francis snapped.

Mr. Kipling hesitated for a moment, then nodded. The guard led Mrs. Francis off the bridge.

"Give up, Kiplink," Schmidt taunted. "You don't stand a chanze mit her. She vants a real man." The helmsman thumped his chest, eliciting a further gale of laughter from the crew. Schmidt's hand was suddenly pinned to the wheel by the slim blade of a stiletto.[53]

"Eeeeeya!" Schmidt screamed. He tugged at the handle of the dagger. The crew fell silent.

"Leave it where it is." Mr. Kipling's soft, cultured voice filled the bridge. "If you remove it, I will gut you like a fish." He smiled at the others. "That goes for the rest of you as well." He looked at the agonized Schmidt. "You may return my knife at the end of your watch. And be sure to clean it first. There's a good fellow." With a final look around the bridge, he turned and left.

---

[53] The stiletto, a thin-bladed knife easily hidden up the sleeve and designed for throwing, was invented by an Italian armourer. He was catering to cultured customers who didn't want to ruin the hang of their clothing by concealing a bulky knife. Alberto Stiletto then went on to produce a line of boots with a long blade concealed in the heel. These were less popular because it isn't very handy to pull one's boot off and hurl it at an enemy. The stiletto became fashionable merely as a piece of footwear and survives to this day.

DOWN IN THE CARGO HOLD, the children huddled together trying to keep warm. The large room was stacked with crates of cheese stolen from the Windcity Orphanage and Cheese Factory and lashed to the bulkheads with thick leather straps to keep them from sliding around. Caribou Blue fumes filled the air, making the children light-headed. The only illumination came from a string of bare bulbs encased in wire cages high on the ceiling. In the corner, a small toilet—or head, as the pirates called it—provided the only creature comfort.[54]

Viggo sat on a crate by the door and wept. His bony shoulders shook with sobs. He was chained to the only two guards to have survived the attack, Pianoface and Tubaface.

"Oh, my beautiful cheese," he wailed. "My beautiful factory! My beautiful life! Why has this happened to me?"

"Quit whining," Tubaface snarled.

"Yeah," Pianoface scowled. "It's bad enough we're stuck here. I don't have to put up with your blubbering."

"You two cowards surrendered at the first sign of trouble. What was I paying you for?"

"Picking on children's one thing," Tubaface shrugged. "Pirates armed with swords and guns—not in my job description."

---

[54] The tradition of calling the toilet on a ship the "head" comes from the 1600s when English sailors were forced to perform their bodily functions while they went about their shipboard duties. Sailors up in the rigging just let go whenever they needed to, often dropping their foul cargo on the head of the ship's Captain. Thus the slang phrase for relieving oneself became "Going on the Captain's head!" later shortened to "Going on the head!" Then, when toilets were installed, the term stuck and the head became the accepted term for a shipboard toilet. In the English navy, captains were better respected. Sailors leaned over the back rail of the ship to do their business. This small raised deck was called the poop for obvious reasons.

"Exactly," Pianoface agreed. "I wonder if they're hiring. We should ask. If you can't beat 'em, join 'em, eh?"

They were interrupted by the sound of the hatch spinning open. As two armed pirates escorted Mrs. Francis into the hold, the children leapt to their feet and swarmed around her. "Oh, my dears," she cried, hugging and kissing every little child she could reach. "Have they been mean to you? Are you hurt?"

The pirates drew out long wooden sticks from their belts.

"Settle down," one of them shouted. "Get back away from the door."

Mrs. Francis turned on the pirates. "How dare you? These children are obviously cold and hungry. Have they been fed since they were so rudely kidnapped? Why are there no blankets in this draughty place? I demand that they be attended to immediately!" She stamped her foot, placed her hands on her hips, and glowered. Though she was only a small, round woman, she seemed to tower over the pirates in her righteous anger. They took an unconscious step back and timidly exchanged a glance.

"We'll take up the matter with the Captain, Mum." The pirates cast down their eyes and backed shamefaced out of the hatch, slamming it shut after them.

"Oh, Mrs. Francis," Viggo cried, "I'm so glad to see you. They've treated me in the most beastly manner, chained me to these simpletons ..."

"Oi," objected Pianoface. "Watch it."

"What's a simpleton?" asked Tubaface.

"I need you to talk to the Captain immediately," Viggo continued. "You will tell him I am a gentleman and not used to such terrible treatment."

Mrs. Francis looked at him with undisguised disdain. "Master Viggo, I suggest you get used to bad treatment because that's all you're likely to get. My mother always told me that in this life you get what you give. You're a mean, cruel man and you're getting exactly what you deserve." She looked at all the little faces of the children gathered around her. "These children deserve better after all you've put them through. If I talk to the Captain, it will be for them, not for you."

Viggo stared, astonished at the little round woman who up until a moment ago he'd thought of as his timid little housekeeper. She seemed different now, resolute and sure. His heart sank. He shrank back against the wall.

"She told *you*," Pianoface sneered.

"Shut up," Viggo said and sat silently watching as Mrs. Francis looked to her small charges. Sitting on the crate, hugging his bony knees to his bony chest, Viggo realized he was truly on his own. He began to think about what the idiotic guards had said. "If you can't beat 'em," he whispered to himself, "join 'em."

Mrs. Francis examined each one of the children for bumps and bruises. The older children she set to care for the youngest, cleaning them with water from the little basin in the corner by the head. She counted every one and sorted each according to age, making sure that all the children were accounted for. Finally, she assigned everyone a place to sleep. She was just finishing up when the hatch opened. The two pirate guards were back. Between them they wheeled a vast pot filled with some kind of stew. They left it by the door and beside it tossed a net bag filled with buns and a box of plastic bowls and spoons.

"The buns are a bit mouldy, but beggars can't be choosers," the first pirate said.

"Indeed," Mrs. Francis said. "Please thank the Captain for me."

"Oh, this ain't from the Captain. Compliments of Mr. Kipling."

Mrs. Francis raised her eyebrows in surprise. She straightened her pink housecoat and ran a hand over her dishevelled hair. "Please offer him our thanks."

"Whatever." The pirates went out the hatch and locked it behind them.

"All right, children." Mrs. Francis clapped her hands. "Form a line, youngest to oldest. There may not be enough bowls and spoons, so we'll have to share." They eagerly scrambled to follow her instructions. Soon Mrs. Francis was dipping bowls into the steaming broth and handing them to hungry children. The soup wasn't exactly hearty, but the buns helped fill up the little bellies.

"What about us?" Viggo demanded. "I'm starving."

"The children first," Mrs. Francis said firmly. "If there's any left when they're done, we'll eat. If not, then we'll go hungry."

All the children had a bowl of stew and half a bun. There was even enough left over for the four adults to have a bowl of soup each. The children began to drop off to sleep, lulled by the sway of the ship and the throb of the engines.

Mrs. Francis sat with her back to the bulkhead, a little boy in her lap, dozing.

"Mrs. Francis?" the boy asked.

"Go to sleep, sweetheart," Mrs. Francis said, stroking his hair.

"I'm afraid," the little boy said, teary-eyed.

"Oh, dear, don't worry. Everything is going to be all right."

"Are you sure?"

"Of course I'm sure," she smiled. "And it's all right to be afraid. It's nothing to be ashamed of. You just go to sleep and we'll see what comes tomorrow."

The little boy's eyelids drooped. "I bet Hamish X wouldn't be afraid," he mumbled softly as his head fell onto Mrs. Francis's shoulder.

"I'm sure he wouldn't be," Mrs. Francis said softly.

Chapter 20

"I'm afraid," Hamish X announced, "that's the last of the food. But thanks to Parveen's firm hand on the stick, we're all in one piece." He heaved the supplies onto the meagre pile. The wreckage of the flyer lay crumpled on the ice, scraps of fabric and piping lying in a tangled heap nearby.

"Can't say the same for this heap o' junk." Mimi sat on a jagged lump of ice, shivering.

"It isn't a heap of junk!" Parveen snapped. He wiped a drop of clear liquid from the tip of his nose with his sleeve. "She was a noble machine and she brought us a long way."

"Sorry," Mimi mumbled. "I didn't mean ..."

Parveen waved her away. He looked at the global-positional satellite compass he had scavenged from the wreck.

"According to this, we are presently located at 72 degrees north by 125 degrees east." He unfurled the laminated map, flattened it on the snowy ground, and held it firmly against the wind's efforts to tear it from his grasp. They all gathered around to look. "We've come over two thousand kilometres. Quite amazing."

"Two thousand kilometres to the middle o' nowhere." Mimi kicked a heap of snow.

"Not nowhere. The Amundsen Gulf. That is definitely somewhere," Parveen pointed out. "We are above the Arctic Circle. Below us, under a few feet of ice, is the Arctic Ocean."[55]

"We're still nowhere!"

"Wrong," Hamish X said. "We're partway to somewhere and that somewhere is the pirate's hideout. Listen, two days ago you never thought we'd leave Windcity. Look at you now."

"Yeah." Mimi threw up her hands. "Look at me. I'm standin' here freezin' on the Arctic Ocean with a busted kite and a bunch o' cans o' beans. We'll never catch them pirates now. We'll never get them kids back or find yer book or rescue Mrs. Francis!"

"Never is a long time, Mimi. I admit we're in a bit of a spot, but we have to look at the positives. We're alive. We have some food. We know which direction the pirates are headed. We'll find the hideout if we continue on the course we were taking prior to the crash."

"Hang on!" Parveen interrupted. He took out a ruler, laying it over the map. He placed it so that the edge ran along a line from Windcity to their current location. The line ran out into the Barents Sea, passing directly over a small brown dot on the map.

"That's where they're going!" Parveen said.

"How can you be so sure?" Hamish X asked.

"It lies right along their current course reading."

---

[55] The Amundsen Gulf is named for Norwegian explorer Roald Amundsen. He was the first man to reach both the North and South Poles. He was the second man to navigate the Northwest Passage. He was the first man to fly over the North Pole. He was also voted most likely to grow a beard by his grade eight class. He died in a plane crash, not while exploring but while searching for a friend who had become lost while exploring. The lesson? Never stop exploring.

"How are we gonna get there? In case you ain't noticed, our only mode of transport is thoroughly broke," Mimi pointed out.

A look of grim determination came over Hamish X's face. He opened his pack and began stuffing cans of beans into it.

"What are you doin'?" Mimi demanded.

Hamish X cinched the rucksack shut and hefted it onto his shoulders. "Exactly what it looks like," he said. "I'm going after them."

"On foot? You'll freeze! And even if ya don't freeze, there are bears[56] and all manner of things to eat ya out there. And it's maybe hunnerts of kilometres!"

Hamish X grinned. "I guess I'd better get started then." He started to tramp in a roughly northward direction.

Mimi leapt to her feet. She ran and stood in front of him, blocking his path. "Are you nuts? You'll never make it walkin'."

"There's no other way." Hamish X tried to push past her.

"Perhaps there is." Parveen's voice stopped them both in their tracks. They turned and looked at the little boy who was on his hands and knees in the snow, digging at something.

Hamish X and Mimi came back and stood over him. They watched as his bemittened hands scraped at something buried in the snow. He finally leaned back to reveal one of the snowmobile engines from the flyer's wing. "It seems to be intact," he explained, wiping steam from his glasses. He pointed at the pile of twisted pipes. "I can use these." He picked up a pipe and squinted down its length.

---

[56] And wolves and Arctic foxes.

Then he laid it down carefully and walked around the wreck. "The porridge vat is still in one piece." He reached down and began tugging on the heavy metal tub, trying to pull it upright.

"What do you have in mind?" Hamish X asked, joining him. Together they managed to loosen the grip of the snow and ice. Mimi lent a hand and they finally wrestled it free.

"Whatcha thinkin'?" Mimi asked.

Parveen walked thoughtfully around the vat. He stopped and reflected for a long moment. Suddenly, he took off his mitten and reached behind his ear for a pencil stub. "I'll need your pocketknife, Hamish X. But first I've got to draw up some plans."

Over the next two hours, Parveen directed their labours as they transformed the flyer into a strange sort of powered sled. Calling the newly created vehicle a snowmobile would be an insult to snowmobiles.[57] It had a snowmobile engine, certainly, and runners made from the aluminum piping scavenged from the flyer. No snowmobile has ever had anything resembling a giant porridge vat for a cockpit, however.

They siphoned all the remaining gas into a tank. Parveen attached the tank to the engine. After coughing twice and belching black smoke, the motor settled into a high-pitched whine. To propel the whole thing, Parveen designed a chain looped around rollers under the length of the machine. The engine turned the rollers that rolled the chain that dug into the ice and pulled the machine forward.

Parveen checked the compass, opened the throttle, and

---

[57] Just a quick note: it is impossible to insult a snowmobile. The author has tried and failed on two separate occasions.

they sped away, once again in pursuit of the pirates. "Good work, Parv," Hamish X laughed as they bumped along the surface of the ice. It was a tooth-rattling ride, but at least they were moving.

"Parveen, please. Yes, it is quite a serviceable vehicle. As long as the fuel holds out."

"How long will the fuel hold out?" Mimi asked.

"By my calculations, just over six hundred kilometres."

Hamish X consulted the map. "But that leaves us six hundred kilometres short of Snow Monkey Island!"

"If that's even where they's headed," Mimi added.

Parveen shrugged. "I can only solve one gigantic crisis at a time."

Hours later, gathering darkness found them on a featureless plain. Blue-white ice lay in crumpled sheets as far as the eye could see. The driving was treacherous, and Parveen was often forced to slow down and weave carefully

through mazes of jagged ice. Once, they saw a polar bear bounding along. The noise of the sled made the huge animal stop, stare, and bolt in the opposite direction.

The sun dropped slowly towards the horizon and the sky filled with flickering colours, a rainbow radiating from the ground ahead.

"It's amazing," Mimi breathed.

"It's beautiful," said Hamish X. "Like a rainbow."

"It's electromagnetic radiation from the sun reflecting off the polar ice cap," Parveen said.

"Boy, you really know how to take the poetry outta somethin'." Mimi shook her head.

"I merely explained what you were seeing," Parveen said. "That shouldn't make anything less beautiful. Perhaps it should make it more so." Mimi was about to interject when the engine chugged, sputtered, and died. The sled continued forward under its own momentum for a few metres and then came to a halt. They stood in the gondola, surrounded by the icy silence.

"I guess we're outta gas," Mimi said finally.

"Good guess," Parveen said flatly, taking off his glasses and cleaning them on his scarf. "What do we do now?

Hamish X grabbed his rucksack and tossed it out onto the ice. "Now, we walk."

"We ain't gonna get far in this cold."

Hamish X jumped out after his rucksack. "We won't get anywhere at all if we stay here. Grab everything you need from the flyer … sled … whatever. Parveen will take a compass reading and off we go."

Mimi tossed her bag out and scrambled down beside Hamish X. Parveen was about to follow when he stopped and stared out across the ice.

"What is it?" Hamish X asked.

"Look over there." Parveen pointed.

Off in the distance to the north, on the very edge of the horizon, a green light shone. It wavered slightly, but it didn't disappear.

"What could it be?" Mimi wondered.

"Let's find out," Hamish X decided. He heaved his rucksack onto his shoulders and Mimi and Parveen followed suit. Soon they were tramping across the ice. Hamish X had no trouble with his huge boots, but the footing was precarious for the others. The light was farther away than it had seemed at first. Hamish X didn't seem to feel the cold as badly as his companions. Before too long, Parveen and Mimi were both suffering, lips blue and breath rasping out in frosty clouds. Hamish X knew he had to get them in out of the cold soon, but the light danced maddeningly ahead, never seeming to get closer.

Finally, after hours of torturous hiking, they crested a rise formed from two huge plates of ice colliding. They looked down into a small valley to see a tent and three snowmobiles. The tent was green and it glowed with light from within. Cold and exhausted as they were, the children felt their hearts leap at the thought of shelter.

"Come on!" Mimi shouted, starting to scramble down the slope. Parveen staggered after her.

"Wait," Hamish X called. "We don't know who they are." They didn't listen but stumbled on towards the tent. Hamish X shook his head and followed. By the time he reached the camp, Mimi and Parveen had already gone inside.

Hamish X stopped and looked around at the frozen expanse of ice. The wind had started to pick up, blowing snow and cutting down visibility. But the snowmobiles were free of snow drifts, leading him to conclude that someone had used them recently. He felt a finger of dread slide along his spine. Quickly, he turned and poked his head into the tent.

It was warm and dry. A portable heater sat on the floor, with Parveen and Mimi hunkered down in front of it. "Close the door!" Mimi grunted. Her eyelids were drooping. Parveen leaned against her, already breathing deeply.

"You can't just go to sleep. We have to be careful," Hamish X pleaded. "We don't know who this camp belongs to." His words fell on deaf ears. Mimi's chin fell forward. She was asleep. Hamish X felt the warmth of the tent beckon, but he forced himself to step back outside. He had to make sure they were safe.

He looked around the camp, but the storm made it impossible to see more than a few metres in any direction. Holding out one of his hands and using the tent to guide him, he made a slow circuit of the shelter. Hamish X had just turned the third corner when his boot struck something on the ground. A rounded, snow-covered lump blocked his path. He crouched down and carefully brushed away the snow.

Hamish X reeled back in horror, falling onto his backside. He had uncovered a skinless face, red muscle frozen solid in a monstrous grimace of pain. At first he thought it was a human face, but after the initial shock he could see that the teeth were far too long and the face had an elongated snout.

"What is that?" Hamish X said out loud.

"A polar bear," came a heavily accented reply. Hamish X turned in time to see a club descend towards his skull. He saw stars and then darkness.

Mr. Candy and Mr. Sweet

Mr. Sweet and Mr. Candy stood looking into the hole that was once the front door of the Windcity Orphanage and Cheese Factory, their helicopter idling behind them on the concrete.

"It would seem there has been some sort of incident, Mr. Candy."

"Well spotted, Mr. Sweet."

Mr. Candy reached down and gingerly lifted the hilt of a broken sword between his thumb and forefinger. "Pirates,

Mr. Sweet. An interesting wrinkle."

"Indeed, Mr. Candy. It would appear that the subject is heading north in pursuit."

"Mother is tracking them as we speak, Mr. Sweet."

"The signs indicate that his development is accelerating, Mr. Candy."

"According to thermal tracking reports, our asset is not alone. He has two companions, Mr. Sweet."

"Companions? He has never before exhibited any willingness to work with others. Could it be he is developing emotionally?"

"The thought is disturbing, Mr. Sweet." Mr. Candy thought for a moment, the wind tearing at his coattails. "We shall have to perform a thorough wipe after retrieval, prior to integration."

"I agree, Mr. Candy."

"Shall we?"

"Let's."

They turned in unison, picked their way fastidiously through the wreckage, and climbed into their helicopter. Minutes later it rose over the slanted roofs of Windcity and swept north.

Mr. Nieuwendyke, the last resident of Windcity, looked out his front window, watching them go. "Meow," he said, for he was dressed as a cat and that was the proper thing for a cat to say.

Chapter 21

Hamish X dreamt he was falling. Below him yawned a black abyss waiting to swallow him up. He could not stop his descent. His arms and feet were bound; he could barely move at all. The lovely voice spoke again, resonating all through his body. It wasn't outside his head but rather inside his mind. "*Hamish X. Wake up.*" The voice was beautiful, feminine, and kind: a mother's voice. His mother's voice. "*You have to wake up now.*"

Hamish X woke to find that he was hanging upside down above a hole cut into the ice. His hands were bound behind his back. He strained to look at his feet and saw that they were tied together with nylon rope. A hook was threaded through that rope and attached via a cable to a tripod winch. Hamish X twisted violently, trying to heave himself off the hook. Suddenly, something long and hard struck him across the back of his thighs, sending an explosion of pain through his body. The area was illuminated by a portable spotlight on a pole rammed into the ice.

"Stop wiggling." It was the same voice he'd heard before being knocked unconscious. He craned his neck around to look at his tormentor.

The owner of the voice wasn't very tall but she was bulky, padded out in a thick down parka. She wore a round fur hat and fur mittens in which she held a long stick. Her face was pale and her cheeks ruddy, whether from the cold or from the bottle she plucked from the snow and guzzled Hamish X couldn't tell. Wisps of white hair framed her blotchy face.

"Where did you come from, leetle boy?" she asked, wiping her mouth on her sleeve. "You and your friends, out on the ice. Spying on us, no?"

"Where are my friends? What have you done with them?" Hamish squirmed but the ropes held him fast. The woman laughed at his efforts, then spat. "Stop struggling or I will hit you once again." She brandished the stick and the dull throbbing of his legs made him decide to bide his time. She cackled and tipped the bottle up again.

"Where are my friends?" he asked once more.

"Don't worry." The woman grinned, displaying brown crumbling teeth. "They will be joining you soon. Ah ..." She looked past Hamish X and cackled, "Here they come now. My strong sons bring them. Yuri! Alexi! Bring them here!"

Hamish X twisted to follow her gaze and saw two men trudging towards him. Each carried a child over his shoulder. Parveen and Mimi were bound in a similar fashion to Hamish X, but Mimi was also gagged. The man carrying her was tall and thin with a narrow face and long nose. A scraggly moustache completed the weasel-like effect. He held up a bare hand. "Mama, she bit me!" The other man giggled in a most disturbing fashion. "It isn't funny, Alexi! Tell him to stop laughing, Mama." He shook a fist at the other man.

Whereas Yuri was a weasel, Alexi was a bear. He wore no hat and his hair was long and matted. His eyes were a little too close together over a broken nose, and the lower half of his face was shrouded in a bushy black beard. A clot of frozen drool crusted the area below his mouth.

"My poor baby Yuri! Let me kiss it better." The woman grabbed the injured hand and planted a slobbery kiss on the wound. Hamish X felt his stomach heave. The two men dropped their burdens on the snow by the open hole in the ice.

"Why are you doing this?" Hamish X cried. "We haven't done anything to you!"

The woman stared at him with hate in her eyes. "You lie. You spy on us! You will tell the government officers and they come and take away our valuable prizes."

"Valuable prizes?"

"Our beautiful bearskins. They fetch a pretty ruble on black market."

"They're Russian poachers,"[58] Parveen said. He had managed to sit up despite his bonds. "They kill polar bears and steal their pelts."

The giggling brother stopped giggling and lashed out with the toe of his boot, catching Parveen in the temple. The little boy fell back, dazed.

"Don't touch him!" Hamish X shouted.

"What are you going to do about it?" the woman chuckled. "You should worry about yourself, leetle boy." She pointed to the open circle of black water below Hamish X. Already the water was beginning to freeze around the edges. The woman's voice grew harder with it. "We hunt the white bears for generations but now they tell us it is illegal! We have to travel farther and farther to find them, but still we come. They tell us we take too many bears. They lie. There will always be bears. And we will always come, as we have for generations. You however …" She jerked her head towards Yuri, who grabbed hold of a crank handle attached to the winch.

---

58 Poachers, despite their name, rarely poach anything. They prefer fried foods, usually in some sort of batter.

"You shall not endure. The sea is cold here. You will freeze before you have time to drown."

"We aren't interested in you," Hamish X cried. "We only want to save our friends. Let us go and we won't tell anyone about you."

"Do you think I can trust them, my sons?" she asked.

"Nyet, Mama," Yuri said. Alexi just giggled and shook his shaggy head.

"Neither do I," she sneered. Her face, upside down, vicious and cruel, was inches from Hamish X's own when she added, "Drop him."

Yuri flipped a lever and Hamish X dropped into the black water.

The cold was instantaneous and all-encompassing. Hamish X screamed out at the intensity of the sensation, receiving a mouthful of salty water for his troubles. Opening his eyes, he saw nothing but blackness broken only by a faint light that was slowly drifting away to his left. He realized that his only chance was to get back to the hole.

He desperately tried to free his hands or his feet but the brothers had bound him well. Panic clawed at his mind as his lungs yearned for oxygen. The light drifted farther away.

Hamish X desperately kicked out for what he hoped was the surface. Swarms of lights chased each other across his vision as his oxygen-starved body screamed for the surface. The cold was disorienting. He was weakening. Hamish X felt the darkness of the water creeping into his body and mind. His struggles lessened. He began to let go. He thought sadly, *I'm dying. I can't save my friends. I can't save myself.*

"*You can, Hamish X. Don't give up.*" The voice spoke to him again within his mind. "*Use your boots.*"

The voice was warm and kind, a woman's voice.

"*I can't move them,*" Hamish thought, and the voice heard him.

"*Concentrate on the boots.*"

Hamish X did as he was told. He pictured the boots in his mind's eye, concentrating as hard as he could with his eyes closed. His lungs cried for air, but he tried to stay calm and hold the image. He saw the boots, glossy and black, and in his mind he saw them begin to pulse with some sort of energy, light, and heat. He felt the heat in his legs creeping up towards his stomach, spreading through his body, renewing his strength. He began to sense a lessening of the darkness around him. He opened his eyes and looked down.

The boots glowed with a blue radiance, illuminating the water around Hamish X. Particles suspended in the water glittered and danced in the glare. The most amazing thing, however, was that the nylon rope binding his boots was melting. He strained and kicked until the rope shredded, drifting away into the darkness.

His hands were still bound behind his back. Precious seconds ticked by as he jackknifed his body, pulling his arms down his back and around up the back of his legs until he could pass them, with some effort, over his large boots. The light and heat were already fading from them. Hamish X pulled at the knots holding his hands with his teeth, swallowing seawater as he did so. The cold was encroaching again as he finally worked his hands free. By the fading light from his boots, he saw the underside of the ice pebbled with small bubbles of air. He swam upward. But in his mind he asked, "Who are you?"

The voice was gone. Hamish X felt its absence in his mind. He bumped the underside of the ice and found a large pocket of air. Pressing his face into it he gasped deeply. Then he saw the pale glow of the hole a few metres away. Hamish X swung himself upside down and, using his boots for traction, began to propel himself in long loping strides, running against the bottom of the ice towards the opening.

Up above, Yuri, Alexis, and their mother had watched in wonder as the glow swelled under the surface.

"What is it, Mama?" Yuri asked. Alexis even stopped giggling.

"I don't know," Mama said as the glow began to fade. She could sense that something wasn't right and decided to get the business over with as fast as possible. "Let's dump these two and get out of here."

Mimi had already been strung upside down on the winch. She strained every fibre of her being but she was bound up tight. Yuri went to the lever and prepared to pull. Alexi began to giggle once more. Mimi resigned herself to her fate, trying to be brave. She looked straight down into the circle of water, black and deep. She saw her terrified reflection, her eyes wide, her hair standing out in a black wiry cloud. Tears fell from her eyes, adding their salt to the sea. Hamish X was dead and soon they would be too.

Then, something odd happened. She saw Hamish X's face in the water beneath her. She blinked, but it didn't disappear. She let out a muffled yelp of sheer joy.

"Look at her," Mama cackled. "She's trying to beg for mercy. Too late."

Mimi saw Hamish X raise his hand. In it, something glittered. The Swiss Army knife! Hamish X pointed to the knife and winked. If the gag hadn't been in her mouth, Mimi would have smiled.

"Drop her!" Mama shouted. Yuri pulled the lever and Mimi plunged into the water with a splash.

Alexi picked up the inert body of Parveen in one hand. He went to place him on the hook, but Mama stopped him. "It's no fun killing someone who isn't awake to enjoy it. Just toss him in and we'll get out of here." Alexi giggled and moved to obey. He didn't get the chance. When he stepped to the edge of the hole, two sets of hands burst from the water and pulled his feet out from under him. The huge man fell backwards, landing flat on his back. Parveen rolled safely away from the hole as Hamish X and Mimi hauled themselves out of the water.

"Shoot them!" Mama shrieked.

Yuri reached for his rifle but Hamish X slammed a boot down on it, driving his other boot into the man's back and knocking him flat. Then he kicked the rifle and it skittered into the hole, sinking out of sight.

"Grab Parveen and run," Hamish called to Mimi. Mimi hesitated. Alexi was struggling to his feet. "Go!" Hamish X shouted. Mimi ducked under a swing of Mama's club and, grabbing the hood of Parveen's parka, began to drag him away. Alexi lumbered to follow her, but Hamish X picked up a chunk of ice and hurled it at him, striking a glancing blow off his skull. Alexi rounded on Hamish X like a bull, snorting and clenching his huge fists.

"Forget them," Mama scowled. "They aren't going anywhere. We kill this one first." Yuri pulled a wicked-looking knife from his belt. Alexi began to giggle. Mama raised her club. They circled Hamish X, waiting for an opening.

Hamish X gritted his teeth, fighting the chill and the exhaustion that threatened to overwhelm him. His mind raced. Three against one wouldn't normally faze him, but he was weak and his limbs were going numb. He looked down at his boots. Could he use them again? Could he call up whatever power was in them one more time? He tried to feel the same strength he had before. He relaxed his mind and tried to connect.

"You should have stayed under the ice, leetle boy," Mama taunted. "What we will do to you will be much more painful now."

There! He felt it: a tickle of heat, a flame of energy coursing up from below. He grabbed hold of it with his will and stoked it in his mind.

Yuri stopped circling, uncertainty flickering in his face. "What's he doing, Mama?"

Hamish X smiled a grim smile. A glow pulsed from his boots, casting a blue radiance over the faces of his attackers. "I am Hamish X."

The three mouths of the poachers dropped open. "Uh-oh!" Alexi said softly.

"And these are my boots!" Hamish X stomped with his right foot. The ice beneath him groaned and popped. He stomped with his left foot and the ice shrieked, fissures erupting outward from where he stood. The ice heaved. Yuri, Alexi, and Mama were thrown to their knees.

"And this is for the bears!" Hamish leapt in the air and brought both boots crashing down.

With a series of loud cracks like firecrackers going off, the ice shattered. Geysers of black seawater erupted from below as the three poachers clung desperately to pitching slabs of ice. The cracks began to radiate farther, with a rumbling like thunder. Alexi slid off a plate of ice like a fried egg off a greased frying pan, disappearing under the water.

"Alexi!" Yuri cried before the ice floe he was clinging to flipped over completely. Mama scrambled to maintain her hold on a piece of ice that crumbled beneath her. When she saw her boys disappear she wailed like a wounded beast. "I'm coming, my babies!" Then she let go of the ice and slid beneath the waves.[59]

Hamish X was too busy leaping from chunk to chunk of bobbing ice to think of anything else. The whole sheet was disintegrating beneath him. He made his way in the direction Mimi had gone, slipping and sliding, his boots providing little purchase. His strength was flagging. He'd dredged up the last of his energy to shatter the ice and now his limbs became leaden. Each step was a labour, his breath rasping in and out of his lungs. He peered ahead and saw Mimi a few metres away. She stood on unbroken ice, waving. A boiling swirl of shattered ice separated them.

"Come on, Hamish!" she shouted. "You can make it."

He tried to conjure up a last burst of speed but the tank was empty. His boots slipped as he tried to jump across from one floe to another. He fell and plunged beneath the water.

At least the others are safe, he thought. *They can help the children ... and Mrs. Francis ... and ... and ...* He gave in to the cold and the darkness.

He didn't know how much time had passed when he felt something coil around his waist. It felt like a thick hose or tentacle. He tried to struggle but he had no strength. The tentacle gripped him tight and he felt himself lifted from

---

[59] Another illustration of the universal fact that even bad, evil, mean, and nasty mothers love their bad, evil, mean, and nasty children.

the water into the freezing air. He blinked the seawater from his eyes and saw a brown, bristly, snakelike appendage wrapped around him, holding him aloft. He followed the appendage to its source and found himself looking into a huge gentle brown eye in the side of a huge furry head.

"What in the world?" That was all he managed to say before he passed out.

Chapter 22

n he awoke, Hamish X found himself warm and dry lying beside a small fire in a room with a white ceiling. e was in a tiny cabin made from stacked blocks of ice. A tove, placed on a round stone, burned in the middle of the cabin. Greasy smoke rose and left the room by way of a little hole in the roof. Through the hole, Hamish X could see a circle of clear blue sky.

Hamish X looked around the little cabin. A couple of rifles leaned against the wall, along with some spears and wickedly sharp knives. He was lying under a pile of soft silvery pelts. He barely had time to wonder where Parveen and Mimi were when Parveen stuck his head through a small opening hung with a similar pelt. He had a bandage over his eye, but he seemed otherwise in one piece.

"Hello Hamish X," Parveen said. "I hope you have slept well. Your clothes are dry." He tossed them in and Hamish X caught them. "Come outside and meet our most extraordinary friends." Parveen left Hamish X to get dressed. He hurried into his clothes and a few minutes later stepped through the door flap.

The sky was endless and blue as a robin's egg. It was cold, but the weak sunlight bounced up off the ice, making the day blindingly bright. Mimi was a few metres away, standing among a group of three short dark-skinned men dressed in down-filled parkas. They were showing her how to hold a spear that ended in a wicked barbed hook. Parveen smiled and waved. Hamish X's mouth gaped in shock when he saw what Parveen sat upon.

The animal looked like an elephant but was much, much bigger. Its entire body was covered in thick brown fur, except for the long leathery trunk that was bare. The trunk ended in a clever little knob with two wet slits in it. Two long tusks protruded from either side of the trunk, curving inward towards the tips.

"Meet Amanda!" Parveen called.

"She's ... She's ..."

"Species *Mammuthus primogenus:* a woolly mammoth. I've ridden elephants before but never of such prodigious size."

"A woolly mammoth? Aren't they extinct?"

"Don't say that too loudly," a voice said. "You'll hurt her feelings." The owner of the voice stepped away from Mimi and the others. He was only slightly taller than Hamish X, but he was a grown man. He had a wisp of a beard on his chin. His face was broad and his features flat. His dark eyes were almond shaped and twinkled with amusement. He smiled at Hamish X. "And here is the boy called Hamish X. You have slept the whole night and day. That is only natural after the adventure you had on the ice."

"You know about that?"

"Your friends told us the tale. Those poachers were bad people. They come from their land to steal the hide of the white bear, our brother. But they do not respect the bear's spirit. They leave the meat to rot and steal only the skin. Our land is better off without them."

"Who are you?"

"I am called Aglucark. This is my band. We are hunters in this land. You are welcome among us for your service in vanquishing the skin stealers."

"I was trying to save my friends."

"Also a deed worthy of praise."

Hamish X looked at the mammoth.

"Come and meet our friend, Amanda," Aglucark said, guiding Hamish X over towards the creature.

"Amanda?"

"That is what we call her. She pulled you from the water. Come. She wants to meet you." They walked towards the beast, who turned her massive head at their approach. She was huge and powerful. She could have easily crushed them all without exerting herself, but she was obviously a gentle creature. Her fur gave off a powerful, musky odour that was strong but not unpleasant, like a barn full of animals. Amanda rolled a gigantic brown eye and her trunk gently wrapped around Hamish X's shoulders. The wet end of the appendage snuffled at his face, tickling him.

"Ha! Ha! Stop that!" Hamish X scratched the side of the trunk, eliciting a happy grunt from Amanda. "How is it possible? I thought mammoths were ..." he caught himself before saying the word. "Where did she come from?"

"Ah yes," Aglucark smiled, "Therein lies a tale. It will be dark soon. Let us eat and we can share our stories."

A half-hour later they sat in the ice cabin around the flickering light of the seal oil stove. Mimi, Parveen, and Hamish X sat on one side. Aglucark and his two companions sat on the other. A meal of roasted seal meat washed down with melted snow sat happily in their stomachs. Seal was strange, heavy and oily, but it filled them up nicely. Mimi was just finishing the story of their quest, starting with Viggo and the Cheese Pirates and ending with the escape from the Russian poachers.

"... Next thing I know, there's Hamish X hollerin' at me to go. So I grab Parveen and drag him outta there and you know the rest."

Aglucark clucked and whistled appreciatively. "An amazing tale. You have done well to survive this far. The Arctic is a harsh realm, difficult even for those who are born here as we are." He indicated his companions, who nodded.

"Now," Hamish X leaned forward, "you have to tell us: Where did you find Amanda?"

Aglucark smiled. "Amanda was a gift from the spirits. I had a dream about her. I heard her call. She was trapped. She was in pain. When I woke, I set off to find her and the spirits guided my steps. I found a cave of ice and she was frozen there, perfectly preserved. I gathered my cousins Angelo and Wilbur ..." Again he indicated his companions, who smiled and nodded once more. "Together we chopped away the ice and exposed the creature to the sun, gently warming her with fans and firepots. Suddenly, she stood up and trumpeted a welcome, alive and well as could be. It was a miracle, a gift from the spirits!"

"Why did you call her Amanda?" Parveen asked suddenly.

"I once had a girlfriend of that name. She reminded me of her."

"A twelve-tonne hairy elephant reminded you of a former girlfriend?"

"They both have big feet."

"Oh."

"Now, we ride her on the hunt. She is cheaper to maintain than three snowmobiles and can forage for herself. We keep her a secret, however, even from our closest friends. If anyone knew she existed, they would come with their scientists and their machines and put her in a zoo or worse." He smiled and made a sign with his hands. "Amanda is a gift from the spirits and so we must cherish her and keep her safe."

Outside the little icehouse, Amanda grunted and stomped. Hamish X looked at the faces of his new friends in the firelight.

"Thank you for your help," he said. "Without you, we'd surely have frozen to death out on the ice. You've already done so much, but I ask you one more favour. You've heard our story. You know we must find our friends. The Cheese Pirates mentioned a place called Snow Monkey Island. Do you know it?"

Aglucark gazed back at Hamish X, his black eyes reflecting the firelight. Finally, he nodded.

"We know it. It is a day's ride from here ... by mammoth, of course."

"Can you take us there?"

Aglucark was silent for a moment. He looked at each of them in turn. Then he spoke for a moment with his cousins in their strange, guttural language. Finally, he addressed the three travellers.

"The island of the snow monkeys is a dangerous place. First, one must get past the snow monkeys. These monkeys are not like normal monkeys. They are not humorous or silly to look at. They are vile and filthy monkeys. They inhabit the cliffs surrounding the pirate stronghold. One must climb past them to reach the plateau where Captain Cheesebeard makes his lair.

"Also, there are a large number of pirates. You must defeat them all in order to escape with your skins intact. Do you have a plan of attack?"

Hamish X shrugged and smiled at his friends. Mimi smiled back and Parveen took off his glasses, polishing them with a piece of cloth. "Why break with tradition?" Parveen said.

"All we need is for you to take us there," Hamish X pleaded. "Can you do that?"

Aglucark looked into the fire as if looking at something only he could see. "I had a dream that you were coming. The Raven spoke and said, 'Be ready: Three will come. One is the Wolf ... loyal and fierce.'" He pointed at Mimi, who blushed and squared her shoulders.

Aglucark continued. "One is the clever beaver, planning and building, dedicated to the good of the clan." He smiled at Parveen, who pursed his lips in mild distaste.

"Fine. She's a big, powerful wolf. I am a large rodent. That's just wonderful."

Aglucark laughed. "Every creature has its task. Every creature has its gifts." He turned to Hamish X, serious once more. "You the Raven could not explain. 'He is a boy but not a boy. He is other. He is alone. He will be called "Big Boots."' He said we must help you, for you have many great deeds to accomplish. You must beware, however. You think you are searching for one thing, Big Boots, but that thing is not exactly what you imagine."

"I'm looking for my mother," Hamish X whispered. He debated with himself for a moment, then added, "I think she's been talking to me … in my mind." He related what had happened under the ice.

"This is puzzling. A spirit voice is guiding you, but it may not be what you think it is. Be cautious," Aglucark said. "You may be disappointed with what you find."

The oil stove popped in the silence. Hamish X sat deep in thought. "Boy who is not a boy," he whispered. "What does it mean?"

"It is not for me to know. It is the place of the Great Spirit and he has chosen to remain silent." The Innu smiled. He reached out and squeezed Hamish X's hand. "You have saved many bears. You have come a long way. This is already a great deed. We will take you to Snow Monkey Island, but there we must part ways."

Aglucark stood. "You must rest now. The way is hard and we leave at dawn."

Later, in the small hours of the night, Mimi woke to discover Hamish X's blanket empty beside her. She carefully got up, picked her way through her sleeping companions, and stepped through the fur hanging that served as a door.

The moon hung low in the sky, casting a pale glow over the ice sheet. The northern lights blazed above, shifting and sliding across the black velvet of the sky. Amanda grunted and raised her trunk when she saw Mimi. Mimi went to her and almost tripped over Hamish X sitting on a lump of ice.

"Hey," she said, sitting down beside him.

"Hey," he answered.

They sat for a while, enjoying the deep silence. Occasionally the ice cracked, sounding like low rumbling thunder. The sky was shockingly full of stars, wheeling slowly against the blackness of space. Finally Hamish X spoke. "I'm afraid," he said.

"Of what? Yer the toughest, smartest, bravest kid I ever saw and that's includin' me. What could possibly scare ya?"

"I'm afraid that if I ever find out who I actually am, I'm going to wish I hadn't. Part of me wants to just leave the book and go away."

"Yeah, I git it. But I think yer gonna go and git that book back and then yer gonna do what ya gotta do. Find yer ma. Figure it all out 'cause that's the only way ya ain't gonna be scared no more."

"The boy who is not a boy ... What does that even mean?"

"Hey, I'm the She-Wolf. How should I know? I do know one thing though ..."

"What's that?"

"I'm freezin'. Get back to bed before the She-Wolf bites ya on the butt."

Hamish X laughed and stood up. Mimi did the same. Suddenly, Hamish X crushed her in a powerful hug. "Thanks, Mimi." Their breath puffed out and mingled, a cloud of mist in the cold night air. He released her and went back towards the ice hut. Mimi stood for a moment on the moon-drenched ice. She looked up at the stars and smiled.

Amanda suddenly snorted.

"Same to you!" Mimi scowled and followed Hamish X back into the cabin.

The next morning at dawn saw the little band climb up onto Amanda's broad back and set off across the ice for Snow Monkey Island.

Chapter 23

Mrs. Francis woke up, forgetting where she was. She reached for her robe and wrapped it around her chubby frame.

"What time is it? The porridge must be boiled. The whey must be strained. The ..."

She stopped short when she realized she was no longer in the cheese factory. She was in a rough stone cell with a cot against the wall and a small wash stand in the corner. A little keyhole set low in the metal slab of a door let in a weak flicker of torchlight from the corridor outside.

She was a prisoner.

It all came flooding back. The airship had arrived two days before at Snow Monkey Island, a cone of black rock jutting out of the frozen sea. When the ship glided over the lip of a large crater she'd seen a scattering of rough buildings. After they docked above a large square structure she and the children were led down through the building, a warehouse of some kind, across the crater floor and into a system of caves. The children were led away to a separate place and Mrs. Francis locked in the cell she occupied now.

A huge, dark-skinned pirate with a high-pitched voice and a cloud of puffy black hair had locked the door. He laughed when she demanded to see the children. "Don't you worry, darlin'," he said as he turned the key in the lock, "they'll be treated as good as they deserve." He ignored her demands to speak to the Captain, laughing harshly as he walked away. Mrs. Francis had slumped onto the little cot and exhaustion claimed her.

When she woke the next day Mr. Kipling was standing at the open door of her cell. In one hand he held some flowers, in the other a plate of steaming bacon and eggs. "You are awake," he said. "I've brought you some breakfast."

Mrs. Francis didn't know what to make of the aloof Mr. Kipling. All through the journey he'd been solicitous of her health, mannerly and decent where the rest of the crew were miserable, rude, loutish, and mean. Still, she had the children to look out for, so she maintained her distance from the tall man. "I can't eat until I see that the children are being properly cared for."

"Madam, you must maintain your strength or you will be no good to anyone."

"Nevertheless, I demand to see the children."

Mr. Kipling sighed, placing the plate of food on a crate by the bed. "Mrs. Francis. I admire your tenacity. However, the Captain is a brutal and ruthless man. The children are beyond your power to help. You must do as you are told. That is the only way to survive. The children will work as they have always done, only now for a harsher master. If you want to have any chance of softening the harshness to come, you must co-operate. Do you understand?"

She thought for a moment.

"What are those?" she asked suddenly.

"What?" Kipling noticed the flowers he was carrying in his hand. He blushed. "What, these? Oh, I, uh ... thought you might like some flowers. Brighten up your cell a bit. I grow them in a little greenhouse. Hobby of mine. Helps me through the long winter nights. You've noticed that the climate is milder here than one might expect?" Mrs. Francis had noticed: the rock itself was faintly warm to the touch. "The whole island is a volcano. Dormant, thankfully. It provides a natural heating system and natural hot springs. Very handy for horticulture. Yes." He stopped babbling and held out the flowers. She looked at them: forget-me-nots, a burst of tiny blue flowers, delicate and sweet.

"What are you doing here, Mr. Kipling?"

"Bringing you breakfast. Please eat."

"No, I mean, what are you doing in this place with these awful pirates? You don't seem to fit in somehow."

Mr. Kipling shrugged. He looked down at the flowers he still held in his hand. "I have nowhere else to go," he said finally. "I owe Cheesebeard my life. Ten years ago, in another life, I was Captain of a ship in the Royal Navy, the destroyer *Duke of Wellington:* lovely ship, excellent crew. We were on a tour in the North Atlantic watching for submarines and what have you. Routine, except for one small thing: my daughter Sarah was on board. She had decided to follow in my footsteps, join the navy, and make me proud. You know how children can be. She was a navigation officer."

He slowly turned the flowers this way and that, studying them minutely.

"To make a long story short, a storm came up, as happens often in those seas. We were sore pressed with fifteen-metre waves sweeping over the bow. I decided we would ride into the storm in hopes of coming out the other side. I could have tried to run before it, head for port, but I chose not to do so. The ship lost power and we were left at the mercy of the sea. We took water and capsized. The ship went down with all hands. I searched frantically for Sarah but eventually succumbed to the icy cold of the water.

"Next thing I knew I was dangling at the end of a rope, being winched up into the pirate ship. They'd found me bobbing in the water, barely alive.

"That day, I became a new person. I am one of the pirates, loathsome and cruel. I owe them my life, such as it is."

He looked up and smiled his sad smile. "Do you want these? I'm fifty-two years old but I feel like a nervous schoolboy." He shifted from one foot to the other. "Please take them. I shall have to throw them out otherwise." He held them out to her again.

Mrs. Francis looked at the tall man with his sad eyes, so lonely and broken. She reached out and took them from his pale, elegant hand.

"They're lovely," she said.

"Yes, they are," he answered, looking her straight in the eye, "Now, eat your breakfast before it gets cold."

He turned on his heel and left.

SNOW MONKEY ISLAND first appeared on the horizon as a shimmering black speck. As Amanda's huge, swaying strides ate up the distance, the speck resolved itself into a black finger of rock jutting up from the plain of ice.

"How long until we get there?" Hamish X asked Aglucark.

"We should arrive in the late afternoon, which is just as well. I am sorry, but when we reach the base of the cliffs that is where we shall part ways, Hamish X. There is no road for Amanda to climb and we must get home to our families."

"You've done more than enough already, Aglucark. We'll have to do the last bit on our own."

Mimi punched Aglucark on the shoulder. "Yer all right, Aggie!"

Aglucark smiled and rubbed his shoulder.

Over the next three hours the island loomed larger and larger. The swinging motion of Amanda's walk lulled the children into some much-needed sleep. When the hunters roused them, the island was much closer. The cliffs soared up into the sky, towering over the little party in an awe-inspiring shimmer of black basalt.[60] White smoke rose lazily from the crown of the island, drifting away on the breeze.

"It's a volcano," Parveen said. "The entire island is the cone of a semi-active volcano!"

The sun was just dipping below the horizon when Amanda finally stopped at the base of the sheer black cliff that was Snow Monkey Island. The fading sun shimmered like oil on the glassy rock. Amanda ponderously lowered her vast bulk until the riders could safely clamber down from her massive back. Hamish X, Mimi, and Parveen caught their packs from the hunters who tossed them down. With majestic slowness, Amanda raised herself back up to her feet.

Aglucark and his companions waved to the children. "Be careful," the Innu hunter said, his black eyes crinkled in his leathery face. "She-Wolf! Guard your pack! Beaver! Trust to your clever brain! And Black Boots! Be true to your friends and to your own heart!" With a final wave, the great mammoth and her riders turned away from the black cliff and set off across the ice. The three children watched them go.

"I'd still rather be something other than a giant rodent," Parveen said, polishing his glasses.

---

[60] Basalt is a form of rock produced in volcanic eruptions. It should not be confused with bath salts, which are lovely and soothing in the bathtub.

"Don't worry, little beaver!" Mimi smacked Parveen on the back. He stumbled under the force of the blow. "You got the She-Wolf watchin' yer back!"

"Breaking it, more like!" Parveen grumbled.

"Enough, you guys," Hamish X interrupted. "We've got a long way to go and it's all in a vertical direction. I suggest we start looking for the easiest way up this thing." They stood back and looked up at the cliff. Three hundred metres of sheer rock face stared back down on them.

"Where do we start?" Mimi asked.

Parveen pulled off his mitten and fished in his pocket for a scrap of paper. He took the stub of pencil from behind his ear and quickly began drawing on the paper as his friends crowded around.

"I've been studying the cliff walls as we approached. Since the island is a volcano, much of the surface will be brittle, volcanic rock. But when a volcano erupts, the lava must flow down channels or chutes. They exist all across the face of the cliff. Our best bet would be to find one of these chutes and use it as a sort of pathway to get up the cliff face."

"Good thinking, Parveen," Hamish X said.

"Do not be having any illusions, Hamish X. It will still be a most treacherous climb. I suggest we rope ourselves together. That way, if one of us should slip, the other two might have a chance of saving such an unlucky person."

"Good idea."

Hamish X quickly fashioned a rope harness that could join the three climbers at the waist, while Parveen, sketched map in hand, set off to locate a suitable chute to climb.

Mimi sat on a stone watching Hamish X craft the sturdy knots he would need. "I can't believe we made it this far," she said.

"We're a great team," Hamish X said. Mimi didn't meet his golden eyes, staring instead at the ground. "What's the matter, Mimi?"

Mimi kicked at some snow. "It was you who got us all this way. And Parveen. I ain't done a single useful thing this whole trip. I ain't been nothin' but extra baggage."

"Mimi! Don't say that!"

"'Strue! I ain't done nothin' good. Without you, we'd be in the pirate dungeon right now, sure as shootin'. And ya saved us from those poachers. Parveen built the flyer and the snow thingy. I ain't done nothin' to help. I'm just a waste o' space."

Hamish X laid the rope aside. "Never talk about yourself that way. Never," he said angrily. "If you don't believe in yourself, how can I? I need you to be tough, Mimi. I need you to be strong. If something happens to me then it's up to you to make sure the kids get out of there."

"Nothin's gonna happen to you."

"Anything could happen," he said. He sat down beside her, lowering his voice. "You've got to believe we can do this. Parveen is a good guy, but he looks up to you. He needs you to be strong. Can you do it?"

Mimi looked into his strange eyes and then nodded.

"Good."

"Hey, come on," Parveen's shout broke in, "I think I've found a way up."

Mr. Candy and Mr. Sweet

Mr. Sweet squatted beside the frozen bear carcass, his head cocked to one side. "It would appear to be Ursus Maritimus."

Mr. Candy stood by the tent as it shuddered, buffeted by the rotating blades of the helicopter. "Polar bear?"

"Indeed." Mr. Sweet rose to his feet. "They ran into some poachers, it would seem. An altercation took place."

The shattered ice had frozen again into a jagged circle where Hamish X's boots had smashed it. Mr. Sweet looked off to the northwest. "The heat signature is very confusing, but they went that way. They were accompanied."

"He is very resourceful, Mr. Sweet."

"As he was designed to be, Mr. Candy."

"Indeed. Shall we continue?"

"Let's."

They climbed back into the cockpit and the helicopter rose above the ice.

Chapter 24

Their ascent was slow. Hamish X led the way, followed by Parveen in the middle and Mimi bringing up the rear. As they carefully picked their way up a narrow funnel of rock the aurora borealis blazed across the night sky above them, obscuring the stars. Moonlight reflecting off the ice field below helped light the way.

They carried only essentials, having left the bulk of their supplies at the foot of the cliff for the last leg of the journey. It was all or nothing from now on. If they weren't successful they'd end up as prisoners themselves, providing they survived the ascent.

The climbing was difficult. The stone was glassy, sharp, and brittle, tearing their clothes and shredding their mittens. But to their surprise, the rock was faintly warm to the touch, allowing them to use their bare hands for climbing. Parveen suggested it was the volcanic nature of the rock that accounted for its warmth. Here and there they saw water gushing out from the rock face, steaming in the cold air. "It comes from hot springs deep in the earth," Parveen explained. They laboured upward, hand over hand, foot over foot. Parveen had the hardest time, being the smallest of the three, but Hamish X and Mimi supported him with the rope and they made progress.

Halfway up the face, they reached a very difficult part of the climb, and stood on a metre-wide shelf gazing up. Directly above them and blocking their way was an overhanging ledge. Hamish X called for a halt. "We can rest here for a few hours. That ledge is going to be hard work and we'll need all our strength."

No one objected. They sat on the slim ledge, legs dangling as they munched on strips of jerky supplied by Aglucark and his cousins. The mountain blocked most of the wind. Their exertions had kept them sweating in their heavy clothes, leaving them moist and uncomfortable, but the rock was warm. They were too tired to talk and merely sat chewing and staring at the seemingly endless sheet of ice stretching away fifty metres below. The ice glowed in the moonlight, perfect and clean.

"Whatever happens," Mimi said suddenly, "I'm glad we saw this together."

Hamish X smiled. "Me too."

When Parveen didn't answer they looked over to find his head tipped back against the rock, fast asleep. Mimi and Hamish X smiled at each other and snuggled in on either side of their friend, immediately falling asleep.

When they woke, stiff and sore, it was still dark. The moon hung low in the sky. The aurora flickered overhead. They ate a quick breakfast of jerky and some seal broth from a flask. Seal broth is extremely salty, and carries a strong taste of seal.

Hamish X studied the seemingly endless ledge of rock that jutted out and blocked their way. They would have to reverse their progress back down the slope before they could shuffle sideways around it.

"It'll take too much time to go back down and around. We'll have to try and climb here," Hamish X pronounced. "I'll go first while you two hold the rope. You'll have to give me plenty of slack. I'll pick my way out and over and I'll find something to fasten the rope onto so that you only have to swing out and climb up."

Mimi and Parveen braced themselves as best they could. When they were ready, Hamish X reached out and grabbed hold of a knob of rock with one hand, then reached out with his other hand and pulled himself out under the rock shelf. He swung his right foot and wedged it in a crack. The soles of his boots seemed to mould themselves to the surface of the rock. Soon, he was clinging like a spider to the underside of the ledge with the rope dangling from his waist. Slowly but surely, he made his way until he reached the lip of the ledge.

Hamish X wrapped his fingers carefully around the rock and let go with his feet. For a moment he was dangling from his fingers alone, looking down through the toes of his black boots at the long drop below. Straining with every fibre of his body, he hauled himself slowly up until he could swing his boot up onto the ledge. He heaved himself up and rolled onto his back, panting and blowing. After a minute of just staring up into the sky, he pushed himself up onto his elbows and looked around.

The ledge he found himself on was about ten metres wide and ran out of sight in both directions. On one side was the vast drop to the ice. On the other was a rock face that looked easier to scale than the one they'd negotiated so far. It was honeycombed, with each opening about a metre across. A path cut through the rock face, sloping up towards the lip of the volcano, their final destination. Hamish X grinned with relief.

He turned his attention back to the strange holes. They were black and impenetrable. A foul stink hung in the air. Hamish X couldn't place it, but it was definitely an animal smell, pungent and rank. And the more he looked at those dark holes, the more a feeling of danger started to grow.

"Hey!" Mimi called. "You all right up there?"

Hamish X wrenched his gaze from the holes and shouted back. "I'm up! There's lots of room here and the climbing looks easier. There's a sort of path that leads to the top."

He scanned the ledge for a good place to attach the rope. "There doesn't seem to be a rock big enough to secure the line. I'll have to hold onto it and brace myself while you climb." He planted his feet and grabbed the rope in both hands. "Okay, come on up. I've got it."

Hamish X felt a tug on the rope and dug his boots into the rock. A few moments later, Parveen scrambled up onto the ledge. He and Hamish held the rope together as Mimi followed. Soon they were all standing on the ledge looking up at the series of holes in the cliff face.

"What do you think they are?" Hamish X asked.

"Beats me," Mimi said.

Parveen removed his glasses and polished them with a square of cloth from his pocket. He replaced them and squinted. "It appears to be a natural formation caused by volcanic activity. We can't be far from the top of the volcanic cone that makes up the island." His nose wrinkled. "That smell ... Ammonia. And something else. I am reminded of a trip to the jungle with my parents when I was a little boy ... Yes. It's monkey."

There is a saying in Ecuador: Speak of the monkey and he's sure to appear. In the dark recesses of the holes, a chittering, rustling sound began to swell. Seconds later, the caves were filled with small, malevolent faces that seemed almost human but with leathery red skin and prominent fangs. As the children watched, the creatures shuffled out into the light. They had dirty white fur all over their bodies except for their faces and hands. The chittering swelled into a chorus of shrieks as the creatures began to

prance from foot to foot, waving their arms in the air.

"Monkeys!" Mimi said in disbelief.

"Snow monkeys," Parveen corrected her.

"So that's why they call it Snow Monkey Island," she said.

"Undoubtedly," Parveen nodded.

"Uh-oh!" Hamish X added.

The monkeys had retreated into their caves and come out again carrying armloads of dark-coloured pellets about the size of golf balls.

"What are they doing?" Hamish X asked. A second later he got his answer when the monkeys began lobbing the pellets at them.

Wherever the balls struck exposed skin the pain was intense, producing a red welt almost instantly. Amid the onslaught Parveen managed to pick up one of the pellets and bring it up to his nose.

"Just as I thought," he said. "Frozen dung!"

"They're throwin' their poo at us!" Mimi shouted, trying to shield her face with her hands.[61]

The three children hunkered down under the rain of dung pellets. The little frozen balls began to pile up around them. The snow monkeys pressed forward, shortening the distance and improving their accuracy.

"We can't stay here!" Hamish X shouted.

"What do you suggest?" Parveen said.

"We've gotta make a break for the summit. There's a rough path to the left up through the caves. See it?"

Mimi lowered her arm and squinted. She had time to see a rough path exactly where Hamish X told her to look. Then a piece of dung rapped off her forehead.

"Ow! That tears it! It's time to kick some monkey butt!"

She reached into her backpack, rummaged around, and came up with a lump of leather: her father's baseball glove! She stuffed her left hand into it then grabbed a handful of pellets and jumped to her feet. "How 'bout a little Texas fastball, you dang ugly monkeys!"

Mimi wound up and drilled a fastball right off the skull of a monkey seven metres away. She began matching the monkeys throw for throw, advancing towards the path step by step. Hamish X and Parveen followed her example, and together they pushed the monkeys back. What the trio

---

[61] Snow monkeys are extremely rare and were thought to be extinct until Hamish X and his companions discovered the colony on Snow Monkey Island. Snow monkeys are the more vicious cousin of the Japanese macaque. They are extremely well adapted to the cold and are renowned for their cleverness. Dung throwing is a common method of attack among snow monkeys, who practise for hours on each other to improve their accuracy. They are the most slovenly of monkeys, rarely engaging in the preening behaviour exhibited by most primates.

lacked in numbers they made up for in accuracy. Mimi's glove flashed like lightning as she caught as many of the monkeys' throws as she could. Soon they'd managed to push their way past the main group of monkeys and were climbing the slope, fighting a rearguard action. Throwing downhill was much easier.

"I think we're gonna make it," Mimi crowed happily.

They were almost at the top of the ridge. A few more steps would put them out of range. Suddenly, all the monkeys stopped throwing. They slapped the rock with the flats of their pink hands, making a sound almost like a drum roll. They looked past the three children and up the slope. A low, rumbling growl rolled down from above.

Hamish X, Mimi, and Parveen turned slowly and looked up at a huge snow monkey. He stood as tall as Hamish X but was far more powerfully muscled. His fur was filthy and matted. Tufts of missing fur highlighted the scars crisscrossing his flesh from old battles. One of his eyes was gone, the socket a mass of puckered scar tissue. He hunched down, glaring at them with his one hateful eye.

"I'm going to try and draw him off," Hamish X whispered. "You and Parveen run for it as soon as the way is clear."

"We ain't leavin' you," Mimi hissed.

"I'll be fine, but you have to take the chance when it comes," Hamish X insisted. He reached over and squeezed Mimi's hand. "Trust me, Mimi." She shook her head but said nothing.

Hamish X stepped forward. The monkey went completely still. The boy pounded a fist into his chest, his golden eyes flashing. "I am Hamish X! Do you hear me, you big stupid monkey?" he shouted. The monkey snarled and bared its teeth. "Get out of the way and let us pass!" Hamish took another step forward. All the smaller monkeys began to hoot derisively. The big one-eyed monkey flexed its huge, gnarled hands.

"Get ready," Hamish X whispered out of the corner of his mouth. He reached down and picked up a ball of dung. Without any warning his arm lashed out, launching the ball through the air to bounce off the forehead of the hulking primate.

The creature bellowed with rage and sprang across the intervening distance, tackling Hamish X before he could make a move. They rolled down the slope, clawing and punching at each other, finally coming to a halt at the very tip of the ledge. The monkey ended up on top of Hamish X, sitting on the boy's chest.

Mimi started down the slope to help her friend, but Hamish X shouted, "Go! RUN!"

Parveen grabbed hold of her arm and tugged her in the opposite direction.

The monkey slammed his fists down, but Hamish X rolled out from under the beast, getting easily to his feet.

"GO!" he shouted again, and launched a kick with his right boot at the belly of the monkey. As Mimi and Parveen watched in horror, the monkey grabbed Hamish X's boot and the momentum of the kick sent both of them tumbling out into space. In an instant, they were gone.

Mimi stood frozen in shock, staring at the place where Hamish X had disappeared.

"NOOO!" Parveen shouted. He tried to head back down the slope, but it was Mimi's turn to grab his arm. "We've got to go," she said.

"But Hamish X is ..."

"He's gone. He gave us a chance! We've got to go!"

The monkeys began to keen, a high-pitched wail. They leapt to the edge and looked over. Then they turned to see the two children high up the slope.

"We gotta go now! Do like he told us. It's up to us now." Mimi pushed Parveen ahead of her up the slope. She stared at the ledge a moment more then turned, tears in her eyes, to scramble up the slope with Parveen. "I'll be brave, Hamish X. I promise."

Chapter 25

Viggo wasn't happy.

He sat on the steps in front of the massive recliner that served as Cheesebeard's throne. His clothes were tattered and filthy, his hair was a greasy mess (nothing unusual), and to compound his misery, Cheesebeard had insisted that Viggo wear a silly orange hat made of thick felt that came to a droopy point. Whenever he moved, it flopped limply from side to side.

"I don't deserve this," Viggo mumbled.

"What's that?" boomed Cheesebeard, who was lounging in his recliner, nibbling on a cheese plate. The Captain's recliner rested on a stone platform opposite the doors to the hall. From his exalted position, he gazed down on his crew. The recliner was of the variety one might see in any middle-class home, only it was covered with cheese and wine stains. It had knobs on the side that controlled its many convenient functions: vibrating, heating, elevating, and reclining. It could even comb his hair, but the Captain rarely used that function. Captain Cheesebeard was currently enjoying the lower-back massage. In his hand was a bottle of very fine wine, which he swigged from time to time, drooling red fluid down his cheese-encrusted beard.[62]

---

[62] The Wine-Tasting Board of France does not recommend drooling wine down one's beard as the proper way to enjoy a good vintage. Beard hair reacts badly with the grapes, producing a very acidic flavour.

"Nothing, sir," Viggo cringed. A metal collar attached to a length of chain kept him from crawling out of range of Cheesebeard's backhanded swipes. He had learned not to make Cheesebeard angry.

Ever since the pirates overran the factory and stole all his beautiful cheese, he had been in a foul mood. What made matters worse was that Cheesebeard enjoyed making Viggo miserable. In fact, the more miserable Viggo was, the more it tickled Captain Cheesebeard.

"Bloody right, it's nothing." The Captain leaned in, blasting Viggo with his foul, cheesy breath. Viggo gagged. (A diet made up almost exclusively of dairy products tended to produce profound halitosis.)[63] "How do you like your new hat, Viggo?"

"It's fine, sir," Viggo said, plastering a grin on his face. The pirates lounging around the hall roared with laughter at that.

The main hall was the size of a small church. The walls were constructed of irregular chunks of volcanic rock fitted together in a very haphazard fashion. Pirates have little patience for bricklaying. The ceiling was made of rough planks laid over one another to keep off the worse of the rain and snow. Electric lights mounted in brackets on the walls provided illumination for the piratical debauch. The pirates were seated on soiled old rugs and cushions stolen long ago in some raid or other. On large slabs of wood, a variety of cheeses waited for grubby hands to lift them into rancid mouths. The pirates took every opportunity to make fun of Viggo.

"It's fine!" they mocked him. "Oooh, it's *fiiiine*! Hee! Hee! Hee!" They slapped each other on the back and

---

63 *Halitosis* is the Greek word for bad breath. It even sounds stinky.

rolled around on the floor. Viggo hugged his knees and rocked back and forth in misery. To complete his humiliation, Pianoface and Tubaface had been taken on as pirates, too. They pointed and laughed with the rest.

"Disloyal oafs," Viggo muttered. "Oh, if I ever get out of here, you'll wish you'd never been born!"

No one paid him any attention. They went back to their merry-making, wolfing down stolen cheese and every so often leaning to one side to release clouds of pungent, cheesy gas from their unwashed bottoms. Viggo was barely able to breathe in the foul atmosphere.

Mr. Kipling strode into the chamber, a clean hankie pressed delicately to his mouth and nose. He advanced to the bottom of the roughly circular platform where Captain Cheesebeard reclined in his recliner.

"Captain," he said, bowing, "I wish you'd look into some sort of ventilation system for the hideout. The buildup of gases is both unpleasant and dangerous." Captain Cheesebeard's response was to lift a buttock and compound the problem.[64] The pirates hooted. Mr. Kipling smiled slightly. "Indeed," he continued. "I have the prisoners assembled as you ordered, sir. Shall I bring them in?"

Captain Cheesebeard wiped his mouth with his sleeve and sat up straighter in his chair, doing his best to strike a commanding pose. "Bring them in," he commanded.

Mr. Kipling bowed slightly and went out, returning in a moment leading a string of shuffling prisoners surrounded by guards. The prisoners included La Comptesse de

---

[64] Dear reader, whatever you do, try not to mention to your parents or anyone else in authority the number of times the characters in this story expel gases. This will lead to a public outcry and the eventual banning of the book. Just giggle where appropriate and keep it our little secret.

Roquefort, Francesco de Maldario, Lord Cheddar, and other cheese masters kidnapped in raids all over the globe. Mr. Kipling had loosely bound Mrs. Francis's hands and guided her in by the elbow. Mrs. Francis had received better treatment than the others, who trudged forward, hollow-eyed and sunken-cheeked, to stand before the bloodshot glare of the pirate Captain.

"Welcome, esteemed cheese masters … and mistress." He winked at La Comptesse, who scowled back. "Welcome to Snow Monkey Island. I'm sorry I haven't welcomed you sooner, but I make it a point to be as rude as possible to everyone." He got up and walked down the shallow steps to stand next to Viggo, who tried to lean out of slapping range. "I'm sure you're all wondering what my plans for you are. I've stolen your cheeses! I've despoiled your factories! I've captured your persons and brought you to this remote and godforsaken place! To what end?

"It is time for you to know your place in my grand scheme. You are at my mercy, so you'll want to get on my good side … which is not this side …" He pointed to the left side of his face, which was heavily scarred. "No! You will want to stay to the right. My right and your left. Whatever! I will tell you how to accomplish the goal of staying alive and pleasing me. It's simple, really: you will make cheese for me." The pirates cheered thunderously and started chanting, "Make us cheese! Make us cheese! Make us cheese!" for a solid minute and a half until Cheesebeard raised his hands for silence. When he had it, he continued.

"My brother Soybeard and I had a dream: one day we would control the flow of all cheese and tofu-based foods in the world. We divided the world in half. I would conquer the cheese-producing facilities of the western hemisphere and he, being lactose intolerant, would subjugate the eastern hemisphere's bean curd factories. Then, together we would bring about a new world order! A glorious Golden Age! A Cheese Empire the likes of which the world has never known—and I would be its Julius Cheeser!!" The pirates clapped furiously at this very bad pun.

The captives were horrified. "You're mad!" exclaimed Maldario. Viggo merely listened in rapt silence.

"Mad." Cheesebeard smiled a vulpine smile. "A visionary is always thought mad until his vision becomes a reality. Sadly, my brother died before he could witness our triumph. Hamish X! Curse his name on all the seven seas and in the sixteen skies!" He shook his fists, his voice a crescendo of rage, his face purple with fury. With great effort he regained control. He smiled at the cringing cheese masters.

"We have all the facilities here. You will be given tools. You will make cheese. But not just any cheese. You will make a cheese even more powerful than Viggo's famed Caribou Blue." Viggo leaned forward, his eyes alight. Just then, a pirate entered pushing a wheeled cart covered in a tattered cloth. Strange chittering sounds emanated from beneath the cloth and the entire cart shook as something thrashed within. Captain Cheesebeard walked proudly over and, with a flourish, whipped the cloth away.

Sitting in a cage was a scabby, forlorn little primate that you are familiar with from the last chapter but that was completely new to the prisoners.

"What in heaven's name is that?" Lord Cheddar gasped, covering his nose with his sleeve.

"That, my dear Cheddar, is a snow monkey for which this island is named." The monkey in question snarled and spat squarely into the face of Francesco de Maldario.

"Filthy beast," Maldario sputtered. "You can't be serious!"

"Oh, I am. All mammals give milk and so all mammals can provide cheese. I believe the cheese of the snow monkey will be the foulest and most pungent ever created. I must have it and you will make it. Take them away."

The pirate guards hustled the protesting prisoners from the room. Mrs. Francis pulled away from Mr. Kipling and stepped in front of Captain Cheesebeard.

"What about the children?" she demanded.

"The children will work for me the same as they did for Master Viggo here. You will feed and tend them."

"I demand to see them right now."

The pirates gasped. No one demanded anything of Cheesebeard. They waited for him to explode. But he didn't. He looked Mrs. Francis up and down and smiled. "I like my women and my cheeses to have a little kick." His smile disappeared. "But don't push me. You'll see them when I say you can see them. You'll do whatever I tell you to do because if you don't ..." He stepped in close until his pockmarked nose was inches from Mrs. Francis's face. "If you don't, I will toss them off the cliff one by one until you learn to do as you're told. Is that clear?" Tears filled Mrs. Francis's eyes, some from frustration, most from the rank stench of Cheesebeard's facial hair. She nodded, pulling her pink dressing gown close about her.

"Excuse me, Captain ..." Viggo's plaintive voice cut through the silence. "A word?"

Cheesebeard turned and glared at Viggo. "Do you want a slapping?"

"NO! Although, a slapping at your hands is a privilege and an honour, sir," Viggo simpered. "I would like to point out that I am ideally suited to the monkey cheese project, having dealt with exotic milk species in the past. I would consider it a tremendous boon to work under you in this grand undertaking." Viggo smiled his most winning smile, displaying yellow, rotting teeth that would have made a baby cry had there been one on hand.

"Boon?" The Captain frowned. "What's a boon?"

"A gift, sir," Viggo explained. "An honour."

"Silly word," Captain Cheesebeard muttered, but he was thinking. He stood completely still, picking absently at his crusty beard as he considered. Mrs. Francis shot such a glare at Viggo that he scuttled as far as his chain could take him away from her. If looks could kill, Viggo would have died right then and there.[65]

"Interesting," Cheesebeard said. "We'll discuss it." He cuffed Viggo brutally.

"Ow! What was that for?"

"Keep you on your toes," Cheesebeard said, climbing the stairs and flopping back into his chair. He turned on the "magic fingers" function. The chair began to vibrate violently. "T-t-t-ake h-h-her a-a-away!"

Mr. Kipling reached out to take Mrs. Francis's arm, but she pulled away and walked out of the chamber alone to the laughter and catcalls of the pirates.

"Monkey cheese?" Pianoface whispered to his friend Tubaface. "That sounds disgusting."

---

[65] There is only one recorded instance of a look actually proving fatal. In 1872, Peter McNeil of Kilkenny, Ireland, died when he stepped out of his house into the path of an angry woman who stared at him very crossly. There were mitigating circumstances, however: the man was suffering from a rare and intense phobia that rendered him deeply terrified of human eyes and had lived his entire life trying to avoid eye contact. The suddenness of the stare caught him by surprise. He suffered a heart attack brought on by the terror and died later in hospital.

“Just keep laughing and don’t rock the boat,” Tubaface hissed back.

As the pirates returned to their drunken debauchery, Viggo sat on the stone floor and allowed himself a little smile. “Things are looking up,” he muttered happily to himself.

Chapter 26

Parveen and Mimi huddled together behind some barrels and peered into the compound below. The wooden scaffold on which they perched served as a walkway around the natural bowl of the volcanic crater, which was roughly circular and about two hundred metres across.

Parveen and Mimi had found the pirates' stronghold at the very centre of Snow Monkey Island. And so they took stock of the situation.

In the centre of the crater was a lake that bubbled and smoked, fed by a hot spring deep in the earth. Huts and rude shelters dotted the floor of the crater around the lake, but two large buildings dominated the scene. One was a rough, square structure built from mismatched slabs of aluminum siding and planks, making it look like a patchwork barn. It was a warehouse of some kind, guarded by two bored pirates squatting by a fire in front of its two mammoth swinging doors. Its peaked roof had a flat platform built onto the apex, evidently reached through a trap door. And hovering just above the warehouse was the pirate airship, attached to the ground by long mooring ropes threaded through blocks of stone. The massive vessel, shielded from the wind on all sides by the crater's high walls, barely shifted.

Every so often, drunken laughter and shouts erupted from within the other large structure, a long rectangle of stone with a peaked wooden roof. Double wooden doors offered the only entrance or exit as far as Mimi and Parveen could see. A nearby hole in the ground yawned.

Wooden stairs had been built leading down into the cave below.

They ducked down behind the barrels to make their plans. Parveen sketched out a rough map of the compound with the nub of his pencil. Mimi watched his hands, but kept thinking about Hamish X tumbling over the ledge into space. She could not get the image out of her mind.

"I assume this is where they store their booty." Parveen pointed to the patchwork warehouse he'd drawn. "They unload their cargo directly from the airship through the hole in the roof. There doesn't seem to be any other way onto the airship, which will work to our advantage." He circled the long rectangular building with his pencil. "This is some kind of meeting hall. All the rest are probably places for the pirates to sleep. The stairs here must lead to natural caverns in the rock." He tapped the cave outline with a finger. "I would bet the prisoners are down in that hole."

As if in answer, the noise from the meeting hall swelled as the double doors swung open and Mrs. Francis marched out. The two children felt their hearts leap. Mrs. Francis looked to be healthy, although her bathrobe was a little bit the worse for wear. The tall, thin pirate called Mr. Kipling followed the little housekeeper. Next came a group of people who were chained together and who the children didn't recognize. Two pirates brought up the rear, prodding the prisoners towards the stairs and then down into the cave.

A little way off, the tall pirate grabbed Mrs. Francis's arm and she whirled to face him. Even though they couldn't hear them, Parveen and Mimi could see they were having a heated argument.

MRS. FRANCIS WAS FURIOUS. "Those children are my responsibility. I demand to see them immediately!"

"Mrs. Francis, I am under orders not to allow it. Surely, you understand ..."

"No, I don't understand. I don't understand how anyone could treat children so badly and I won't be a party to it."

"But the Windcity Orphanage and Cheese Factory is hardly an orphan's paradise, Mrs. Francis. You didn't seem to mind working for Viggo regardless of his poor treatment of the children."

Mrs. Francis opened her mouth to make a retort, but instead she hung her head. "You're right, Mr. Kipling. I see that now. I would do anything to change the way things were, but that is in the past." She suddenly stepped close to Mr. Kipling, clutching his hand. Tears stood in her eyes.. "You're just like me, you know. You pretend to be one of these horrible, ruthless pirates but you aren't, are you?"

"Please, Mrs. Francis, I ..."

"There's kindness in you. I can see it, Mr. Kipling. Help me help these children. For your daughter. For yourself."

They stood looking into each other's eyes for a long, long moment. Mr. Kipling finally dropped his gaze and stepped away.

"I must take you back to your cell, ma'am."

Crestfallen, Mrs. Francis turned to go. But out of the corner of her eye she saw a flicker of movement high up on the crater wall. Stacks of barrels lined the walkway, presumably to collect snow for drinking water. Her eyesight had always been excellent, and she trained it on one group of barrels in particular. For an instant, she saw a flash of frizzy black hair and a reflection of sunlight off a pair of eyeglasses. She stared in wonder for a moment, but forced her face to be calm.

Mr. Kipling noticed her hesitation and followed her gaze. "What is it?"

"Hmm? Oh, I thought I saw a duck." It was all her panicked brain could think of.

"A duck?" Mr. Kipling repeated, thoughtfully. He scanned the area carefully. "Unlikely.[66] Shall we go, ma'am?" He took her arm and steered her to the cave entrance. They disappeared down the stairs.

MIMI COULD BARELY CONCEAL HER DELIGHT. She hugged a startled Parveen with such ferocity that all the air came out of him in a sharp bleat. She grabbed his shoulders and shook him.

"Mrs. Francis is alive! And she knows we're here! Oh, I could just bust a gut, I'm so happy!"

"I share your excitement, but please refrain from injuring me!"

"Sorry," she said, letting go of him and hugging herself instead. "We made it! I can't believe it." She stopped suddenly, tears filling her eyes as she remembered. "I just wish Hamish X was here to see it."

"He would not want us to be crying and wasting time. We are lucky these pirates believe they are completely safe and so are spending no effort on keeping watch. We must

---

[66] A duck isn't such a bad choice for Mrs. Francis to have made. There are several species of duck that inhabit the region: the Arctic duck, the tundra mallard, and the volcanic lava duck. The lava duck is especially rare. Its bottom half is impervious to heat, allowing it to float in molten lava pools common in volcanic areas. This trait also makes lava duck very difficult to cook.

get right to work and get out before they know what is happening."

Mimi nodded and wiped her eyes. She poked her head up and took another look at the compound. After a moment, she ducked back down and held up the map so that both could see it. "We gotta do two things. One: free the prisoners. Two: steal the blimp …"

"Zeppelin. There's a difference."[67]

"Whatever!" She pointed at the warehouse on the map. "Here's the deal. You go git the thing ready to go. Warm up the engines 'n such. I go git the prisoners and bring 'em to ya and then we hightail it."

"A simple plan." Parveen chewed his pencil.

"Simple's best. We wait till it's dark, then we go."

"We could both be caught and imprisoned ourselves."

They sat for a moment in silence.

Mimi spoke. "Are you scared?"

"Indeed."

"That's okay." Mimi smiled and squeezed his hand. "When you're doing something good and important, you're supposed to be scared."

"If you say so," Parveen shrugged. He pushed up his glasses and looked at the weak sun low in the sky. "It'll be dark in a few hours. We'd better get some sleep."

Huddled together for warmth in their hiding place, they took turns watching and dozing fitfully.

---

[67] Indeed, there is a difference. A Zeppelin's gas bags are contained within a rigid framework whereas a blimp has a soft hull made entirely of fabric. The Zeppelin is named after Graf Von Zeppelin, who owned the company that manufactured the first commercial airships. The blimp gets its name from the sound it makes whenever it collides with a hard surface.

Finally, the two infiltrators deemed the darkness deep enough to cover their assault. They finalized their sketchy plan, checked their gear, and prepared themselves for what was to come.

The escape from Snow Monkey Island had begun.

Part 3

ESCAPE FROM SNOW MONKEY ISLAND[68]

[68] Well, obviously. I just said it at the end of the last chapter.

Yet Another Note from the Narrator

Me again. We're on to Part 3 and I think things are going very well. Parveen and Mimi have seemingly hopeless tasks ahead of them and Hamish X is dead after a long fall down a nasty cliff.

What? That doesn't sit well with you? How dare you question my authority as narrator of this story? I was appointed by the Guild and you have no right to insinuate that I don't know what I'm doing. In fact, I know exactly what I'm doing. It's you who don't know how these things are supposed to work. Have faith! I wouldn't let the story go so horribly wrong and kill off the main character! That would be negligent! Criminal even! And worst of all, it wouldn't be what actually happened. Changing the story would get me into deep trouble. Believe me, I have no desire to go back to Storyteller's Prison. Horrible place! Nothing makes any sense there. You're trapped in a cell without a coherent plotline for years on end. No! I won't go back! Never!

You're forgiven for thinking, like Mimi and Parveen, that when Hamish X fell over the ledge with the big angry snow monkey hanging onto his boot he was doomed. One would expect that the best he could hope for was a long fall and a sudden stop on the rocks below, all in the company of a smelly, vicious monkey. But you should know better by now that you can't write off Hamish X so easily. When will you learn? It's time to return to the story to show you the error of your ways.

Chapter 27

Hamish X hung from a ledge with a screaming, one-eyed snow monkey dangling from his right boot, trying desperately to pull himself to safety. No matter how hard he pulled, he couldn't seem to lever himself up. His own weight, combined with that of his attacker, was proving to be too much. To make matters worse, the panicked monkey wouldn't keep still. It thrashed and clawed at his leg, swinging them both wildly in space like a giant monkey–boy pendulum. Hamish X's arms strained to maintain his grip on the crumbling rock.

"Voice?" Hamish X muttered. "Are you there? I could

use a little help right now." But there was no reply. He was on his own. The monkey down below shrieked and flailed, almost dislodging Hamish X's fingers from the stone.

"Knock it off!" Hamish X shouted. He looked down at the snow monkey. The ugly, one-eyed face was twisted in terror. Hamish knew he had to get the creature to let go if he had any hope of pulling himself to safety. He raised his left boot to smash the pink, leathery fingers.

The snow monkey saw the boot going up and realized what was coming. It looked up, and the expression on the primate's face made Hamish X stop short. Though the horrible creature had only moments before been bent on his destruction, the look of piteous entreaty on the disgusting visage was so human that Hamish X was moved to stay the blow. He wasn't a cruel person, and so he couldn't send the snow monkey plummeting to its death.

He looked down into that terrified eye and saw something of himself there. You might think Hamish X mad, but mercy is never a bad thing. Sometimes, showing a little kindness can reap huge rewards. Wait and see.

"I don't know if you can understand me, you big ugly thing," Hamish X said to the monkey, "but I need you to stop thrashing around."

The monkey hooted loudly.

"Shhhh! Relax." Hamish X used his most soothing tones. "Relax! Shhh! Calm down. Shhhh!"

The monkey seemed to understand. It stopped wriggling and hung quietly.

"All right." Hamish X smiled at the monkey, who bared its teeth in return. "We have to get up on the ledge. I have an idea." Hamish X started to swing himself to one side, then the other, slowly at first, then as the momentum grew the arc became wider and wider, taking the monkey closer and closer to the level of the ledge. At first the monkey was terrified, but after a few swings it began to figure out what Hamish X was up to.

"Grab the ledge," Hamish X shouted, grinding his teeth against the pain in his shoulders and arms.

The monkey held onto Hamish X's boot with one strong arm and reached out with the other, trying to grab hold of the ledge at the top of every swing. When the boy felt he couldn't hold on any longer, the monkey finally grasped the ledge, letting go of Hamish X's leg and pulling itself to safety.

Hamish X's arms quivered with exhaustion. Even without the added weight of the monkey, he found he didn't have the strength to even try to pull himself up. He felt his fingers losing their grip. A shadow fell over him. He looked up into the pink leathery face of the monkey, gazing down with its one brown eye. The creature sat on its haunches, staring at the boy with its furry head cocked to one side.

"Help me," Hamish X begged. "Please!"

The monkey didn't move. At last, Hamish X felt his strength give out. He let go of the ledge and prepared himself for the end. In that instant, the monkey's long arm shot out and grabbed the front of the boy's woolly jacket in an iron grip. He hauled Hamish X up onto the ledge.

For several minutes Hamish X just lay on his back, panting as the terror left his body. *I'm alive,* was all he thought, listening to the racing of his heart and the blood singing in his veins. *I'm alive and anything is possible*. Finally, he sat up and looked around him.

He was on a small stone outcrop a few metres square. To his right lay the edge and the drop. To his left was the mouth of a cave. The opening was narrow but high enough for him to stand upright. Sitting in the mouth of the cave was the snow monkey.

Hamish X immediately tensed. The monkey squatted on its haunches, looking at him. Suddenly, it leapt across the intervening distance and grabbed him, crushing him in its powerful arms. Hamish X began to struggle, but he soon realized it wasn't an attack but a show of affection. The creature hooted softly, running its large hands over Hamish X's head, picking at his scalp.

"Hey now, settle down," Hamish X chuckled. "Whew, you need a bath, monkey! Whoa."

The monkey hooted loudly and tossed Hamish X onto the ground, tickling him furiously.

"No! No! Stop!" Hamish gasped helplessly. Finally, the monkey allowed him to get up. It sat back on its haunches and grinned, baring his huge fangs in what seemed to be a laugh.

"Well, here we are. But where is here?"

The monkey hooted and slapped the rock between them.

"I don't suppose you understand anything I'm saying, do you monkey?" Hamish X smiled. "Well, I suppose I can't just keep calling you monkey. What should I call you?" Hamish X scratched his head. "You don't look like a Dave or a Ron. Hmm." The monkey sat in silence, watching Hamish X with its one brown eye. "I know." Hamish X snapped his fingers. "I'll call you Winkie on account of your permanent wink. Winkie! Does that suit you?"

The monkey hooted and hopped up and down, slapping its chest with open palms. Suddenly, it lunged out, grabbed him by the arm, and began pulling him towards the open mouth of the cave.

"Hey." Hamish X dug in his boots. "I have to find my

friends. Winkie!" Winkie tugged harder, and finally Hamish X had no choice. He allowed himself to be dragged into the mouth of the cave.

The cave led into a narrow, winding tunnel. Hamish X tried to keep up with Winkie, tripping over unseen rocks on the uneven floor. The darkness was complete, but the walls were covered with a variety of glowing fungus that cast a pale green light.[69] Eventually, his eyes adjusted. He probably could have followed Winkie by smell alone, so profound was his monkey stench.

Winkie led him on a winding course through the glowing bowels[70] of the island. Soon, Hamish X had lost all sense of direction, but he was fairly sure they were steadily climbing. At one point they entered a vast cavern lit by the glimmer of a lava pool far below. A narrow path curved precariously over the seething rock. "Parveen was right," Hamish X whispered to himself. "It is a volcano."

They left the lava pool and followed a steep tunnel up, up, up until Hamish X saw a faint glow ahead. Winkie stopped and laid a smelly hand over Hamish X's mouth. Hamish nodded. They crept forward softly until the tunnel ended in an opening awash in a glare of light. Hamish X heard human voices. Cautiously, he crept up and peered around the corner.

The opening looked out over a vast cavern lit by strings of electric torches. Huge metal machinery stood silent under the lights: a vat, a press, a cutting machine.

---

69 Glowing fungi are common in subterranean environments. The Ancient Egyptians used to cultivate glowing fungus that they would make into little glowing hats. They wore their glowing hats whenever foreigners visited just to show off. Everyone agrees that the Ancient Egyptians were extremely immature.

70 I hope no one is offended by the concept of glowing bowels.

"It's a cheese factory," Hamish X breathed. Covering three of the four walls were rows and rows of cages stuffed with miserable snow monkeys hooting and screeching. They barely had enough room to sit down in their cramped quarters. Ranged in front of the cages were small glittering cylinders with hoses sprouting from them.

"This machinery seems to be in excellent working order," a familiar voice said. "As soon as we can begin the milking process, our first batch will be ready for consumption in under a year."

When he saw who spoke, Hamish X almost shouted out loud in fury.

Viggo Schmatz, wearing a ridiculous orange hat, was examining the cheese press. The cheese maker's clothes were ragged and filthy and he had a leather collar around his neck. Beside him, Captain Cheesebeard, flanked by two pirates holding swords, rubbed his hands together gleefully.

Hamish X would have leapt down right then and there, but Winkie restrained him with his powerful paws.

"Good! Excellent! Wonderful!" Cheesebeard gestured to the caged monkeys with one filthy hand. "Who would have thought these useless, ridiculous creatures would be the source of such an exquisite, delightful cheese?" He strutted up to one of the cages, banging his fist on the bars. All the monkeys inside cringed back fearfully. "We'll milk them dry! And when they wear out and die, there are plenty more where they came from. An endless supply!" Cheesebeard laughed and the pirates dutifully joined in. The monkeys started hooting and soon the din was tremendous. Finally, the chaos died down.

"It will be my pleasure to serve under a man of your

incredible vision, Captain Cheesebeard," Viggo simpered. "With your leadership and my humble expertise, the world of cheese will tremble!"

"Will your children perform their duties as required?" Cheesebeard asked.

"They will do as they are told. They have no choice. Keep them hungry and tired and you won't have any problems. And when they wear out, I have contacts in the ODA who will be happy to provide us with more."

"What about the woman? She seems like a handful."

"Don't worry about that idiot Mrs. Francis," Viggo tutted, waving a hand dismissively. "All you have to do is threaten the children and she'll fall into line."

"I like you, Viggo Schmatz," Cheesebeard leered. "You have a cruel streak and a spiteful nature. We have so much in common. Let's chat some more over a bottle of wine."

"Delighted, Captain!" Viggo bowed deeply, an evil grin on his nasty face.

Cheesebeard and Viggo linked arms and walked towards the doorway that led out of the cavern.

"You can take the hat off now," Cheesebeard said.

"Thank you, sir." Viggo whipped the ridiculous orange hat off his greasy head. He clapped it on the head of one of the pirates. "There. You wear it. Ha! You look stupid!"

"He does, doesn't he? Ha!" Cheesebeard laughed.

Cackling, they left the cavern with the two pirates trailing behind.

When they were sure the cavern was clear, Hamish X and Winkie dropped down from their vantage point. As soon as the monkeys saw Winkie they started hooting and shrieking whilst grabbing hold of the bars and rattling the cages. Winkie hooted back in long, low notes, trying to soothe them. At last, the hooting subsided.

"I can see you have a bone to pick with these pirates, too," Hamish X said. Winkie snarled.

"Let me take a look around."

Hamish X walked up and down the cavern, his big boots scraping on the rock floor. He examined the cages. They were arranged in rows, one on top of the other. The monkeys looked miserable. Winkie went up to one cage and pressed his face to the bars. The monkey inside pressed her lips to the opposite side, hooting mournfully.

"Is she your ..." Hamish X was about to say "wife" but he wasn't sure if monkeys married.[71] "Partner?" Winkie hooted and sighed. Hamish X suddenly realized something. "It's all the lady monkeys who are are locked up. That's so sad." He crossed to Winkie and scratched his head. "You poor guys must be so lonely." He felt anger start to rise in his heart. "It isn't right."

He looked closely at the locking mechanism. Each row had a lever that one had to pull to release the doors. They were all locked electronically, connected to a computer on the cheesing floor.

Hamish X studied the locks. He studied the computer. Finally, he sat down at the keyboard. "I wonder." He laid his fingers on the keyboard, and as if under someone else's control, they started to dance across the lettered keys. Hamish X laughed out loud. "I guess I know about computers! Your lady friends will be free in no time."

---

71 Monkey marriage is not scientifically documented, but there is evidence of wedding shower activity among some bands of gibbons observed in the wild. Nests filled with blenders, toasters, and ugly lamps lead researchers to believe that wedding guests in the monkey world have no more taste than their human counterparts.

Chapter 28

Mimi darted between the little shanties, making her way across the floor of the crater to the cave opening she hoped led to the prisoners. Twice she had to stop and press herself up against a wall, hiding in the shadows as pirates lurched past. Once they passed so close to her that she could smell wine and the sweat of their unwashed bodies. Luckily, they were too drunk to notice her in the darkness. After a seemingly endless amount of crouching and running, she came to the opening in the ground that they'd watched Mr. Kipling and Mrs. Francis disappear into.

She crouched at the opening and looked down. The steps were roughly carved out of the black rock of the island. They stretched down a long way. Lights glowed below. Mimi couldn't see anyone but felt horribly exposed as she crept down the stairs, keeping up against the stone wall.

At the bottom, she found herself in a roughly square cavern with tunnels leading away on either side. Electric lightbulbs were strung along the ceiling of the tunnels, providing weak illumination.

"Which way?" Mimi whispered to herself. "Left or right?" She couldn't make up her mind. She decided to go right, but after just a couple of steps Mimi heard shuffling noises coming from that direction. She ducked into the left corridor and pressed herself up against the wall, willing herself to be invisible.

A pirate shuffled into the chamber, a cutlass at his side and a dirty scarf around his head. He turned and yelled back down the way he came.

"Kipling says I've gotta get the prisoners some bread."

Mimi's heart jumped. She was going the right way.

"I'll be back in a few minutes. Youse want summink to eat or what?"

"Cheese! And some buns," a deep voice echoed up the tunnel.

"And some cake," another voice added.

"All right! All right!" Dirty Scarf hitched up his greasy trousers and started up the steps, passing within a metre of Mimi's hiding place. "Guard duty! What a pain," he muttered as he climbed out of sight. Mimi waited a full minute before she relaxed.

"The prisoners," she smiled grimly and set off as quietly as a shadow down the right-hand tunnel.

After only a few metres she reached an opening on the right side. Smoke drifted out in blue swirls around the naked lightbulb. Mimi crept to the edge of the opening.

"Ha! Quinzalp!" a deep voice crowed triumphantly. "That's twenty-six points and a triple word score, which makes a delicious seventy-eight!"

"That's not a real word, Tom," a squeaky voice complained.

"It is so, Tim!" the deep voice boomed indignantly.

Mimi peeked into the opening and saw two pirates sitting at a folding table. One was huge, with dark skin and a cloud of puffy black hair sticking out from his huge head. The other was tiny, barely bigger than an eight-year-old boy. Apart from his luxuriously oiled moustache he was completely bald, his shiny scalp criss-crossed with scars. He danced on top of the stool and pointed at a Scrabble board spread out on the table between them.

Oddly, it was the big man who had the high voice. "Tom, you're cheating. It isn't a real word."

"Tim, I don't cheat! It is," the little man boomed in his deep voice.

"Is not!"

"Is!"

Suddenly, Tim swept the table out of the way and leapt on the smaller Tom. While they wrestled, Mimi took her chance and darted past the doorway and off down the corridor.

The tunnel sloped slightly downward, a bare electric bulb shining weakly every few metres. Mimi kept to the wall but still felt horribly exposed. Should she meet anyone coming up the other way, there was nowhere to hide. She would have to fight or run.

After a harrowing minute and a half she came to the top of a stairway that had been hacked out of the living rock. She crept down. Directly in front of her at the foot of the stairs was an empty cell. A door made of heavy iron bars stood open. To her left, the corridor ran ten metres, with three doors on each side and a heavy metal door at the end. The corridor to the right also had three metal doors shut tight—but the door at the end was slightly ajar. Voices echoed down the corridor.

Mimi could hardly contain her excitement when she heard Mrs. Francis shout, "You have to help me, Mr. Kipling. I know you're not like them. Think of your own daughter."

"I am," he replied. "I will do what I can to see that the children and you yourself are well treated. That's the best I can do."

"No." Mrs. Francis's voice was cold. "It's the least you can do."

"I must be going."

To Mimi's horror, the door opened wide and Mr. Kipling

stepped into the corridor. She cast around for a place to hide as he took a key from his jacket pocket and turned his back to her, locking the door. Mimi leapt from the bottom step into the empty cell directly across the corridor, pressing her body flat against its cold stone wall.

She held her breath as the approaching footsteps echoed outside. To her horror, they stopped right outside the cell. For an endless moment she waited. Then another. When Mr. Kipling didn't call her out of her hiding place, she screwed up her courage and peeked around the edge of the door.

He stood under the bare bulb at the base of the stairs, light shining down on his worn peaked cap. His body was turned away from Mimi's hiding place, his back to the cell, looking down at a small tattered photograph in his hand. The picture showed a smiling young woman with short blond hair.

Mimi scarcely breathed. Silently, she willed him to leave. *You have to go to the bathroom*, she urged silently. *You left the stove on! The bathtub is overflowing!*

Mr. Kipling didn't budge.

Please! Please! Please! Mimi pleaded. *Move!*

As often happens when one is desperate to be quiet, the body is determined to be heard. Perhaps it was the tension. Perhaps it was a cramp from standing so still. Perhaps it was a diet of canned food interrupted only by the odd morsel of seal jerky, but at the worst possible moment, Mimi's stomach decided to gurgle. Not loudly. Not long. Just one, distinct blort.

Mr. Kipling raised his eyes from the photo. He stood still as a post, his head tilted to the side. Mimi waited, tension coiled in every limb, ready to launch herself at him should he turn to look into the cell.

For a long moment, nothing happened. Mimi's stomach didn't offer any more comment. Mr. Kipling didn't move. Mimi clenched her fists, ready to spring.

At last, he shook his head, tucked the photo into his threadbare peacoat, and trudged slowly up the stairs.

Mimi waited a full five minutes just to be certain. Satisfied, she edged out of her hiding place and into the hall. Nothing stirred. She set off quickly down the corridor and stopped at Mrs. Francis's door, pressing her ear to the steel blackened with years of soot. A metal ring hung on one side in lieu of a doorknob, with a huge keyhole piercing the metal below the handle. A flicker of light showed through the keyhole. Mimi crouched down and looked in.

She saw a lamp sitting on a crate. Beside it, she made out the end of a lumpy cot. On the floor in front of the cot, a foot was on display. A fuzzy pink slipper adorned the foot.

"Mrs. Francis," Mimi hissed. The slipper didn't budge. Mimi tapped lightly on the door. "Mrs. Francis."

The slipper shifted, to be joined by another slipper. Mrs. Francis stood up and rubbed her eyes. She'd been crying. She pulled her housecoat around her and stood looking at the door.

"Who's there?"

"Mrs. Francis! It's me, Mimi!" Mimi could barely contain her excitement. "We've come to get you out."

Mrs. Francis couldn't believe her ears. She ran to the door and pressed her hands to it. "Is it really you? I can't believe it. I thought I saw you outside but … oh, Mimi! How is it possible! Is Parveen with you? And Hamish X?"

Mimi felt the excitement drain away at the mention of her lost friend. But she pushed aside her sadness and got down to business. "We're here to get you and the children. Where are they?"

"Down below, I think. They're all together. You have to get me out of here. You need the key."

"Who has it?" Mimi asked.

"I do."

Mimi whirled to see Mr. Kipling. A ring of keys dangled from the end of one long, elegant finger. He arched an eyebrow in amusement. On either side of him stood Tim and Tom, grinning evilly.

Chapter 29

Parveen crouched behind a pile of foul-smelling garbage. After a meandering transit of the pirate camp he'd at last arrived at the hut nearest the warehouse, and now he looked across at the two guards who leaned drunkenly against its door. They were passing a bottle back and forth between them, but Parveen doubted they were drunk enough to fall asleep in the next hour or so. He looked closer and realized the two men were none other than Pianoface and Tubaface.

"I'm thinking I should get my own website," Pianoface said, belching loudly to punctuate his thought.

"Website," scoffed Tubaface. "What do you need a website for? You're a pirate."

"All the more reason. I need to get my name out there, promote myself."

"What, like www.pirate.com?"

"Exactly! Then people could reach me for the odd side job, pillaging and whatnot."

"I bet someone already has www.pirate.com, though."[72]

"Good point. I could try getting www.pirate.org."[73]

"Naw, that's only for nonprofit companies."

And on and on. Parveen had to find a way past them. He studied the patchwork warehouse, cobbled together

---

[72] Indeed, pirate.com is already taken.

[73] Pirate.org is also taken. It's a nonprofit organization dedicated to providing adequate housing and medical care for retired pirates.

out of pieces of aluminum siding, planks of wood, and sheets of corrugated tin.

He carefully retraced his steps and crept around the side of the hut. When he was out of the guards' sight he cut straight for the warehouse, huddling down in its shadow. After a short search, he found a loose board in the wall. With a little effort, he wiggled it till he'd created a gap large enough for him to slip through.

Inside he couldn't even see his hand in front of his face. He paused, waiting for his eyes to adjust to the darkness. The air in the warehouse was heavy and stale, rich with the stink of rare cheeses. After a moment, Parveen was able to make out row upon row of precariously stacked crates. He jogged along a corridor made of boxes and came out into a square space in the centre of the warehouse. A ladder, attached to a support beam, led up to a square of pale moonlight. Parveen checked to make sure no one was about. Satisfied, he ran to the ladder and swiftly climbed up.

The ladder emerged in the middle of the platform atop the warehouse. Directly above him loomed the vast bulk of the airship, with a retractable staircase leading up into its open cargo bay.

"Well," Parveen whispered to himself. "Onwards and upwards."

He tiptoed up the steps, his heart beating so loudly he was sure the guards below would hear it, and peeked into the hold.

It was empty save for a pile of coiled ropes on the floor and some long poles with hooks on the end hanging on the walls. The poles were used to guide the ship into its moorings and to push her off again during launch. Parveen hopped into the empty bay and moved to the nearest hatchway.

It was the engine room. In the dim light of emergency lamps overhead, the dark, bulky humps of engines glistened like great animals sweating in their sleep. The engine controls were probably in the bridge. He had to find it.

Parveen strode back across the cargo bay to the opposite hatch, and stepped through it into a corridor panelled in dark wood. At one time the panelling might have been quite handsome, varnished and polished. The pirates didn't place varnishing and polishing high on their list of priorities, however. The wood was scuffed and scratched. Someone had carved "Jimmy Loves Feta" in crude letters at eye level. Small wooden doors punctuated the corridor every three metres. Parveen looked in one that was open: a small cabin with a bunk and a tiny table. Dust swirled on the floor and the bunk was unmade, but otherwise it looked quite cozy.

Parveen padded softly along the worn carpet that ran the length of the corridor and stepped out into a wider room. Rows of tables and benches: the mess hall.[74] Once again, the room was empty. Obviously the pirates didn't think there was any need for guards on the airship while they were safe at home.

Parveen passed through the mess and into a tidy little kitchen. Pots and pans hung overhead. A stove took up one corner and cupboards covered every bit of space. In the corner opposite the stove was a steep metal hatchway

---

[74] The "mess" is the traditional name for the place where sailors eat aboard ship. It was originally referred to as the "tidy" by superior officers in an effort to instill the urge to clean in the crew. Sailors are notoriously messy, however, mainly because while they eat, their food is sliding back and forth across the table and often ends up on the floor.

leading forward. A wooden chopping block stood in the centre of the room with a very sharp knife sticking out of it. On the block was a loaf of bread cut in slices, of which several were missing, and a chunk of cheese.

Parveen froze. Someone had evidently made a sandwich. He reached over and poked the loaf of bread. It was still soft. He stood still and listened, hearing nothing but the sound of his own heart thumping. Gathering his courage, he walked over to the hatchway, pushed it carefully open, and stepped through.

He stood on a catwalk running all the way down the ship in both directions. Bare bulbs cast a yellow light. Surrounding the catwalks and supported by aluminum beams, giant gasbags crowded in overhead. Vast nets attached to the beams held the hydrogen envelopes in place. Parveen looked down towards the front of the ship. Light shone from an open hatch about twenty metres away. As softly as he could, he padded down to the hatchway and peered through.

He was looking into the bridge. On one side was a bank of levers attached to cables, on the other an array of monitors. Parveen recognized a radar screen and a sonar panel. In the middle of the floor facing a panoramic window that wrapped around the cabin, a helmsman's wheel sprouted from the deck. The Captain's chair was directly behind the wheel on a raised step.

Sitting in the Captain's chair was a stringy man with a scabby bald scalp. The scabby bald scalp tilted back so that the man could drink deeply from a heavy earthenware jug. He placed the jug on the arm of the chair and picked up a cheese sandwich in his left hand, his right being swaddled in a grimy bandage. He waved his sandwich as he ranted to himself.

"Mr. Kiplink sinks he's soooo much better zan me, but he isn't. No. He'd better vatch his back or I'll schtick a knife in it." He leapt to his feet, throwing his sandwich at the wall in a sudden burst of fury. "I, Schmidt, should be ze first mate. I'm a better sailor. I'm certainly better lookink, zat's for sure! Forget first mate! I should be Captain. Ja! Captain!" He struck a pose, hands on his hips.

"Check ze trim, zere! Look lively! If you don't do as I say you'll valk the plank!"

As Parveen watched the strange display he wracked his brain for a way to neutralize Schmidt. He had to get him out of the way if he was going to steal the ship. But try as he might, he couldn't think of what to do.

"Wotzat, Mr. Kiplink?" Schmidt shouted, making Parveen jump. The man pointed at an imaginary figure only he could see. "You sink you are man enough to tell me, Helmut Schmidt, vot to do? Never! Do you understand? Nobody tells me vot to do!" He reached for the jug and shook it. "Empty! Bah!" He turned to the hatchway and, to Parveen's horror, began to stagger drunkenly towards him, stuffing the heavy jug under his right arm.

Parveen froze. He watched the scabby scalp bobbing closer and closer. He knew he should run, but he couldn't make his terrified body budge.

The pirate opened the hatch and looked straight at Parveen, blinking blearily.

"Fill zat, vill you?" he said, shoving the empty jug at Parveen, who took it in his hands. "Vell, vat are you vaiting for, boy?" Then his eyes bugged out as he saw Parveen clearly. "Who are ..."

He didn't get to finish. Parveen swung the heavy jug by its handle with all his strength, smashing it on the side of

Schmidt's skull. The jug shattered and Schmidt fell heavily onto the deck. Parveen looked down at the inert pirate. "Sometimes it's best to think on your feet." When he was sure the man wasn't getting up, he shrugged and walked into the bridge. All he had to do now was start the engines and be ready when Mimi freed the prisoners. "If she frees the prisoners," he whispered to himself.

MIMI BOUNCED on the balls of her feet, ready for a fight. "Okay, Kipling. Gimme them keys or yer gonna be in a world o' hurt."

"Is that so? And who, pray tell, are you, my young hellion?" Mr. Kipling asked.

"My name is Mimi Catastrophe Jones. And yer gonna gimme that key or I'll lay a beatin' on ya."

Mr. Kipling looked at the thin girl with her fierce green eyes blazing and fists cocked. Her hair was a mess and her clothes were tattered but there she was, ready to go toe to toe with three grown men. He looked at her and he did something he hadn't done for many years. He laughed. "Miss Jones, please ..."

"I'll take care of this," Tim chuckled. He took a leisurely step towards Mimi. "Come on, girlie. Let's not make things difficult ... Ow!"

Mimi drove her fist into the man's nose, then spun and drove her heel into his belly. Tim folded over and fell to his knees.

"Why you little ..." Tom pulled a pistol from his belt and brought it up. The murderous mouth of the barrel looked like a cannon in his tiny hand. He aimed it straight at Mimi, but before he had a chance to fire it Mr. Kipling's sword swept out of its sheath, batting the barrel upward. The shot reverberated loudly in the close quarters of the stone corridor, striking the ceiling and bringing down a rain of stone shards.

The shocked pirate had only time to say "Oi, Kipling! What's the big idea?" before Kipling brought the hilt of his sword down on the little man's head. Tom's eyes crossed, closed, then he fell onto his face.

Mimi stared at Mr. Kipling in shock. "What did you do that fer?"

Mr. Kipling sighed. "I really don't know what came over me. Perhaps I've grown tired of cheese." Tim tried to stand up, got the same treatment from Kipling's sword hilt, and fell heavily on top of his Scrabble partner. Mr. Kipling sheathed his sword and fumbled with the keys, selecting one and plunging it into the lock of Mrs. Francis's cell door. As soon as the door opened Mimi was crushed in a fuzzy pink embrace.

"Oh, Mimi! Mimi! Mimi! Darling Mimi!" The chubby lady smothered the squirming girl with kisses.

"C'mon Mrs. Francis," Mimi complained. "Can all the mushy stuff. We ain't got time! We've gotta get the other prisoners out. Mr. Kipling here's got the keys."

Mrs. Francis allowed Mimi to escape her clutches as she looked at Mr. Kipling.

"Mr. Kipling," she said softly, "I knew you were a good man deep down." Mrs. Francis stood up on her toes and gave him a kiss on the cheek. Mr. Kipling blushed, covering his embarrassment by plucking his handkerchief from his sleeve and blowing his nose. "Yes. Quite. Well, uh ... let's toss these two into the cell vacated by the lovely, um ... Mrs. Francis, shall we?"

Mimi looked back and forth between the two adults and shook her head. "Grownups," she snorted. She grabbed the small man by the feet and dragged him into the cell while Mrs. Francis helped Mr. Kipling drag the heavier one. Once the guards were inside, Mr. Kipling swung the door shut and locked it.

"Right," he said, "I guess there's no going back now."

"Where are the children?" Mrs. Francis asked.

"Follow me." He turned and led them back down the tunnel.

Chapter 30

Hamish X concentrated as hard as he could on the job at hand. Screen after screen flashed by as his fingers danced over the keyboard. The trick was not to think about what he was doing, and just let whatever part of his mind knew about computers take over. The sensation was very strange: like letting someone else operate your body while you were asleep.

He was in such a state of intense meditation he didn't notice when the snow monkeys started to fill the room. First one at a time, then in bunches. Somehow, the word had spread through the caverns and corridors of Snow Monkey Island. All the male monkeys who for so long had been without their mates began to flock to the cavern where their loved ones were imprisoned. They gathered by the hundreds, tiny black eyes blinking in the glare of the lights, waiting to see if the strange boy with the black boots would succeed.

When at last the bolts on the cages slid back with a heavy thud Hamish X sagged with relief. But he almost leapt out of his chair when the monkeys began to celebrate their freedom.

Immediately there were monkeys everywhere, hugging, nuzzling, swinging and screeching, hopping and howling.

"No! No! Be quiet! Calm down!" Hamish X waved his arms ineffectually. "The pirates are going to hear you! Oh, what am I doing? You're monkeys! You don't understand a word I'm saying."[75]

"Eeeeeak." The authoritative shriek pierced through the cacophony of monkey noise. Silence filled the cavern. Winkie stood atop the cheese press with his arms raised, looking for all the world like a politician calling for silence at a rally. Only he was covered in fur and only had one eye. All the monkeys sat silently, their beady little eyes blinking.

"Thank you, Winkie. I'm glad I could help you all, but I have another job to do. I have to save my friends." Hamish X reached up and took Winkie's leathery paw in his hand. "You saved me and you brought me here. I doubt you can understand me, but thank you. Go and be free. I've got an appointment with some pirates. Goodbye and thanks again."

Hamish X squeezed the paw once and let go. He turned and headed for the door Captain Cheesebeard and Viggo had exited through moments before. But he hadn't gone five steps when he heard Winkie hooting.

He turned to see the big snow monkey gesticulating wildly, swinging his massive arms and pounding his chest. The monkeys responded by pounding theirs. Winkie pointed at Hamish X and pantomimed falling off a cliff. The monkeys hooted as he re-enacted Hamish X swinging him to safety.

As the incredulous boy watched, the monkeys began hopping up and down, pointing at him and hooting with their yellow teeth bared fiercely. Winkie pointed at the doorway and, as if responding to an order, the monkeys

---

[75] It's true. Monkeys never understand a word you're saying. Many European explorers in Africa and the New World went horribly wrong by asking monkeys for directions.

swarmed past Hamish X, sweeping the startled boy up a stone tunnel towards the surface. Hamish X laughed and ran as fast as he could until he was leading the monkey wave. As they rose through the broad tunnel, more monkeys joined them from holes in the walls and side corridors. The walls echoed with the cries of monkey vengeance.

"YOU'LL NEVER GET AVAY viss it, you know," Mr. Schmidt taunted Parveen as the boy studied the controls of the airship, looking for a way to start the engines. Parveen had taken the precaution of tying Schmidt to the Captain's chair.

"There must be an ignition switch of some kind."

"Oh there is, but you'll never find it."

"Why do you doubt I will find it?" Parveen asked. "I'm actually quite good at figuring things out."

"Because it isn't on ze bridge. It's in ze engine room, schtupid. Oh darn!" The pirate banged his head against the wooden chairback in frustration. "I just told you vere it vas, didn't I?"

"Yes, you have. Thank you."

Parveen quickly ran out the hatchway, leaving Schmidt to curse in his chair. He dashed down the length of the ship, retracing his route from the cargo bay and into the engineering room. It didn't take him long to find the switch. Crossing the fingers of one hand, he flipped the switch with the other. The engines coughed once, twice, then caught, roaring to life. Parveen ran back through the ship, hoping that Mimi had been able to free the children and Mrs. Francis, too.

Now, you might be thinking, *Oh, that Schmidt. What an absolute nincompoop! First he lets Parveen brain him with his own jug, and then he gives away the location of the ignition switch!* Certainly, you might be forgiven for thinking he is a nincompoop. You'd be playing right into his hands.

He only told Parveen where the ignition switch was so that he could have an opportunity to free himself from his bonds. Parveen had done the best he could to tie the ropes tightly around Schmidt's wrists, but he couldn't have known that before he became a pirate Schmidt was a chiropractor.[76] He knew the limits to which the human skeleton might be pushed in an extremity and he knew the limits of his extremities. Grimacing in pain, he dislocated his thumbs, allowing his hands to slip through the ropes. He was free.

Schmidt popped his thumbs back into their sockets, the joints cracking like gunshots. Then he felt the engines thrum to life through the deck and he grinned evilly.

"Now we'll see."

MR. KIPLING OPENED THE GATE to the cavern that served as a prison for the orphans of Windcity. The hapless children huddled together against the far wall, fearing the worst. But when Mimi and Mrs. Francis stepped into the door, a cheer went up!

"Look! It's Mimi," some shouted.

"Mrs. Francis! Hurray!" cried others.

"Door open. Yay! Blort!" shouted some toddlers who hadn't truly grasped sentence structure or grammar.

The children crowded around their rescuers, crying, hugging, and dancing for joy.

---

[76] A chiropractor is a physician who is concerned with the alignment of the bones and muscles in the body. The first chiropractor came from the Egyptian city of Cairo, where he helped workers suffering from back pain after they were forced to lift huge blocks to build pyramids.

"Settle down! Settle down!" Mimi tried to restore some order.

"Quiet, children!" At those two words from Mrs. Francis, silence fell.

"Children," Mrs. Francis said, "we are being rescued. That doesn't mean there shall be pushing, shoving, and horseplay. We must follow Mimi and Mr. Kipling."

"We'd better be going." Mr. Kipling leaned in the door. The children cowered at the sight of him.

"He's with us," Mimi assured the frightened children. "Now let's git the heck outta here. Parveen is waitin' on us."

Mrs. Francis led the children out the door, two by two, holding hands. Mr. Kipling started up the corridor, sword drawn. Mimi brought up the rear. As they passed another cell door, they heard voices inside.

"Let us out! Help! Help!"

"Who's in there?" Mrs. Francis asked.

"The other cheese masters that Captain Cheesebeard kidnapped," Kipling said. "We must hurry."

Mrs. Francis shook her head. "Let them out. They're coming with us."

"There isn't time!"

"No one should be left at the hands of these dastardly ruffians."

Mr. Kipling was about to protest, but Mimi pointed at the door. "She's right. Let 'em out!"

So, a moment later, a gaggle of orphans and a confused but grateful pack of cheese masters marched up the corridor past Mrs. Francis's old cell. The two unfortunate pirates pounded at the door and cursed, but to no avail. Mr. Kipling guided them to the foot of the staircase that led to the outside, and there they stopped short.

Standing at the top of the stairs in the light of the moon was a shocked pirate carrying a basket of food and drink.

"What the ..." the pirate gasped. Taking in the sight of the children, Mrs. Francis, Mimi, and the naked blade in Mr. Kipling's hand, he did what human beings have always done when faced with insurmountable sensory input. He dropped the basket and fled.

"Oh, dear!" Mr. Kipling sprinted up the stairs after the man, shouting over his shoulder as he went, "Get them to the airship!"

He reached the top of the steps, came out into the night air—and caught sight of the pirate making a beeline for the great hall. Knowing he'd never catch him in time, Mr. Kipling turned to the children emerging from the stairs and bellowed, "Hurry! Hurry!"

Mimi and Mrs. Francis hustled the children up the stairs, helping the youngest ones to climb faster. The adults picked up the smallest children. Reaching the top, Mimi and Mrs. Francis joined Mr. Kipling. He had removed his heavy woollen peacoat and his peaked cap, placing them in a little pile on the ground at his feet. He drew his knife. Now he had a sword in one hand and the knife in the other.

"What are you doing?" Mrs. Francis demanded, tugging at his arm. "We have to get to the airship."

"They will be coming any moment. I'll hold them off as long as I can while you get the others to the ship."

Mimi picked up a sharp stone. "I'll stay with ya."

"No." Mr. Kipling smiled and laid a hand on her head, ruffling her hair. His tired blue eyes gazed down kindly into her fierce green ones. "You have to go, my dear. Someone must take care of Mrs. Francis." He turned to the chubby little woman in her now tattered pink dressing gown.

"He's right, Mimi," Mrs. Francis said, wiping her eyes. "Let's get going."

Mimi reluctantly turned away. "C'mon everybody," she shouted, "Parveen cain't wait forever!" She took off in the direction of the warehouse with the cheese masters herding the crowd of children after her.

Mrs. Francis squeezed Mr. Kipling's arm. "Goodbye," she said. "I told you … It's never too late to do something good with your life."

A roar went up in the great hall.

"Time to go," Mr. Kipling said. He smiled sadly and turned to face the swarm of pirates pouring out of the doors into the night. Mrs. Francis suddenly flung her arms around Mr. Kipling's neck and planted a huge kiss on his lips. "Never too late!" she whispered, and ran off as fast as her little legs could carry her.

"Kipling!" Cheesebeard's voice boomed across the open ground, echoing off the walls of the crater. Mr. Kipling shook off Mrs. Francis's kiss and faced the Captain. Cheesebeard stood about fifty metres away. The pirates ranged out behind him, waiting for instructions.

Mr. Kipling took a few steps until he stood directly in the path of anyone trying to skirt the lake and pursue the escaping children. The pirates could go around the other way, but it was a longer route and might buy the children more time.

"Captain Cheesebeard," Mr. Kipling said in a friendly tone, "I've decided to tender my resignation."

"What are you talking about?" Cheesebeard demanded, his face growing red above his greasy facial carpet. "No one resigns from piracy. You're a pirate and then you die. There's no resigning."

Mr. Kipling sliced the air with his sword, taking a couple of practice cuts, then stood in the ready position and smiled. "I guess if resigning isn't an option, I'll have to die."

"You're a fool, Kipling," Cheesebeard laughed. "You'll die for nothing. There's no way those children will escape. They'll never even get the airship started!" he laughed loudly and all the pirates joined in.

The engines of the airship chose that instant to roar to life. The laughter stopped.

"Kill the traitor. Then capture the prisoners," Cheesebeard ordered.

A pirate beside him raised his hand.

"What?" Cheesebeard grated.

"Technically, they aren't prisoners, Captain. They're escapees. If they were prisoners they'd still be imprisoned and not escaping and we wouldn't have to capture them. You follow my logic, Captain?"

Cheesebeard pulled out his sword and ran the man through.

"Point taken," Cheesebeard smiled, pulling his sword free and directing the dripping blade at Mr. Kipling. "Kill the traitor. Then capture the former prisoners!" he shouted.

"Better," the dying pirate said and collapsed in a heap.

Mr. Kipling prepared to sell his life dearly as the pirates swiftly closed the distance.

Chapter 31

Mimi dashed towards the warehouse and the airship moored above it. By the time she reached the doors she was easily a hundred metres ahead of the pack. The doors were flung open wide and the two guards she'd seen earlier were nowhere in sight.

"Mimi! Help!" Parveen's familiar voice sounded from within. Mimi dashed through the doors and looked frantically around.

"Mimi!" The voice came from above. She looked up and saw the hole in the roof and the ladder. By now the others were almost at the warehouse, so she ran to the ladder and scrambled up.

At the top of the ladder she stepped out onto a platform to see Pianoface and Tubaface with their swords out, trying to climb into the airship's cargo hold. Parveen was desperately attempting to hold them at bay with a long boathook. He sighed with relief when he saw Mimi. Unfortunately, he alerted the guards to her presence. They turned and saw her.

"Look it's that crazy girl from the orphanage. Where are all these kids coming from?" Tubaface asked in exasperation.

Pianoface shoved him towards Mimi. "Never mind! You get her, and I'll take care of this one."

Mimi didn't wait. She ran straight at him and drove one of her feet into his chest. He staggered back from the impact, teetering on the edge of the platform and pinwheeling his arms, trying to maintain his balance. Parveen took the opportunity to jab him with the boathook, sending him plunging backwards. Tubaface fell ten metres and crashed through the roof into the warehouse below. His fall was broken by a large wheel of brie.

Pianoface took advantage of Parveen overextending himself with the pole and grabbed hold of it. He pulled with all his strength, tugging Parveen off his feet. The little boy fell down the steps and rolled to a stop at Pianoface's feet.

"Now I've got you!" Pianoface raised his sword above Parveen, preparing to chop the helpless child in two.

Fortunately, Mimi remembered she'd picked up a sharp stone in the last chapter.[77] She cocked her arm and fired the missile as hard as she could. THOK! Pianoface's forehead made a hollow sound like a hammer hitting a coconut. He stood quite still for a moment, then his eyes rolled up into his skull and he thumped onto his back unconscious.

Mimi stepped over to Parveen and extended her hand to him.

"Get up! We've gotta get outta here." She pulled him to his feet.

"What took you so long?" He brushed the dust off his parka.

"Parveen?"

Mrs. Francis had reached the top of the ladder. She practically leapt across the intervening distance and swept Parveen into a crushing hug.

"Oh my little genius! Are you all right?"

"I was," came the muffled reply. "However, I may be asphyxiated." Parveen was saved from further mauling by

---

[77] Sometimes characters can forget things in the heat of a good story.

the arrival of the first child. Mrs. Francis reluctantly let go of Parveen. "Everyone aboard as carefully as possible. No pushing. No shoving. There's plenty of time."

"I don't know about that," Mimi said, looking out towards where Mr. Kipling stood facing the pirates. The tall man was shouting something. The Captain shouted back. The distance was too great for Mimi to hear what was said, but the Captain seemed annoyed. He stabbed the man next to him and then the pirates charged. Mr. Kipling wouldn't last long.

"Let's git everybody aboard," Mimi said urgently. "Mr. Kipling's bought us a minute or two at most."

MR. KIPLING CALMLY AWAITED the wave of attackers boiling towards him. He held his weapons ready and tried to pick out whom he would take down first. Captain Cheesebeard hadn't joined the attack, leaving the death of his first mate to his underlings as a final insult. The loathsome Viggo stood beside the Captain, grinning and whispering into his ear.

Suddenly, the pirate charge faltered. The wave shambled to a stop, with each filthy, greasy face turning to look at something behind Mr. Kipling. He stole a glance over his shoulder and saw a boy walking towards him. The boy wore a torn and tattered woollen coat, a broad smile, and a pair of huge, shining black boots. The boy stopped beside him and held out his hand.

"Hello there," the boy said, "I'm Hamish X."

"Mr. Kipling." He shook the proffered hand and sketched a bow. "I've heard a lot about you from Mrs. Francis. Magnificent boots."

"Thanks," Hamish X grinned. He cocked a thumb at the pirates. "Looks like you could use a hand."

"Always! However, your friends are already on the airship. You should join them and leave this to me."

"Very thoughtful of you, but I'll stay just the same," Hamish X answered. He turned to the pirates. "Surrender!"

At the sight of the boy, a fury swept over Cheesebeard. He raised his sword and pointed at Hamish X. "You!" he howled, "Hamish X!"

Hamish X merely looked at him in mild curiosity. "Yes. I'm Hamish X."

"You killed Soybeard, my dear brother," Cheesebeard bellowed.

"He tried to kill me first," Hamish X answered, "and he tried to sink the boat I was in along with forty-two orphans I was helping to escape from a running shoe factory."

"You call that an excuse?"

"Yes, I do," Hamish X said sadly. "It was self-defence. He was an evil, vicious murderer, and so are you."

At this, Cheesebeard howled with fury. "I am going to kill you right now and I promise you ..." Cheesebeard licked his lips, "it will be slow and painful."

"It's nice to have a goal in life, even if it can never be realized," Hamish smiled. "Surrender." The pirates looked at each other incredulously, then started to laugh.

Cheesebeard's beard shook with his own scornful laughter, raining crumbs down upon the ground. "There's only two of you."

"I'm impressed that you can count so high. I'm giving you one chance to give up, and it's more than you deserve. You're a vicious pirate, a thief, and a kidnapper, but more importantly, you stole something that belongs to me."

"What's that?"

"A book."

Cheesebeard picked at his beard, thinking. "You mean that horribly boring book about plumbers? It's terrible!"

"Nonetheless, it's mine and I want it back. Give it to me and we'll leave you in peace. Otherwise, I'll take it from you by force."

The Captain barked out a laugh. "By force! You'll take it by force? You and what army?"

"This one," Hamish X said. "Winkie!"

At the sound of his name, the huge snow monkey burst out of the stairway from the caverns below. At his back swarmed hundreds of his fellow monkeys, shrieking, hooting, and bent on destruction.

"Sweet mother of all primates!" Cheesebeard gasped, astonished at the tide of angry monkey flesh rolling over the front rank of disbelieving pirates. The men barely had a chance to raise their weapons before the deluge overwhelmed them.

Hamish X and Mr. Kipling lent their support to the monkey onslaught. Mr. Kipling lay about with his sword and dagger, spinning and striking with devastating grace. Hamish X lashed out with his powerful boots, somersaulting, pirouetting, cartwheeling his way towards the foe, attempting to clear a path to the pirate Captain.

The bewildered pirates didn't know what to do. Sheer weight of numbers and the ferocity of the attack forced them to retreat towards the great hall. They tried to rally, to organize some kind of defence, but the monkey attack was too intense. One by one, gangs of angry simians began to drag them down. Perhaps with better leadership they might have had a chance, but Cheesebeard only shouted insults at his men, all the while edging towards the hall behind him. "Hold them, men! Hold them! Have you no pride? Are you no match for a gang of dirty monkeys?"

Clearly, the pirates were not. Between the monkeys, Mr. Kipling, and Hamish X, Cheesebeard's men were losing their stomach for the fight. First one turned and fled. Then another. In seconds, the entire pirate force was in full retreat, catching the monkeys by surprise with the suddenness of their flight.

"To the hall!" Cheesebeard shouted. He stood by the open doors waving his sword. "This way!"

Viggo had seen which way the battle was going and was hiding behind the door watching the battle unfold. When Hamish X had emerged from the caverns he could hardly believe his eyes. And now he felt such a surge of hatred that he almost ran out of his hiding place to confront the boy with the big boots.

First he has the nerve to escape from my orphanage, Viggo fumed. *Then he has the temerity to survive a pirate attack!*

And now he comes here and ruins my wonderful new partnership with Cheesebeard!

Unfortunately, coming out into the open would expose Viggo to personal danger and monkey vengeance. His natural cowardice won out and he stayed huddled in the shelter of the doorway.

The pirates ran as fast as their legs could carry them towards the open doors of the hall, the monkeys hooting in hot pursuit. Fear fuelled the pirates' steps, but fury drove the monkeys faster. Cheesebeard assessed the situation and, realizing that his men would never reach the doors in time, he decided to do what all true leaders of pirates have done throughout the ages: he saved himself. He leapt into the hall and pushed the doors closed in the faces of his henchmen. Viggo quickly slammed down the bar, effectively locking the monkeys and pirates out while locking himself and the Captain in.

The pirates howled in frustration, pounding in vain at the wood with the butts of their weapons. Defeated, they turned to face the onrushing monkey horde and did the only sensible thing: they threw down their weapons and surrendered.

"Stop!" Hamish X cried. Winkie hooted and the monkeys reluctantly reined themselves in. Hooting and shrieking, they pounded their chests and slapped the ground with the palms of their hands, making such a ferocious din that some of the pirates began to cry like little children.

"Don't kill us," they begged. "We give up! We was just followin' orders."

"I don't even like being a pirate!" one man cried.

"I don't even like cheese," added another.

"I'm easily led," said another. "My guidance counsellor in high school said so."

Hamish X and Mr. Kipling made their way through the ring of monkeys to stand in front of the captives. Hamish X looked at the pathetic men on their knees wringing their hands.

"Should we kill them?" Mr. Kipling asked.

Hamish X thought for a moment. "No," he said at last. "Then we'd be no better than they are. I have no quarrel with them any more. It's Cheesebeard I want, and the book."

"Good boy," said Mr. Kipling, sheathing his weapons.

"You go to the airship and make sure everyone's aboard," Hamish X said to Mr. Kipling. "I'll deal with Cheesebeard."

"Be careful, lad," Mr. Kipling said, laying a hand on Hamish X's shoulder before trotting away.

Hamish X watched him go, then turned and glared at the pirates. "Out of the way."

They parted like a flock of sheep for a wolf as he walked up to the doors. He kicked them once. A resounding boom echoed from the crater walls.

"Cheesebeard!"

"We don't want any," came the muffled response. "Come back later!"

"Very funny," Hamish X called back. "Open the door right now or else I'll kick it down!"

"I'd like to see you try! It's made of solid oak reinforced with steel."

"You asked for it!"

Hamish backed up a few steps. He concentrated on the boots. It was becoming easier now to connect with the strange energy they held. The familiar tickle of power coursed up his legs.

He stamped one foot. "One." The power swelled.

He stamped the other. "Two!" The boots began to glow.

He leapt, striking the doors where they met in the centre with both boots together.

"Three!" The power surged as he made contact. With a crack like a cannon blast, the doors burst inward. The bar broke in two pieces and fell to the floor. Hamish X tucked and rolled in a somersault, coming to his feet ready for action.

Standing on the raised step in front of a huge recliner was Cheesebeard, grinning like a maniac. One of his arms was wrapped around Viggo's neck and the other held a knife to the cheese master's throat.

"Don't come any closer," Viggo whimpered piteously. "He'll kill me."

Chapter 32

The cheese master cringed in terror as Captain Cheesebeard pressed the knife harder into the wattle of loose skin covering his Adam's apple.

"Why should I care if he kills you?" said Hamish X. "You never did a good thing for anyone in your life."

"Please," Viggo whined, "I know you have no reason to care about what happens to me, but I know you're a kind-hearted boy. You were so nice to little what's-his-name with the glasses and whosit ..."

"Parveen and Mimi."

"Exactly! What would they think of you if you let someone die in cold blood?"

Hamish X clenched his jaw. According to Cheesebeard, he'd killed the pirate Soybeard. But he felt sure he'd been justified in ridding the world of an evil pirate who'd killed so many people and was probably bent on killing him, too. Viggo was helpless, however, and at Cheesebeard's mercy. Hamish X searched his heart and found that he couldn't let the cheese master die like this. Despite Viggo's horrible behaviour towards himself and his friends, Hamish X discovered he felt sorry for the miserable man. Perhaps this would be the act of kindness Viggo needed to see the light.

"All right, Cheesebeard. Let him go and I promise you won't be harmed. All I want is the book. Give it to me and I'll go."

"You promise?" Cheesebeard laughed. "What good is a promise from you? How do I know the moment I let him go you won't give me a boot massage with those massive clodhoppers?"

"What do you want me to promise by?"

"The International Pirate Code!" A gasp went up from the pirates who had surrendered outside. They had gathered in the doorway to watch the confrontation between the Captain and the strange little boy.

"International Pirate Code?" Hamish X asked.

"Is there an echo in here? Yes the International Pirate Code!" Cheesebeard pressed the knife deeper into the flesh of Viggo's neck.

Hamish X sighed. "I promise by the International Pirate Code that I shall not harm you if you let him go."

Cheesebeard's eyes narrowed. "The IPC, eh?"

"You heard me."

"You promise by the International Pirate Code not to harm me or Viggo here?"

"You're the one with a knife at his throat."

"Just promise!" He pressed the knife harder.

"Fine. I promise!"

Cheesebeard hesitated a moment longer, then smiled. "You were right, Viggo. He's an altogether gullible boy." He removed the knife from Viggo's neck.

"I told you, Captain," Viggo grinned, "I can read him like a book." He looked at Hamish X's shocked expression. "Of course it was just a ruse, Hamish X. You are such a little fool."

"Why you rotten ..." Hamish X snarled and lunged at Viggo. The thin man yelped and darted behind Cheesebeard.

"We had a deal," Cheesebeard said smugly. "IPC!"

With supreme effort, Hamish X curbed his anger. "All right. You fooled me. Once! You've taken advantage of my kindness. Once! You won't be given a second chance. Now, where's the book?"

"That wasn't part of the deal. I said I wouldn't harm Viggo. I didn't say I'd tell you where the book is."

"Give it to me! Now!" Hamish stamped his foot. Bottles jumped on the table and fell crashing to the floor.

"Temper! Temper!" Cheesebeard tutted. "You really have to control yourself. You won't get anywhere being so rude." He walked easily up the steps and sat in his recliner, crossing his legs. "What's so important about this book anyway?"

"It's none of your business."

"I'm making it my business."

Hamish clenched his fists. "It was my mother's. She meant for me to have it."

"She couldn't have cared that much if she left you with strangers and with the most boring book ever written as a final slap in the face. I don't mind saying, it's obvious to me she didn't care too much about you at all."

Hamish X's sudden leap caught Cheesebeard by surprise. The boy launched himself through the air, landing with one big black boot on the arm of the recliner and the other big black boot pressed against the pirate Captain's throat.

"Say one more word about my mother ... one more word and IPC or no, I'll crush you like a grape." Cheesebeard's face went red and then purple as Hamish X leaned on his windpipe. Finally, Hamish X hopped down from the chair and stood waiting for Cheesebeard to regain his breath.

"The book," Hamish X said simply.

"I have it somewhere safe. You'll never find it if you kill me. But I'll tell you what we'll do ..." Cheesebeard's eyes glittered with malice. “We’ll have a challenge according to the code. If you win, I’ll give you the book. If I win …” he smiled like a crocodile, yellow teeth gleaming in the lamplight. “If I win, then you have to come and work for me. Is it a deal?”

Hamish X was silent. Working for Cheesebeard was an impossible scenario, but so was leaving without the book. *Great Plumbers and Their Exploits* was the only connection he had with his mother. Each time he held it he felt closer to the truth. He had to have it back.

“All right,” he sighed at last. “But I choose the challenge.”

“It can’t be anything to do with boots or kicking,” Cheesebeard said quickly.

“Good one, Captain,” Viggo simpered.

Hamish X glared at the cheese maker, who ducked behind the recliner. Hamish X thought for a moment. Then he smiled.

“I know,” he said. “We’ll have an eating contest. Whoever can eat the most Caribou Blue wins.”

A triumphant light filled Cheesebeard’s eyes. He crowed to the ceiling. “Ho! Ho! Ho! You’re on, my little friend. No one can eat more cheese than I. No one! Especially not a sawed-off little runt like you. Ho! Ho! Ho!”

Hamish X smiled grimly and crossed his arms. “Any time you’re ready.”

“Bring in the Caribou Blue,” Cheesebeard snarled.

“Right away.” Viggo bowed and scraped, backing away.

HAMISH X AND THE PIRATE CAPTAIN sat on the platform. Cheesebeard occupied his recliner while Hamish X sat on a low stool facing him. A small table separated them.

Viggo painstakingly measured each cube so that each weighed a uniform ounce. The fumes were so powerful

around the block he cut them from that he was forced to wear a gas mask. Hamish X watched the process like a hawk, keen to catch Viggo in case he cheated with the measurements.

At last, the two combatants announced they were satisfied. Two plates piled with one-ounce cubes of Caribou Blue rested on the table. Everyone stood back a good distance, but many complained of watery eyes and dizziness.

Hamish X and Cheesebeard didn't flinch. They stared at each other over the mounds of cheese, the tension so palpable one could have cut it with a knife. The stench of the cheese was so palpable one could have used the same knife to cut it, too.[78] But neither of the combatants showed any sign of weakness.

Cheesebeard raised his buttock, expelled some trapped gas, smiled and spread his hands. "As challenger, you should go first."

"If you insist," Hamish X said.

Hamish X reached out and plucked a cube of cheese from the top of his pile. He popped it into his mouth and chewed it with gusto. The crowd of pirates standing all

---

78 Of course, one should rinse cutlery thoroughly between uses to avoid food poisoning.

around gasped. The monkeys clinging to the walls hooted. Hamish X swallowed, opened his mouth, and displayed the empty cavity.

"Your turn," he said.

Cheesebeard reached out, plucked the top piece of cheese off his plate, and with a nonchalant flick of the wrist tossed it into his mouth. This time the pirates hooted and the monkeys gasped. He chewed, swallowed, and smiled.

"You know you haven't got a chance, don't you?" Cheesebeard said as Hamish picked up his next morsel. "I'm going to win and you'll be my slave."

"Don't be so sure," Hamish X said, placing the cheese in his mouth.

"It's a matter of fact that I am easily three times the size of you. I've been eating cheese my whole life. There's no cheese that can get the better of me," Cheesebeard laughed.

Hamish X shrugged, opening his mouth to display that he had swallowed. His golden eyes watered slightly, but otherwise he showed no ill effects. "That may be true. But Caribou Blue is a powerful cheese. The fumes alone can induce madness. No one has ever eaten more than three ounces and survived. Those consuming two ounces have been known to experience hallucinations, blindness, and paralysis."

Cheesebeard popped another ounce into his mouth, chewing as he answered. "Umph, yes, indeed. So how can you hope to defeat me? I'll eat you under the table. Yumph." Beads of sweat stood out on Cheesebeard's brow. He blinked again and again. "Feeling it yet, Hamish X?"

"No. I think you are though. Look at your hands."

Cheesebeard held up his hands. They were trembling violently. "It's nothing ... just the cold ... and I haven't been sleeping well lately ... Mommy?" He turned his head sharply to look at an empty space. "Is that you, Mommy?" Suddenly his right arm went rigid. He banged it on the tabletop. "Mommy my arm's all stiff!"

Viggo darted in to Cheesebeard's side, whispering into the pirate's ear. "Captain? You're hallucinating. The cheese is too powerful for you."

Cheesebeard swung his stiff arm, smashing Viggo to the ground. The plate of cheese cubes spilled across the table. "You're not my mommy!" The pirate's face was red with rage. "Stop pretending you're my mommy!" The moment of violence seemed to clear his head. He looked at Hamish X sitting quietly on his stool. The boy didn't seem to be suffering in the least. "All right! All right! Your turn again."

Hamish X smiled. "Viggo says that no one has ever eaten four ounces and survived." He picked up a piece of cheese in each hand, holding the greasy blue-white squares between his thumb and forefinger. "Hallucination. Paralysis. Death. Are you up to the challenge, Captain Cheesebeard?"

Hamish X stuck out his tongue and placed the two chunks of cheese onto it. He drew his tongue in and chewed grimly, staring into the awestruck eyes of the pirate Captain. The collected audience of men and monkeys looked on in wonder as he opened his mouth to evidence its emptiness. Cheesebeard's chin quivered. Tears formed in his terrified eyes.

"Well?" said Hamish X, crossing his arms. "Your turn, Cheesebeard. Or do you admit defeat? Give me my book and let us go in peace."

"NEVER!" Cheesebeard thundered, his foul breath blasting over Hamish X, who fanned a hand in disgust.

Viggo laid a bony hand on Cheesebeard's wrist as the Captain reached for his plate. "Captain, I must beg you not to do it. No one knows better than I how potent this cheese is. I don't know how he's able to survive, but I must advise caution."

Cheesebeard tore his arm out of Viggo's grasp. "Stop touching me, Queen Elizabeth! I'm trying to win this game!" (For indeed, the cheese was working on his mind in such a way as to make him think Viggo was actually Queen Elizabeth the First, complete with starched ruffle collar and Renaissance ball gown.) "I'll eat this fellow under the table and then invade Spain, your majesty!" He snatched up two cubes of cheese and rammed them in his mouth, chewing furiously. "I'm like a little teapot. Here's my handle and here's my spout!" He got up and posed with one arm extended and the other bent to touch his hip. "Look at me! I'm all full of tea!" Suddenly, he started hopping and pointing at the floor, terror in his eyes. "Look out for the fire toads! They're leaping. LEAPING!" He climbed up onto his recliner, perching on the headrest and flapping his arms. "Caw! Caw! Birds like worms! Get me worms!"

The pirates exchanged looks of confusion. The Captain was completely mad. Even the monkeys looked perplexed, and monkeys are difficult to perplex considering they understand very little in the first place.

"Cheesebeard," Hamish X said soothingly, holding out his hand to the pirate who was now pecking at his own arm with his nose. "It's over. We don't need to continue. Just tell me where the book is and I'll go."

Cheesebeard suddenly went very still. His eyes, wild and watery, fixed on Hamish X and for a moment he seemed completely lucid and sane. He stared hard at the boy for a long moment.

"I want my mommy," the pirate Captain said. "Right now!" And with that final request, he fell backwards with a loud crash, taking the chair with him. His heavy, cheese-encrusted beard lay on his scarred face. Hamish X held two fingers against the man's neck.

"He's dead," Hamish X pronounced to the gathered spectators. He stood up and looked at the floor where the chair had been. There, on the floor, was his book.

Chapter 33

Hamish X bent and picked up the book. He let out a sigh of relief. As soon as his hands came in contact with the book he felt calmer, more complete.

"How did you do it?" asked Viggo. "How? No one could eat that much cheese and feel no effects."

Hamish X turned to look at Viggo. "Easy, really. I built up my resistance. Every day I was at the orphanage, I stole a little cheese and ate it."

Viggo stabbed a pointy finger at Hamish X. "You were the thief!"

"Yes, although I prefer the term 'pilferer.' Slowly, over the weeks, I increased the amount I ate each day. I can eat about six ounces now without any ill effects." Hamish X hugged his book to his chest. "Now that I have my book, I'll be on my way."

"No you won't." Viggo turned and shouted at the pirates, "He's killed your Captain. You can't let him walk away!"

"It's the International Pirate Code," one of the pirates shrugged. "We have to honour the agreement. Besides, nobody really liked the Captain anyway." The rest of the pirates nodded and mumbled in agreement.

"Sorry Viggo," Hamish X said. "Hate to disappoint you. I must be going. My friends are waiting for me."

The crowd of pirates and monkeys parted respectfully as the little boy in the big boots walked through the hall and out the big doors into the early morning light.

Winkie waited outside. As Hamish X emerged from the doors, the snow monkeys made such a racket of monkey noise that Hamish X was forced to cover his ears. Winkie lifted Hamish X off his feet, crushing him in a vicelike hug with his long ropy arms.

"All right! All right, Winkie! Let me down!"

Winkie obeyed, gently placing Hamish X back on his feet. The big monkey's eye glowed with happiness.

"I don't know if you understand me, but thank you for your help. I have to go now, back to my friends."

Winkie hooted mournfully, slapping his hands gently on the ground. The other monkeys joined in, a soft ululating call.

"Don't be sad, Winkie. You're free now. Go and find a new place to live. I'm sure there's a place for you somewhere, just as there's a place for me." Hamish X reached up and scratched Winkie behind the ear. The huge monkey grinned, showing his long canines, and thumped his right foot against the ground. He looked like a big, happy dog.

"Take me with you!" The whining voice cut through the joyful moment. Viggo stood at the door of the hall, wringing his bony hands. "You can't leave me here with these ... moronic, cretinous criminals."

"Hey. Not nice," one of the pirates objected.

"Sorry," Hamish X said. "I think you should stay with your new friends. We don't need you back in Windcity. We can manage fine without you."

"It's my factory! My money! My cheese!"

"Built on the backs of poor orphan children. It's time they had a better life. Without you!" Hamish X tucked his massive book under his arm and gave a little bow. "Goodbye Viggo. Goodbye pirates! Goodbye monkeys!"

"No! No! You can't leave me here!" Viggo threw himself at Hamish X's feet, sobbing and begging, but

Hamish X shook his head. Pulling his boot out of Viggo's bony grasp, he turned and trotted off towards the waiting airship.

The monkeys hooted in farewell until Hamish X disappeared into the warehouse. Then, led by Winkie, they bounded off down the steps into the caverns below. They rushed down through the winding tunnels of the volcano and poured out onto the arctic plain. A long stream of monkeys set off in a westerly direction, searching for a new home.

MR. KIPLING had brought the happy news that Hamish X was alive and well. And now the tall man stood with Mimi, Parveen, and Mrs. Francis on the landing platform, all watching the doors of the hall with bated breath.

When Mimi saw Hamish X trot out into the morning light she leapt for joy, pumping her fist in the air. "It's him! He's comin'!" she shouted. The children collected in the cargo bay cheered. Mrs. Francis's eyes filled with tears.

"Remarkable boy," Mr. Kipling muttered.

When Hamish X emerged from the warehouse, climbing up the ladder to the docking platform, the cheering grew thunderously loud. Mrs. Francis practically hauled him up the last few rungs.

"Oh, my dear boy!" She covered his face with kisses. "Oh, I was so worried about you! Are you all right?"

"I'll be fine if you don't suffocate me," Hamish X laughed. He sauntered over to where Mimi and Parveen stood with Mr. Kipling and wrapped his arms around his two friends. "Good work, Mimi. I knew you could do it."

"I'm just glad yer okay." Mimi hugged him back. "I thought you were a goner when that ugly monkey pulled you over the cliff."

Hamish X finally let his friends loose. Mr. Kipling cleared his throat. "Well done," he said, offering his hand. "And Cheesebeard?"

"Dead," Hamish X said, shaking Kipling's hand. "Cheese poisoning."

"Poetic justice, some might say. Allow me to make a more formal introduction. I am Mr. Kipling, formerly first mate aboard the airship *Vulture*. Currently without a commission."

"You're welcome to come to Windcity, sir," said Hamish X. "We have plenty of room."

Mr. Kipling smiled at Mrs. Francis. "I could think of no better place to be." Mrs. Francis blushed. "Now, I think we should get underway. I'll head up to the bridge. If you would be so good as to cast off, Chief Engineer Parveen?"

Parveen nodded and pushed his glasses firmly up on his nose. Mr. Kipling went up into the ship and through the forward hatch. Parveen moved to climb up but Hamish X grabbed his arm. "Thanks, Parveen. You did so much with so little."

Parveen's mouth twitched slightly, but he didn't smile. He shrugged and scampered up into the ship towards the engine room.

"I'll check on the children," Mrs. Francis announced and headed up after Parveen, leaving Hamish X and Mimi alone on the platform.

"I guess we better untie the lines," Mimi said.

"Yes, we should," Hamish X agreed. "Mimi?"

She stopped and looked at him. "Uh huh?"

"You really kicked butt."

She grinned. "I know!"

PARVEEN PRIMED THE ENGINES, checking the fuel lines and the engine temperature. Satisfied, he headed to the bridge, meeting Hamish X and Mimi in the cargo hold. They had just finished winching the doors shut. The ship was now floating free, the deck swaying slightly with the gentle roll of the huge vessel. Mr. Kipling obviously had the wheel and was turning them southeast, pointing the airship's nose in the direction of Windcity.

"What a trip," Hamish X said.

"It's good to be going home," Mimi said.

They made their way forward, through the crew quarters and into the galley where Mrs. Francis was settling the children into their cabins for the journey. She smiled when she saw the trio.

"I thought I'd never see you again after I had to leave you in that vat." She gathered them all in a hug that strained the limits of even her ample bosom. "Who would ever have thought you'd be saving me?"

"Uh … Mrs. Francis," Parveen said hesitantly. "About your porridge vat. I'm afraid we lost it." He recounted the many services the vat had performed in the air and on the ice. "We left it somewhere south of here. I'm sure we could find it if we try."

Mrs. Francis shook her head and laughed. "No, my dear. As of today, I won't need that vat any more. I don't plan on making porridge ever again." A cheer went up from Mimi and Hamish X and the children. Parveen frowned. "I kind of like porridge."

"Then I'll make some especially for you." Mrs. Francis kissed him on the crown of his head. "Now, go up and tell Mr. Kipling I'm making some breakfast. I'll bring him up a pot of tea directly."

Hamish X, Parveen, and Mimi continued forward to the bridge. They found Mr. Kipling at the wheel, adjusting course with the help of the compass fastened to the steering column.

"Hello, children! We have a course set for Windcity. Barring any adverse weather conditions we should arrive in two days."

"Fantastic." Hamish X moved to the panoramic window at the front of the bridge and looked out on the expanse of white ice and blue sky stretching out into the distance. Mimi and Parveen joined him, standing at either side. They merely looked out, each wrapped in their own thoughts. Such a long journey, so many adventures, and now it was all coming to an end. Here in the sky they found it hard to believe that the earth with all its danger and fear and trouble was real at all.

Their reverie was broken by a gasp of pain. They whirled around to see Mr. Kipling clutching at the handle of a knife, its blade buried in his shoulder. He slumped to the ground. Mimi rushed to his side.

"Schtay vere you is!" Schmidt stood in the doorway, a heavy black cannon of a pistol in his hand. Blood from his head wound was matted in his hair. His eyes were filled with hatred. "Schmack me in de head, vill you? Not so schmart now vit Herr Schmidt holding a pistol in your face, hmmm?"

"You haven't got a chance," Hamish X said. "Put down the pistol and we'll take you back to the island. We won't hurt you."

"Ha! I'm not schtupid!" He waved the gun. "Hands up, kinder! You, little girlie! Stand up and get avay from him!" Reluctantly, Mimi stood and joined Hamish X and Parveen, hands in the air.

"Schmidt," Mr. Kipling said reasonably, though it hurt him to speak, "let the children go. This is between you and me."

"Not ze high and mighty Mr. Kiplink now, are you? Mr. Schmidt is in charge now! I'm turning ziss vessel around. We'll go back and pick up ze crew and I vill be Kapitan. Kapitan Schmidt." He laughed and puffed out his chest. He grinned hideously and raised the pistol, aiming at Mr. Kipling's heart. "Ze first sing I'm going to do is get rid of you, Herr Kiplink." His finger tightened on the trigger. Mimi and Hamish X tensed to fling themselves at him, but there was no chance they could reach him in time. It was at that instant that Mrs. Francis smashed the teapot down on his head.

"Ugh! Zat's tvice in von day," Schmidt mumbled, folding into a boneless heap on the ground. The gun rattled to the floor and Hamish X kicked it away from the pirate. Mrs. Francis dropped the broken handle of the teapot and rushed to Mr. Kipling. She knelt down at his side, pressing a corner of her apron into the wound at his shoulder.

"Way to go, Mrs. Francis!" Mimi said, pumping her fist in triumph.

"Indeed," Mrs. Francis scolded. "That's no way for a lady to behave, Mimi. Help me get Mr. Kipling into bed."

BACK ON SNOW MONKEY ISLAND, now happily devoid of snow monkeys, Viggo ranted and raved. He marched back and forth, tugging at his greasy hair and cursing Hamish X.

"I'll kill him! I'll kill him. I'll hunt him down and kill him. If it's the last thing I ever do, I'll have my revenge. He's a thief! He stole everything from me. I'll kill him, I swear!" The pirates watched this display with a mixture of confusion and dread.

"This guy's got a lot of unresolved anger issues," said one pirate.

"I agree," said the man beside him. "But he might make a good replacement for Cheesebeard. He's got that homicidal rage that comes in handy in the pirate industry."

Mr. Candy and Mr. Sweet

As Viggo ranted and the pirates discussed his attributes, a helicopter rose above the edge of the volcanic crater. In the cockpit sat Mr. Sweet and Mr. Candy wrapped in grey parkas trimmed with grey fur.

"The subject performed remarkably well, Mr. Sweet," said Mr. Candy. "His level of ingenuity and mental improvisation indicates that his development is on schedule."

"Indeed, Mr. Candy," Mr. Sweet nodded. "He is progressing well. I suggest we tie up this loose end and move on to the next level of the program. Integration is imminent. He is almost ready for harvesting. It's been a long time coming, but our goal is in sight."

"Given a few more weeks with the book, he should be completely ripe." Mr. Candy's face registered the slightest displeasure. "The only thing that disturbs me is the subject's emotional development. He is exhibiting a surprising level of psychological attachment to these friends of his. It may lead to disturbances in his information matrix."

"We will have to be particularly meticulous when we perform the memory wipe before integrating him."

"Agreed. Now, let us remove these witnesses and return to Providence HQ. Detonate the geothermal charge."

Mr. Candy reached down and pushed a red button on the control panel of the helicopter. Deep in the mountain, a thunderous explosion smashed through layers of brittle volcanic rock, releasing the molten lava that had festered like an abscess for centuries beneath the surface. The explosion thundered on and on, rumbling up through the mountain as the volcano, dormant for many years, erupted violently.

"We'll head back to Providence. The Board will be eager for our report." The helicopter peeled away as ash, rock, lava, and smoke blasted miles into the air. "We must prepare Mother for the Integration."

THE ISLAND TORE itself apart, melting the ice for miles around. When the eruption finally died down, Snow Monkey Island was gone, leaving only a steaming hole in the frozen ocean to indicate it had ever existed.

Chapter 34

Aglucark and his cousins, sitting on the back of Amanda, witnessed the blast. They were forced to build a shelter to hide from the rain of fine ash that covered the snow with dust.

Winkie and the snow monkeys paused in their exodus, burrowing into the snow for protection. When they emerged after two days, they found the ice caked in soot and ash that made it difficult to breathe as they moved west towards their ancient home.

Pianoface and Tubaface sat on the ice sharing a can of beans. They had crept away down the mountain when they realized the pirates were out of business.

"Would you look at that," Tubaface said. "If we hadn't left right away, we'd have been killed."

"I guess we're just lucky," Pianoface grinned.

A huge hunk of rock expelled from the volcano fell on Tubaface. The stone obliterated the ugly man, leaving a gaping puncture in the ice sloshing with black seawater.

Pianoface looked at the yawning black hole with astonishment. "Holy cow. A few more inches and I'd be dead, too. I guess I'm just lucky. Ha!" He giggled and danced around in a circle. "I'm lucky! I'm lucky! I'm still alive."

A strange sound stopped him short. A low growl followed by soft barking yaps came from all around him. Slinking out of hiding places all around him were tiny white doglike creatures with bushy white tails and glittering black eyes. They formed a ring around him and began to converge, licking their sharp teeth hungrily with long pink tongues.

Pianoface whispered in terror, "Arctic foxes. Just my luck."[79] And then they were on him.

Parveen and Mimi saw the eruption from the bridge of the airship. The red glow was visible in the sky from an incredible distance.

"Wow. That was close," Mimi said in a voice tinged with awe.

"One more hour and we'd have been killed for certain," Parveen said, chewing on his pencil. "It makes me wonder ..."

"What?"

Parveen frowned. "Was that really a coincidence? It seems a little too close to be anything but deliberate."

"But who has the power to make a volcano erupt at will?" Mimi asked.

"I don't know." Parveen shook his head. "But I find the notion extremely disturbing."

"Know what I find disturbin'?" Mimi asked.

"What?"

Mimi pointed at Hamish X, who sat cross-legged on the floor in the corner of the bridge. He hadn't moved in the whole time since the Schmidt incident. His face was buried in the book as he read page after page with a feverish intensity. Nothing of the Hamish X they knew was present in his eyes. It was as though he'd become a machine of some kind designed only to read the book.

---

[79] I told you.

“It’s creepy,” Mimi whispered.

Parveen silently agreed.

The airship sailed southward through the arctic morning.

EPILOGUE

If you happened to come to Windcity a month later, you would hardly have recognized the Windcity Orphanage and Cheese Factory. The electric fences were gone. The gates stood open. The brick walls were painted a cheerful green and white. The airship, newly rechristened *The Orphan Queen*, bobbed above the factory roof. The greatest change of all, however, was that children played in front of the factory. Certainly, they were tethered to the ground to prevent them from blowing away in the stiff gale, but they were happy. They were smiling. They were playing. They were doing exactly what children should be doing: having fun!

Mr. Kipling was finally up and around after weeks of recovering from the wound inflicted by Mr. Schmidt. He was still the same tall and elegant gentleman, only his clothes were cleaner and lovingly mended. He spent a lot of time with Mimi. She taught him how to throw a knuckleball and a slider. He taught her the finer points of fencing. If one didn't know better, one would have mistaken the tall girl with the wild hair for Mr. Kipling's daughter, a mistake that would have delighted them both.

Parveen spent long hours in the common room drawing plans and making blueprints. He had converted the space into a workshop where he tinkered day and night with his inventions. He dedicated himself to finding ways to streamline the cheese-making process, making it safer and more profitable and allowing the children to work shorter hours. They now had more time to play and to learn, just as children ought to do. Parveen also tinkered with *The Orphan Queen*, making improvements here and there, keeping the giant gasbags inflated and generally figuring out how it all worked.

Hamish X spent almost every waking hour poring over the book. Parveen and Mimi tried to lure him into games with the other children, begged him to tell them the tale of their journey north across the ice. Though he could be coaxed away from it for an hour or more, he would always be drawn back to its pages, sitting on his cot with the book on his lap. Mrs. Francis became worried when she saw the dark circles under his eyes. He wasn't eating well and he barely went outside. The pull of the book was disturbing and unnatural.

One night, as the children sat down to dinner, Mr. Kipling asked for silence. The children always ate together now, and Mrs. Francis outdid herself in the kitchen to provide the most delicious food imaginable for every meal. Porridge was never on the menu (except for Parveen). Today, southern fried chicken, mashed potatoes, and sweet corn steamed on huge platters. The children's stomachs rumbled in anticipation. Even Hamish X had been enticed into the newly painted cafeteria (now sky blue rather than goat's-intestine pink). He poked at his food, the book resting by his plate.

Mr. Kipling tapped on his glass with a fork until all the children were silent. He stood and cleared his throat awkwardly. For the first time anyone could remember, the tall, elegant man looked nervous.

"Ahem," he cleared his throat again. "Thank you for your attention. I won't take long. I know you are all hungry so I'll get straight to the point." He fumbled with his napkin for a moment, then continued. "I would like to thank you all for being so kind to me. If it weren't for the efforts of Parveen, Hamish X, and of course Mimi," he smiled at her and she grinned back, "I would be a pirate still, or worse, I might have perished in the eruption. You've all become the family I thought I'd lost forever, and I thank you." Everyone clapped and cheered. "Yes. Well. I think we are creating a very nice life for ourselves here, and there is one person in particular who deserves a large part of the credit."

He turned to Mrs. Francis. Since she'd returned home she'd taken to dressing in more colourful clothing, taking care to do her hair up nice. Her cheeks were very red as she felt everyone looking at her.

"A toast," Mr. Kipling said, raising a glass of sparkling grape juice. All the children raised their glasses. "To Mrs. Francis: a truly kind and wonderful woman." Everyone clinked their glasses together and repeated the toast. Mrs. Kipling went even redder in the face. Mr. Kipling then knelt down by her side and looked into her eyes.

"Mrs. Francis," he said softly. "Isobel ... You have saved me in more ways than one and I want to know if you would consent to becoming, um, Mrs. Kipling." He produced a golden ring from his pocket and held it out to her. Everyone gasped in astonishment.

Mrs. Francis couldn't speak. Her eyes filled with tears. Finally, she threw her chubby arms around Mr. Kipling's neck.

"Rupert!" she cried. "Yes! Yes! Of course, yes!"

All the children started clapping and cheering again. (Some of the younger ones were frightened by the noise, but the older children soothed them.)

Mimi, Hamish X, and Parveen sat in the midst of the celebration.

"It's kinda wonderful, ain't it?" Mimi said.

Hamish X smiled, his face drawn but happy. "I should have known."

"They've been all goo-goo since we got back." Mimi stuck out her tongue in mock disgust. "Yer face has just been stuck in that book all day and night!"

"I know." Hamish X hung his head, fingers straying to the green leather cover. "I just can't seem to put it down …" He shook his head as if to clear it. "Where'd Mr. Kipling get the ring?"

"I made it," Parveen piped up.

"And you didn't tell us?" Mimi demanded.

Parveen shrugged. "He told me not to." And then Parveen did something they'd never seen before. His dark face broke into the brightest smile, full of white teeth.

"Parv! You're smiling!" Mimi whispered.

"Indeed!" Parveen said, smiling even wider. "Like my mother always told me: Smile, you're home now."

Mimi hugged the little boy, knocking his glasses askew. Even Hamish X smiled and ruffled Parveen's hair. Mrs. Francis and Mr. Kipling held each other close and kissed in a shy way, eliciting choruses of "Yayy!" and "Ewwwww!" in equal measure. Such a moment of happiness had never before been felt in Windcity Orphanage and Cheese Factory.

IF ONLY THE STORY ENDED HERE! But it doesn't. This story is a lot like life: you can't make it stop at a good part and stay there forever. Those who try to do that end up miserable in the end. Don't be afraid. Embrace change in this story, and in life. Change is what makes everything interesting. But I digress ...

THE EXPLOSION KNOCKED EVERYONE to the floor. Dishes shattered. Chunks of plaster rained down from the ceiling.

Mr. Kipling managed to haul himself up. A cut over his eye dripped blood down the side of his face. "Isobel! Get the children under the tables! We're under attack!"

"Oh, dear!" Mrs. Francis began to herd the children to the relative safety of the tables. They all waited for the next explosion, tense and fearful. None came. Instead, into the anxious silence blared an amplified voice. The voice was soothing and feminine.

"Hamish X."

Hamish X stood up. He had a beatific smile on his face.[80] "Mother."

---

[80] *Beatific* is a fancy word for very, very happy. I just like that word and I thought you should know about it.

"Hamish X," the voice continued, "come to me now."

"Yes, Mother." Hamish X picked up his book and walked towards the door.

"Hamish X. Don't ..." Mr. Kipling laid a hand on the boy's shoulder. Instantly, Hamish X spun and drove his right boot into the tall man's stomach. There was flash of light and a smell like burning rubber. Mr. Kipling sailed through the air and crashed into the far wall, his shirt front smouldering with a scorch mark in the shape of a boot print.

"Rupert!" Mrs. Francis cried, rushing to Mr. Kipling's side. Hamish X stood looking down on them. His face showed no emotion.

"Hamish X!" Mimi cried.

The boy turned to her and she gasped. His face held no recognition.

"It's me! It's Mimi!"

His golden eyes seemed to look right through her. They glowed faintly with an inner light, making him seem bizarre and inhuman. "I must go to Mother now," he said in a flat, lifeless voice.

Hamish X turned without looking back and pushed through the doors of the cafeteria.

Mimi and Parveen dashed after him.

They caught up to him as he stepped through the ruined front doors of the factory. They were a smoking wreck, destroyed by a blast of some kind. The wind was swirling into the front, carrying sleet onto Mrs. Francis's meticulously vacuumed carpet.

"Hamish X." Mimi reached for him but Parveen grabbed her arm.

"Don't touch him," Parveen warned. "He's not himself. He'll hurt you and won't know he's doing it."

They followed him out into the freezing rain.

"Hamish X," the voice of the woman cooed loudly, cutting through the gale. "Come to me. Come to Mother."

Hamish X smiled and looked up into the sky. Bright lights lanced down from above, bathing him in a bluish glare. "Mother!" he cried.

Parveen and Mimi followed his gaze and saw a black helicopter hovering above, its glossy black surface glittering with frozen rain. In the narrow glass cockpit, two grey figures sat side by side in grey coats, grey fedoras on their heads and goggles over their eyes. They looked like a pair of insects huddled in the belly of a dragonfly. From speakers on the craft's undercarriage, the voice thrummed.

"Come to me, Hamish X." The voice was rich and clear, full of love and motherly concern. Mimi felt its pull even though it wasn't aimed at her.

The helicopter lowered itself towards the earth. Hamish X moved forward and stood waiting for it to alight. He clutched the book in his arms and smiled as though he were seeing the most beautiful thing imaginable. Mimi stared in helpless horror as the helicopter landed. The noise of the rotors blotted out everything but the woman's voice.

Mr. Candy and Mr. Sweet stepped out into the freezing rain. The wind tore at their coats but, oddly, their hats didn't blow off. They stepped towards Hamish X, stopping a few metres in front of him.

"Come, Hamish X," said Mr. Sweet, holding out a gloved hand.

"Mother is waiting," Mr. Candy added.

ACKNOWLEDGMENTS

I'd like to thank everyone who had a hand in this book:

Barbara and Helen for their encouragement and excellent criticism. Lorne, my agent, who gives me so many opportunities to succeed.

My mother, father, sisters and brother, nieces and nephews, each and every.

Mrs. Lonergan for teaching me to love stories.

And the Narrator's Guild of Helsinki for the loan of their excellent narrator.